THE EXTRAORDINARY ADVENTURES OF

ORDINARY BOY

BOOK TWO
THE RETURN OF
METEOR BOY?

WILLIAM BONIFACE

ILLUSTRATIONS BY STEPHEN GILPIN

HarperTrophy®
An Imprint of HarperCollins*Publishers*

The Extraordinary Adventures of Ordinary Boy, Book Two:
The Return of Meteor Boy?
Text copyright © 2007 by William Boniface
Illustrations copyright © 2007 by Stephen Gilpin
All rights reserved. Printed in the United States of America.
No part of this book may be used or reproduced in any manner whatsoever
without written permission except in the case of brief quotations embodied in
critical articles and reviews. For information address HarperCollins Children's
Books, a division of HarperCollins Publishers, 195 Broadway, New York,
NY 10007.
www.harpercollinschildrens.com

Library of Congress Cataloging-in-Publication Data
Boniface, William.
  The return of Meteor Boy? / William Boniface. — 1st ed.
    p.   cm. — (Extraordinary adventures of ordinary boy ; bk. 2)
  Summary: While working on a time machine for the Spring Science Fair,
Ordinary Boy discovers the true identity of long lost Superopolis hero Meteor
Boy.
  ISBN 978-0-06-077469-1 (pbk.)
  [1. Heroes—Fiction. 2. Time travel—Fiction. 3. Science fair projects—
Fiction. 4. Humorous stories.] I. Title.
PZ7.B6416Ret 2007   2006029877
  [Fic]—dc22   CIP

Typography by R. Hult
14 CG/OPM 10 9 8 7 6
❖
First Harper Trophy edition, 2008

For my brother Jim,
whose love of comics and cartoons
helped warp my mind, too.

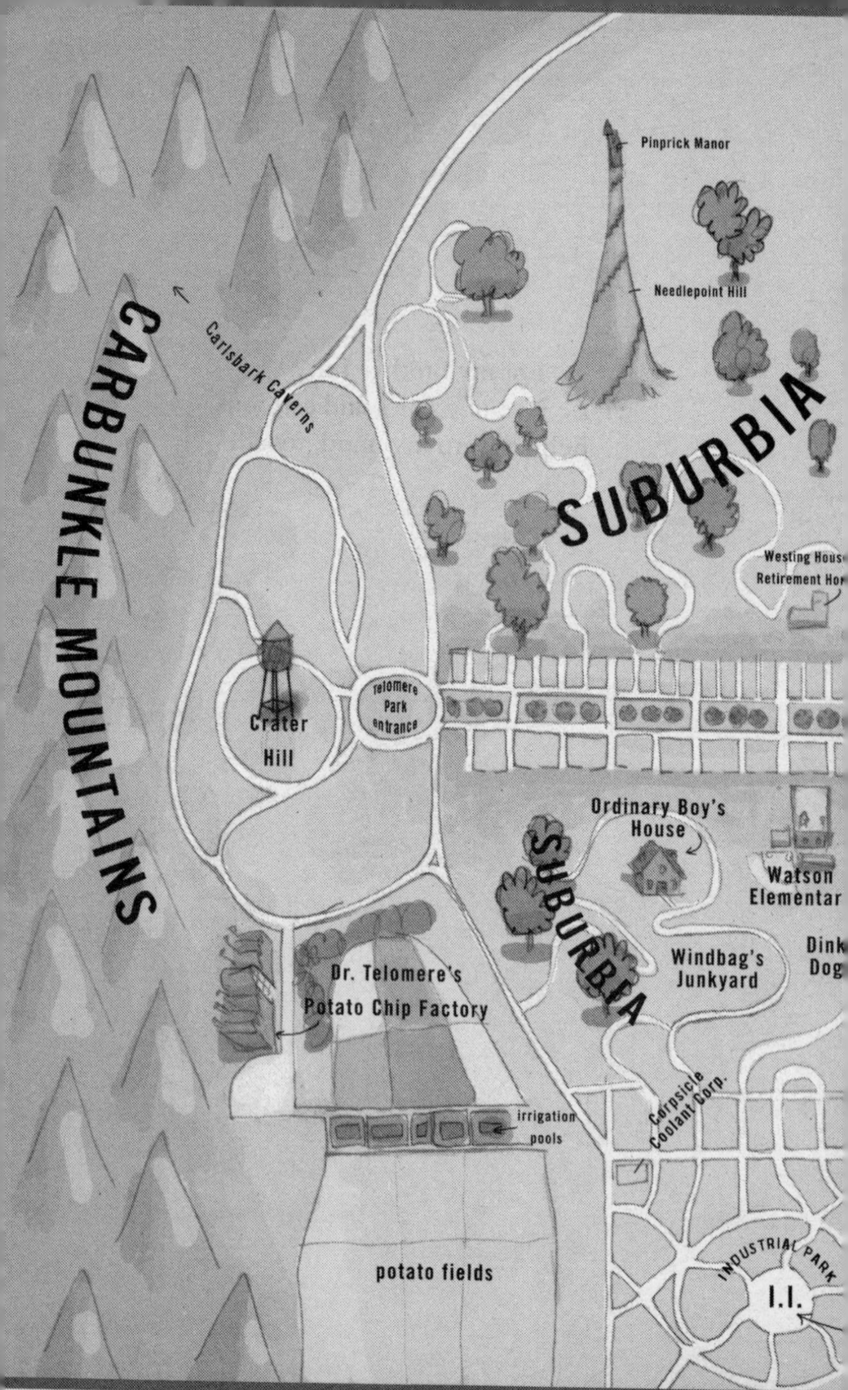

CARBUNKLE MOUNTAINS
Carlsbark Caverns
Pinprick Manor
Needlepoint Hill
SUBURBIA
Westing House
Retirement Hom
Telomere Park entrance
Crater Hill
Ordinary Boy's House
SUBURBIA
Watson Elementar
Dr. Telomere's Potato Chip Factory
Windbag's Junkyard
Dink Dog
irrigation pools
Corpsicle Coolant Corp.
INDUSTRIAL PARK
I.I.
potato fields

SUPEROPOLIS
(AND ITS ENVIRONS)

ORNERY

retail area

City Hall

lighthouse

HOITY-TOITY ROW

Hero's Cape

warehouse district

SUPEROPOLIS HARBOR

Mt. Reliable

LAVA PARK

museum

MEGAMANLY BEACH

SS Befuddlement wreck

Cavalcade of Candy

BOARDWALK amusement park

retail area

DOWNTOWN

VERTIGO BUILDING

OCEAN

peropolis Zoo

opera

TREMOR PARK

INDESTRUCTO INDUSTRIES

RESIDENTIAL

PROLOGUE

With Just a Little Oomph

The fact of the matter is I was lucky to be alive. Only one day earlier, I had been at the mercy of Professor Brain-Drain himself, the most powerful villain of them all. Like everyone else in Superopolis, Professor Brain-Drain had a superpower. In his case, it was the ability to drain the intelligence from anyone he could get close enough to touch.

Wait a minute. I said that everyone in Superopolis has a power, but that's not quite true. Everyone has a power—except me. Don't ask me why, because I don't have a clue. My own theory is that my parents' powers canceled each other out. My dad, Thermo, can make his hands incredibly hot, and my mom, Snowflake, can freeze anything solid just by looking at it.

But anyway, back to Professor Brain-Drain. He had been attempting to destroy Superopolis by burying it under trillions of collector cards with his face on them.

1

He was able to do this for two reasons. One: he had invented a small, handheld device called an Oomphlifier that could magnify anyone's power a million times. Two: he had drained the brain of another villain, called the Multiplier, to whom he had given the Oomphlifier in order to make the cards.

Fortunately, Professor Brain-Drain's plan was thwarted, and Superopolis was saved, thanks to me.

Okay . . . so that's not exactly true. In reality a whole bunch of heroes worked together to put an end to his criminal reign of terror.

For example, there was the brand-new team my dad had just formed. They're calling themselves the New New Crusaders because their team when they were younger was called the New Crusaders. I really think he could have come up with something a little cleverer, personally. Here's their old entry from the *Li'l Hero's Handbook*:

The handbook is great. It's full of all sorts of handy information about the people, places, and things in Superopolis.

My own team helped bring down Professor Brain-Drain, too. We call ourselves the Junior Leaguers. It includes my best friend, Stench, who's stronger than just about anything. Unfortunately, that strength extends to other bodily functions, as well. His name probably gives you a hint as to what I mean. Then there's Tadpole, who can extend his tongue almost twenty feet. Next is Halogen Boy, who can make himself glow really brightly depending on how much apple

TEAM NAME: The New Crusaders. **MEMBERS:** Thermo, the Big Bouncer, Windbag, the Levitator, Snowflake, Chrysanthemum. **PROFILE:** One of the more successful groups of up-and-coming heroes. Managed to burn brightly for several years (due in many cases to Thermo's inability to control his power), at least until they had to get real jobs. **CAREER HIGHLIGHT:** Both Thermo and Windbag met their wives on the team, doing each of them a world of good. **STATUS:** Inactive.

juice he's had to drink. Sadly, although Halogen Boy can make himself incredibly bright, the truth is he's just not very . . . well . . . bright. And then there's Plasma Girl. We never expected to have a girl on our team, but she's pretty cool. Sure, she loves all that typical girly stuff like dolls and tea parties, but she can also turn herself into a bubbling mass of gelatinous goo. You have to admire a girl like that.

Far less impressive, but also present, were five members of the League of Ultimate Goodness. They're Superopolis's premier team of superheroes . . . which is a little odd since they're also Superopolis's most incompetent team of superheroes. They're famous mainly because of their lead member—the Amazing Indestructo. The Amazing Indestructo is an incredible hero. I mean, think about it. The guy is totally indestructible. Absolutely nothing can harm him. Up until recently he was hands down my favorite hero. I—and every other kid I know, for that matter—would have loved to be him. That was until I actually met him.

In reality, AI is kind of a creep. He's more interested in licensing arrangements and endorsement deals than he is in being a great superhero. My teammates and I saw it all firsthand. But who's going to believe a bunch of kids, right? Of course, he ended up getting all the credit for defeating Brain-Drain.

Still, he did help save me from a fate worse than death. You see, Professor Brain-Drain was determined to drain away all my intelligence. The last thing I

THE SUPEROPOLIS TIMES

A.I. PULLS PLUG ON BRAIN-DRAIN

PROFESSOR PROBABLY PERISHES

UNKNOWN GROUP AIDS A.I.

needed was some crazy old man leaving me high and dry in the smarts department. But my dad, with some reluctant help from AI, saved me from that fate, while Professor Brain-Drain and his blimp were destroyed in the volcanic fires of Mount Reliable.

Not everything had been destroyed, though. I had come away from the adventure with a small souvenir. Hesitantly, I opened my hand and looked down at the Oomphlifier resting in my palm. I had picked it up during the final battle with Professor Brain-Drain and the Multiplier. It could magnify someone's power a million times. Maybe even a person who appeared to have *no* power would show one if it were amplified enough. I pressed my thumb down on the button. I waited almost a full minute for something—anything!—to happen . . . but I didn't feel a thing.

With a resigned sigh, I tossed the device onto the

top of my dresser and then crawled into bed and shut off the light. What would it be like to have a power? I would never know. I pulled my blanket up to my chin, closed my eyes, and did my best to fall asleep.

CHAPTER ONE

The Picking Order

Being a kid with no superpower in a town where *everyone* has a superpower can make you feel bad enough all by itself. I guess gym class was invented to rip away any remaining shred of dignity. At least that's how I felt on Friday afternoon as Coach Inflato lined us up for his twice-weekly ritual of humiliation.

Don't get me wrong. I'm not saying I'm no good at sports. In a fair game I can hold my own pretty well. The problem is, where do you find a fair game when everybody else has some sort of power? The truth is that a lot of the kids in my class have pretty useless powers. Still, guess who almost always gets picked last when it comes time to choose teams?

I prepared myself for the worst as the coach bunched us together in one corner of the school gymnasium. It was a typical basketball court sort of setup, with a stage at one end that was used for school plays and presentations.

I would tell you that Coach Inflato is your typical muscle-bound jock, but that would only give you part of the picture. In fact, his muscles are so enormous he looks like he would burst, but usually the only thing to explode is his temper.

"All right, kids," he hollered as he fished a handful of uninflated soccer balls from a canvas bag. "Today you're gonna keep yourselves out of my hair by playing dodgeball."

"But—but—" I started to sputter. Dodgeball had been eliminated from grade school gym classes years ago because the already violent game only got worse when kids with superpowers were added to the mix.

"No buts," Coach Inflato said. "Dodgeball it is."

I groaned as I saw Cannonball and the Quake grinning. They knew that this gave them free rein to pummel other kids. To make matters worse, Coach Inflato's normal routine was to get a game going and then disappear until the end of class. With no adult supervision, things always got out of hand.

"Today's team captains will be—" The coach paused for a moment as he brought one of the deflated balls to his lips and then in one quick burst filled it to capacity with air. "Cannonball . . . and—"

"Chooth me! Chooth me!" I heard Melonhead, the most annoying kid in my class, shout as he splattered seeds against the back of my neck.

"Stench."

What a relief! With my buddy as one of the captains,

NAME: Coach Inflato. **POWER:** The ability to pump himself up to impressive proportions. **LIMITATIONS:** Which mostly turn out to be a lot of hot air. **CAREER:** Exaggerated claims of heroics have never been verified. **CLASSIFICATION:** One of the greatest athletes in the history of Superopolis—at least according to him.

I wouldn't be in any danger of being picked last.

"Now choose your teams," Coach Inflato instructed. "Stench, you go first."

To no one's surprise, Stench's first choice was our fellow Junior Leaguer, Tadpole. It was a smart choice. If there's anything Tadpole hated, it was losing.

Cannonball's first choice, however, was a complete surprise.

"I choose Sparkplug," he said, a confident smirk on his face.

An agitated murmur spread through my classmates as Cannonball's best friend, Lobster Boy, spoke up. "But what about me?" Lobster Boy's claws clenched and unclenched as a shocked look of betrayal spread across his face.

But the selection process went on. For the next round the captains had to choose a girl.

"I'll take Plasma Girl," Stench said immediately.

Another member of our team and another excellent choice.

"Transparent Girl," Cannonball countered.

Tadpole snorted.

"Halogen Boy," Stench responded.

While it would have been nice to be the next person selected, I had to admit that it made more sense to choose Hal. Stench knew that there would be no danger of me being picked by Cannonball, so why not first choose the remaining member of the Junior Leaguers who had a power? I knew that he would pick me next time.

"Foggybottom," Cannonball said next.

A hushed silence fell over everyone. None of us wanted to look over at Lobster Boy, but we could all sense his dismay.

Foggybottom was sort of a mysterious kid who never really spoke much. He had the ability to create a cloud of fog around himself. I'm not certain how he produced it, but based on his name I had a pretty good guess.

As the choosing continued, with Stench taking Limber Lass and Cannonball picking the Quake, it suddenly became clear to me what Cannonball's strategy was. His choices all had powers that gave them an enormous advantage in dodgeball. Sparkplug could generate a magnetic force field to protect himself. Transparent Girl could make herself practically invisible. Foggybottom could disappear into a cloud of fog. The Quake could knock anyone off balance who tried to aim a ball at her. And then I realized why Cannonball was not going to choose Lobster Boy.

I was eager for Tadpole and Stench to choose me so I could warn them about Cannonball's strategy. Unfortunately, Stench's choice was not what I predicted.

"I'll take Lobster Boy," he said cockily, as if he had managed to pull one over on Cannonball.

I could tell by the grin on Cannonball's face that Stench and Tadpole had walked right into his trap.

And here I was, still unpicked. Then I noticed that Cannonball's gaze had stopped on me. I could feel his beady eyes boring into me, and I suddenly got the sense that he was going to choose me. I was so horrified that I think I even stopped breathing for a second. Looking straight at me, he made his next choice.

"I'll take the Spore."

My breath rushed back out with relief. A second later, I also realized I was incredibly insulted that he hadn't considered me worthy of being picked. I know that sounds contradictory, but I never claimed to be Logical Boy. As I stood there and fumed, I barely heard Stench make his next choice. But after Cannonball picked the Banshee, I was up again.

"Thelect me, Thtenth," Melonhead began slobbering. "I'm an athet in any thituathion."

Despite Melonhead's self-promotion, Stench didn't hesitate this time.

"I choose O Boy," he said guiltily.

I stalked over to join my "team." I was really annoyed.

"Lobster Boy can't hold the ball with his claws," I whispered curtly.

I got only a small sense of satisfaction from the pained looks of realization that spread across their faces. Stench went on with his next selections, which included Little Miss Bubbles and the Human Sponge. That left only Puddle Boy and Melonhead. Stench just shrugged and picked Puddle Boy.

"Tho that'th the thituathion, ith it?" Melonhead laughed as he sprayed seeds everywhere. "Thaving the betht for latht."

The funny thing about Melonhead was that he actually believed this. Cannonball just rolled his eyes and waved over the final (and most confident) member of his team.

"All right," Coach Inflato hollered. "Just in case you've forgotten the rules: If you get hit by the ball, move your butt back to the jail behind the opposing team. If the ball hits the ground before it hits you, you don't go to jail. If a person catches a ball, the person who threw it goes to jail. The only way to get out of jail is to get a ball and hit someone on the other team with it. The first team to get all their opponents into jail wins."

Each of the teams began to spread out on either side of the gym's center court line. Cannonball's team took the side near the stage.

"When I blow the whistle, the game begins," Coach Inflato instructed as he tossed two balls each to both teams. "I'll be in my office if anyone needs me. However, if anyone disturbs me, they automatically flunk this class."

This hardly struck me as the type of behavior that would be recommended in any legitimate teaching manual, but I didn't have time to think about it for long.

The whistle had just blown.

CHAPTER TWO

The Artful Dodger

I barely had a chance to blink before Cannonball launched a ball in my direction with all the propulsive force he could manage. Luckily, I saw it just in time to duck. Lobster Boy was standing behind me, though, and Cannonball's ball smacked him right in the chest, flinging him back almost eight feet.

I glared at Cannonball as he laughed, then I picked up the ball that had hit Lobster Boy and hurled it back at Cannonball. It was too fast for him to catch, but he easily stepped aside.

It was no mystery why he had gone after me first. Ever since the first day of kindergarten, when he had tried to beat me up but was instead clobbered by Stench, he had wanted revenge. He knew he couldn't come right out and smack me because Stench would give it back to him a dozen times over. But a dodgeball game was a rare

NAME: Cannonball. **POWER:** Human projectile able to hurl himself with destructive results. **LIMITATIONS:** Does not fare well against immovable objects. **CAREER:** Currently enrolled at Watson Elementary, excels at bowling. **CLASSIFICATION:** Juvenile record still under seal.

chance to hurt me, and he wasn't about to waste it.

I glanced at Coach Inflato under the delusion that he might do something to prevent any of us suffering serious harm. It was as if he knew what I was thinking.

"Dodgeball builds character," he said before he turned and headed for his office, strutting like the muscle-bound jock that he was.

I quickly shifted my eyes back to the game, and saw the Quake running toward the center line, a ball cocked back in her arm. Each of her footsteps caused the floor to shake as she rumbled forward. Her target, Little Miss Bubbles, turned and ran screaming in the opposite direction.

"Zigzag!" I hollered after her.

But she ran shrieking toward the back in a straight line and the ball hit her squarely in the back. On impact, bubbles erupted everywhere and were soon floating throughout the gym.

The distraction was short, but it was all Cannonball needed to get me back in his sights. I dove forward onto the ground as his ball came speeding at me. I could feel the rush of air as the ball missed the back of my head by inches.

I looked back up instantly, and I was glad I did. Almost the second Cannonball had gone for me, Stench had aimed a ball squarely at him. I was just in time to see it smack him right in the middle of his big, round belly.

"All this does is change the position that I'm going to be clobbering you from, Powerless Boy." He said as he passed me on his way to jail. "Your team is rotten, and we're gonna cream you."

I could hardly disagree as I gazed around at a scene of utter confusion and panic.

Cannonball's team currently controlled three of the balls. Sparkplug had one, and Transparent Girl had another. They both were targeting Puddle Boy, who froze in place, blocking his face with his hands. A huge puddle formed beneath his feet, just as both balls hit him.

Cannonball, behind us in the jail, had the third ball. I know he wanted to hit me, but I zipped one way and then another, making it impossible for him to get a clear shot. Instead, he focused on the Human Sponge, who let out a shriek when she noticed. Her first reaction was to run, but she didn't see where she was going and she tripped and landed right in the middle of the liquid that Puddle Boy had just left on the floor.

"EEEWWWW!" she screamed as the liquid was instantly absorbed. Even worse, her head quickly expanded to double its normal size, creating a target that Cannonball couldn't have missed if he'd tried. Sure enough, the ball squished into her head moments later.

"You're next, Odd Boy." Cannonball laughed, clearly impressed by what in reality was a fairly poor ability to make up insulting names.

The trouble was even our good players couldn't hit most of Cannonball's players. I watched Tadpole use his fully extended tongue to whip one of the balls right into a cloud of fog, but it passed through to the other side. Stench kept throwing balls at Sparkplug but the balls bounced off his force field an inch before touching him. And while Plasma Girl was doing a great job avoiding getting hit (after all, she could dissolve into a pile of protoplasm at the first sign of trouble), she was having no luck finding Transparent Girl to hit her.

Back with his team, Cannonball got his hands on a ball and wasted no time getting me in his sights.

I braced myself for the impact . . . and then something amazing happened. The ball barreled into my chest . . . and I caught it!

"You might as well get used to jail, you creep," I taunted as he passed me on his way to jail. "You'll be spending plenty of time there when you're older."

I was so proud of both my catch and my comment that I almost didn't notice that an adult was standing on the sidelines observing us. It was as if he had appeared from nowhere.

"Principal Doppelganger!" I said in surprise.

I was relieved. Surely he would put a stop to this unsanctioned dodgeball game before anyone was harmed further. Unfortunately, I thought wrong.

"Don't mind me," he said in his usual humorless tone. "I'm just watching for a few minutes. Go on with your game."

No one wanted to chance playing at full brutality with the principal standing there. This was especially true since none of us really knew what Principal Doppelganger's power was, and that always kept us on guard.

As the game resumed, I was still holding the ball Cannonball had hurled at me. I turned to throw it at someone else, but in the middle of the ball's arc toward Sparkplug, it suddenly came to a halt. Only then did I notice the faint outline of the person who'd caught it.

"Transparent Girl!" I hollered.

"Get your behind to jail," she ridiculed. "You . . . are . . . out!"

How humiliating. My throw was so feeble even a girl could catch it. Thank goodness she was nearly invisible. Maybe nobody else saw it. Then I glanced at Principal Doppelganger. It was impossible to make out his face, but I got the distinct impression he was smirking at me.

"Ha-ha!" Lobster Boy laughed as I arrived in jail. "O Boy got knocked out by a girl."

"Just ignore him," a voice said behind me.

I turned to see Plasma Girl, also on her way to jail.

NAME: Principal Doppelganger. **POWER:** Classified. But it's probably not what you think it is. **LIMITATIONS:** Hard to say—which is exactly why he keeps it a secret from his intimidated students at Watson Elementary. **CAREER:** Little is known about Doppelganger prior to his employment as principal, possibly due to his ability to come and go remarkably quickly. **CLASSIFICATION:** Possibly a major power—if it ever becomes known.

Moving away from Lobster Boy, the two of us went over by Hal.

"We're getting clobbered," he commented quietly.

He was right. The only members of our team still alive were Tadpole, Stench, Limber Lass and . . . Puddle Boy? How did he get out of jail? Well, I guess anything was possible.

"Let's get back over there and help them!" Plasma Girl insisted.

"First we've got to get a ball back here," I said.

"Stench," she hollered across the gym. "Throw a ball back."

Stench had one, but he threw it to deflect one coming straight at him from Foggybottom. Then it rolled out of bounds, coming to rest at the feet of Principal Doppelganger. He picked it up and turned in my direction. Without saying a word, he cocked his arm and threw the ball right toward me. But it passed clear over my head and up onto the stage.

"I'll get it," I volunteered. I jumped onto the platform to chase it and caught a glimpse of the white ball as it disappeared into the shadows, rolling toward some curtains at the back of the stage.

I shifted the curtains aside and noticed a small hole in the back wall of the stage. Kneeling down, I peered inside and saw light coming from somewhere. As my hand pressed against the wall alongside the hole, it budged slightly, and I realized it was actually a hatch cover of some kind.

I stood up and felt around the edge of the hatch.

With a firm grip on both sides, I yanked it, and it easily came loose.

Crouching back down, I crawled into the space. Thanks to the mysterious light source, what should have been total darkness was brighter than I expected. Then I noticed that the illumination was coming in through a grate at the base of the wall. I crawled over and looked through the grate. What I saw there was utterly fascinating.

CHAPTER THREE

A Peek into the Past

I barely noticed as Hal and Plasma Girl crawled up behind me. I was transfixed by what I was seeing through the slits of the grate.

"Gosh," Halogen Boy whispered. "We can see into Coach Inflato's office."

"Shhh!" I instructed. Hal was right, though. We were situated above the coach's office, and we could see right down into it.

Plasma Girl looked over at Hal and me with an expression that basically said, *Isn't this SO cool?* We would have nodded in agreement, but just then Coach Inflato did something that left us dumbstruck. He slumped down in his chair, and then he let out his breath as if he'd been holding it for hours. Not only did his muscle-bound body deflate like an empty balloon, but he actually flew up out of his chair and briefly ricocheted around the room. After settling to the ground, he got back up on his now-skinny and wobbly legs and reseated himself in his chair.

"He's all hot air!" I mouthed to my two teammates, who were equally astounded.

We watched as our now deflated coach reached for a bag of Dr. Telomere's Caramel-Coated Potato Chips and struggled mightily to tear it open. Just when we thought that the bag was going to win the battle, it suddenly ripped all the way down the front and potato chips went flying everywhere.

"Can you believe that Coach Inflato is really a deflated wimp?" I whispered.

"Why would anyone pretend to be something he's not?" Plasma Girl asked seriously. She hasn't figured out yet that guys almost always pretend to be something they're not.

I turned to Halogen Boy and found him practically doubled over in hysterics. He was doing a great job of keeping his laughter silent.

The only problem was that he was getting brighter and brighter the more he tried to hold it in. It wasn't exactly a blinding light, but the last thing we needed was for Coach Inflato to realize we were spying on him.

I backed up against the grate in an attempt to block the light, and that's when I noticed our surroundings. The first thing that caught my eye was a poster on one of the walls. It was hand lettered as if it had been created by a kid. It said THE JUNIOR LEAGUERS. My friends noticed the astonishment on my face and turned to look.

"Who could have put up a sign for the Junior Leaguers?" I whispered. "*We're* the Junior Leaguers!"

"I've never been in here before," Plasma Girl said with equal conviction. "And look! There's even a Hall of Trophies, just like ours!"

Sure enough, in a corner of the space was an upside-down shoe box with the words "Hall of Trophies" sloppily written on it in marker. Sitting on top of the box were a couple of odd items like a knitting needle and a packet of flower seeds. But one object in particular caught my eye. It was a rock the size of a large fist, partially wrapped in a piece of newspaper. And the part of the rock that was exposed was glowing. In fact it appeared to be getting even brighter.

Then I looked up and realized it was Halogen Boy who was getting brighter. He had been doing it so that he and Plasma Girl could look more closely at the team's handmade sign.

"There's more written here," Hal informed us. "It also lists the group's members."

"Who are they?" Plasma Girl probed.

"It says, 'Friends Forever,'" he read slowly and deliberately, "'Funnel Boy, InvisiBoy, the Great Inflato, and . . . Meteor Boy!"

"Meteor Boy?!" Plasma Girl and I said in unison.

I wished we'd said it more quietly, but I took a quick peek through the grate and saw that the coach was still crawling around under his desk in an attempt to retrieve his scattered potato chips.

A week ago, the name Meteor Boy would have meant nothing to us. We hadn't known about him because the Amazing Indestructo had gone to great lengths to keep the name from ever being mentioned. You see, Meteor Boy had briefly been his sidekick. That was at the start of AI's own career, when having a kid as a partner was considered a trendy thing to do. Unfortunately, Meteor Boy, despite his awesome ability to fly as fast as a meteor, vanished in a mysterious explosion the first time he and AI took on Professor Brain-Drain.

From that day on, AI, who was racked with guilt over his failure to protect his young sidekick, did everything he could to make sure the public never saw any further reminders of Meteor Boy. And for over two decades he was successful. People who had been around at the time hadn't completely forgotten him, but with nothing to remind them, their memories faded. Then something happened that AI hadn't expected. The Amazing Indestructo's business partner, a guy named the Tycoon, allowed Meteor Boy to be included in the set of AI collector cards that my friends and I had spent the entire past week searching for. The Tycoon had printed only ten of the cards, but that small number had had a large effect. They had become collector's items, and now Meteor Boy was once again fresh in people's minds. AI had been furious . . . and guilt-ridden . . . just not both at the same time.

"Coach Inflato and Meteor Boy were on a team together as kids?" Plasma Girl hissed under her breath.

"Along with some kids named Funnel Boy and InvisiBoy," Halogen Boy added helpfully. "Who are they?"

"I've never heard of InvisiBoy," I admitted, "but I think I know who Funnel Boy was." I fished my copy of the *Li'l Hero's Handbook* from my back pocket. "My dad mentioned him to me once. I think he was a junior sidekick to Zephyr, one of the founding members of the League of Ultimate Goodness."

I flipped through the pages and soon came to Funnel Boy. It said: *See* Cyclotron. I flipped back a bunch of pages and found an entry about a villain named Cyclotron.

"Wow, a kid who fought alongside the original League of Ultimate Goodness ended up going bad." Plasma Girl shook her head in amazement. "It just goes to show that you never know how you're going to turn out."

I was about to look up InvisiBoy, when I heard

NAME: Cyclotron. **POWER:** The ability to whip up tornado-like funnels of wind. **LIMITATIONS:** About category three in strength. **CAREER:** As Funnel Boy, Cyclotron battled crime as Zephyr's sidekick. He later turned to crime, working occasionally with Professor Brain-Drain against the Amazing Indestructo. **CLASSIFICATION:** A powerful villain, with a fixation on humiliating AI.

shouting from the gymnasium and remembered our dodgeball game. Our teammates had to be missing us.

"Come on," I said to Hal and Plasma Girl, "let's get back to the game."

Following my two friends, I was about to crawl back through the hole, but then I stopped. Don't ask me why, but I turned and grabbed the glowing stone wrapped in newspaper from the Hall of Trophies.

Back on the stage, I shoved the rock into my pocket, and quickly moved one of the curtains to cover the hole. Without looking back, I ran to get into my team's jail just in time to see our final humiliation. Every one of our players was there except Stench.

"What happened?" I asked Tadpole, who was hollering for Stench to throw him a ball.

"They clobbered us!" he said in disgust.

I watched with admiration as Stench successfully avoided one ball after another. But there was just no way he could keep avoiding four balls.

Sure enough, the inevitable happened when Cannonball and the Quake caught him in a triangulation move along with . . . Melonhead? . . . who was back in jail. Even with Melonhead's lack of athletic ability, Stench didn't have a chance with all three balls headed for him at once. The first smacked against the back of his shoulder, the second missed him altogether, and the third skimmed off the top of his head from the front.

The other team's jubilation was short-lived, however, as Stench momentarily lost control and an invisible cloud of noxious gas drifted toward the victors.

"That is so disgusting!" Transparent Girl's jubilation was replaced by a shriek of horror. Like a canary in a coal mine, she served as an early warning for her teammates, who all ran to the opposite side of the court in an attempt to get out of harm's way.

At that moment Coach Inflato returned, once again fully inflated, just as the bell rang signaling the end of class.

CHAPTER FOUR

Half-baked Science

All the way back from gym class, Stench and Tadpole grumbled over our embarrassing dodgeball defeat. Cannonball couldn't resist hurling taunts and insults at us right up to the door of Miss Marble's classroom.

They were quickly silenced, however, when we found Principal Doppelganger standing with Miss Marble at the front of the room. In a sudden burst of wishful thinking, I imagined that he was here to tell us that he was firing Coach Inflato for gross incompetence and dereliction of duty. Silently and calmly we filed in and took our seats.

"Sure, you all shut up for him," Miss Marble vented, "but if it were just me, you'd be screaming your heads off."

Miss Marble has some issues, but she's really a pretty good teacher. I'm not sure how old she is. My friends and I generally lump everyone who's between twenty and sixty into one big group (old) and everyone above sixty into another (really old). But if I had to guess, I'd say she's somewhere in her late forties. She has a power that comes in pretty handy for her. She can freeze anyone she wants in a brief state of suspended animation. With a class full of unruly fifth graders, she ends up using her power quite a bit.

"Principal Doppelganger is here today to tell us all about a very exciting upcoming event," Miss Marble continued without a trace of excitement in her voice. "Despite the fact that it's only October, it involves the school's annual spring science fair and bake sale."

This piqued my curiosity. The science fair always took place in the spring. About five years ago they had begun holding it jointly with the school bake sale. It made a lot of sense. The baked goods weren't even remotely good enough to draw people in by themselves. But if they were offered at the science fair (which most parents felt obligated to attend), people would end up flocking to the cakes and pies just to get away from the inevitable pea plant experiments and baking soda volcanoes. Bake sale sales skyrocketed the first year, and stayed that way ever since.

"First of all, how many of you kids are familiar with the famous artist Crispo?" the principal asked. His use of the adjective *famous* was his hint that he expected us all to know who Crispo is. I started to raise my hand, but when I noticed that nobody else's hands were moving, I discreetly slipped mine back under my desk.

"Nobody, eh?" he said as his black mask of a face appeared to look directly at me. "Well, let me just give you a brief biography of Superopolis's greatest artist.

"Crispo began his career nearly twenty-five years ago by making art out of potato chips. In fact, that's how he got his name. Of course I'm not saying he used potato chips to create the art. What he did was use potato chips as the *subject* of his art. Initially, he did paintings of potato chips. From there he moved onto his famous potato chip mobiles and eventually to his potato chip sculptures, which I'm sure you've all seen throughout Superopolis."

Even the dumbest kids in my class had seen the potato chip sculptures all over town, but I guess nobody else had wondered where they came from. I had been fascinated by them as a little kid, so I was familiar with Crispo's potato chip period, even though I didn't know that much about the artist himself. But it was some of the projects that came later that most impressed me. Principal Doppelganger must have read my mind.

"Of course, it was the works that came later that were most impressive. Projects such as filling Superopolis Harbor with giant rubber ducks and covering MegaManly Beach with millions of miniature cocktail umbrellas; and of course you all remember his most recent extravaganza, decorating Mount Reliable to resemble a giant fudge sundae."

Everyone in my class remembered that one! After all, how many times in a kid's life does an active volcano erupt whipped cream?

"Well," Principal Doppelganger continued, "the exciting news is that Crispo is once again at work on another enormous project. I can't tell you where or what it is just yet, but given Crispo's reputation, it's sure to be exciting!

"What's even more thrilling," the principal continued, "is that I've made a proposal to stage our science fair and bake sale on the same day that Crispo will unveil his new creation—and that proposal has been accepted!"

He paused for what he expected to be a spontaneous outburst of excitement, but he had seriously overestimated my classmates' interest in the arts. Everyone sat silent.

"And with so many people attending these multiple events," he continued in an attempt to spur the sort of hubbub he wanted, "we expect our bake sale to bring in at least triple what it normally does."

"Yippee!"

We all turned in surprise to look at Miss Marble. I guess her excitement was understandable since the money from the bake sale goes to help the teachers buy school supplies. Of course, school supplies, according to our teachers' definition of the term, meant things like fully stocked refrigerators and snack cupboards in the teachers' lounge. But back to Principal Doppelganger. So far, with the exception of me and Miss Marble, his big announcement had been a big flop.

"And did I mention the celebrity judges who will be reviewing your science experiments?" he announced with an air of desperation. "They'll include Crispo himself . . ."

My classmates all sat as still as five rows of Crispo potato chip sculptures.

". . . And the Amazing Indestructo."

The class erupted in a frenzy of cheers and applause, but I was looking at my teammates, none of whom was joining in the commotion. Don't get me wrong. A week ago, all of us would have been cheering, too. But we had all recently seen firsthand how unworthy of admiration the Amazing Indestructo really was. None of our classmates knew this, though, and frankly, none of them would have believed us even if we'd told them. As a result, the noise continued to grow even as the principal tried to keep talking.

"Let me handle this," I heard Miss Marble shout to her flustered boss.

I got as comfortable as I could in my seat and waited for the inevitable. Sure enough, seconds later I felt my body tense and freeze up as Miss Marble exercised her power on my unsuspecting classmates. Of course I couldn't turn my head to see what had happened behind me, but the kids within my line of sight had been caught in some incredibly uncomfortable-looking poses.

"There you go," she said to the principal, who

looked us over with a combination of what I can only imagine was relief and pity.

"Uh, thank you," he said. "As I was saying, this is an exciting opportunity. Of course, it will require some additional effort on all our parts."

Uh-oh, I thought.

"In this case," he continued, "the challenge will be the amount of time that we have to prepare for this big event. I know that in the past you've had as much as four weeks to prepare your projects. Unfortunately, Crispo's new masterpiece is set to be unveiled next Thursday, October seventeenth."

"Are you insane?!" Miss Marble exploded in surprise.

She would have had lots of backup from us, if we weren't all still in a state of suspended animation.

"Oh, I'm sure they can do it," Principal Doppelganger said. "And just keep thinking about that bake sale."

He then leaned in and whispered something in Miss Marble's ear. Despite her shock, she nodded numbly in response. Then, returning his attention to the class of statues, he added, "Miss Marble will now group you all in teams of two. And let me just tell you all how proud I know you'll make me."

We all began to come out of our suspended states, but were still stunned by the amount of work that would be expected of us in order to get our projects completed in just six days. Little did I know that for me, things were about to get even worse.

"However," the principal interrupted, "I need to speak with one of you privately. Melonhead, could you come with me?"

"Thertainly, thir," he splattered. He never missed a chance to suck up to a school official. "It'th my pleathure!"

"Before you come with me, though, I think Miss Marble should tell you your partner," he added, tipping his head toward our teacher.

At first, I thought this was a good thing. With Melonhead's partner being picked from the entire class, there was only a one-in-twenty-one chance of getting stuck with him. One poor sucker would have to deal with his ego and incompetence, not to mention an uncontrollable output of watermelon seeds. Thankfully, the chance that I might be that unlucky individual was slim.

Then I noticed Miss Marble looking directly at me.

CHAPTER FIVE

A Double-Dip Disaster

Man, I couldn't believe my bad luck getting stuck with Melonhead as my science fair partner!

Plasma Girl had ended up with Little Miss Bubbles as her partner, and the two of them were already giggling with each other as they discussed a variety of girly projects ranging from flower anatomy to the use of snowflake patterns as tea doilies. I suggested they should use some of their dolls to demonstrate the amputation and reattachment of limbs, but they just glared at me.

Stench and Tadpole had been lucky enough to be partnered. They were currently huddled in a way that made it look like they were planning their project, but in reality I knew they were discussing dodgeball strategy.

The only member of my team that I think was in a position equal to my own was Halogen Boy. His partner was Cannonball. Even now I could see Hal brightening and dimming himself at Cannonball's command, and I could tell the fat creep was up to no good.

While I waited for Melonhead to return, my mind turned back to the mystery of Meteor Boy and the rock I had discovered. I retrieved the rock from my pocket and carefully unwrapped the piece of newspaper that partially covered it. Unfolding it, I was startled to see that it was a photo of Funnel Boy, Inflato, Meteor Boy, and InvisiBoy. They were holding a much larger version of the rock I now held in my hands. Shoving his way into the middle of this group of kids was none other than the Amazing Indestructo—a much younger Amazing Indestructo. The caption for the photo identified the four boys but didn't mention AI at all. The kids had apparently foiled the robbery of a rare prodigium

meteorite from the Superopolis Museum.

I considered the rock, mentally weighing it and wondering what exactly it was. I had never heard of prodigium before. Could that be what this was? If only I could go back in time and ask these kids what the deal was.

Then an idea struck me. A time machine! Why not invent a time machine for our science fair project? Of course, the realist in me said, *Are you nuts? No one has ever invented a time machine and there's no way you're going to be the first—especially with Melonhead as your partner.*

As if on cue, Melonhead returned from Principal Doppelganger's office. "Ithn't thith ekthiting, O Boy?" he splattered as he sat down next to me. "All thortth of famouth people will be able to thee firththand how thmart I am."

Melonhead's sense of his own importance was so delusional that I was left speechless.

"And gueth what?" he continued without pause. "I've already chothen an idea for uth."

"What do you mean, *you've* chosen?" I sat up. I wasn't going to let this go by unchallenged. "This is a team project. We choose the subject together."

"Thimmer down, thilly," Melonhead said, clucking soothingly, as if he were trying to calm down a half-wit. "I'll thee to all the complekth thtuff mythelf."

Trying to argue with Melonhead was a lot like trying to say a tongue twister with a mouthful of peanut butter—no matter what you said, he heard something totally different. So I decided to ignore his misguided opinion of his abilities and jump right to the heart of the matter.

"So what is this brilliant idea of yours?" I asked.

"It'th thimple, really," he said with a smirk. "I'm going to conthtruct uth a time mathine."

The shock of hearing him suggest exactly what I had been thinking was drowned out by the sound of the last bell of the day ringing. Melonhead got up and began gathering his books. As I watched in amazement he turned to leave without another word.

"Where are you going, seed brain?" I hollered.

"When the latht bell ringth it meanth we can go," he explained as if this were my first day of school.

"What about the project?" I blurted. "We only have six days. We're going to need to work on it this weekend."

Melonhead looked at me as if I was the only obstacle between him and scientific immortality.

"Fine," he said with a sigh. "I thupothe you can come over to my houthe tomorrow morning if you feel you mutht."

It was clear to me that Melonhead would have been more than happy to take on this project all on his own and that he perceived me as an annoyance at best.

"I'll be there at eleven," I said.

As Melonhead walked off in a huff, I turned to find the rest of my team standing there waiting for me.

"We're so sorry," Plasma Girl said. "It's not fair that anyone gets stuck with Melonhead as a partner. Do you really have to meet with him tomorrow?"

"Why?" I asked.

"We thought we would move our normal Sunday meeting of the Junior Leaguers to Saturday," Stench said.

"Little Miss Bubbles and I have already agreed to meet about our project on Sunday," Plasma Girl explained.

"And Cannonball told me to be at his house then, or else," Hal added softly.

I can join you in the morning for a little while." I shrugged. "Even if we don't get any science fair work done, we can at least develop some dodgeball strategy."

"Definitely," promised Stench, "and I just wanted to apologize for picking Lobster Boy this afternoon when I should have picked you."

"That's okay. I know you thought you were doing the right thing," I said. "But we have to figure out some way to beat those guys next time."

"Just like I said," Tadpole jumped in, already working himself into a state of agitation. "That creep Cannonball has gotta be taught a lesson or we're never gonna hear the end of it."

Tadpole continued to rant and fume about our loss as we made our way out of school. We were barely past the front door when we all came to an immediate halt.

"Look at that!" Halogen Boy interrupted with a touch of awe in his voice.

There ahead of us, parked on the street right in front of school, was a big truck with what looked like a giant ice cream cone stuck on the top of it. Its bell rang and we all began moving toward it.

"Mmm, ice cream," Hal muttered. I looked around and noticed that the ice cream truck was attracting kids like mosquitoes to a blood bank. Moving closer I noticed that it had a window on the side, but the inside of the window looked like it was coated with frost. Then, suddenly, the window slid open to reveal . . .

"Uncle Fluster?" I said with complete surprise.

"OB?" He looked momentarily perplexed. "What are you doing here?"

"Umm . . . this is my school." I answered.

"Of course." He laughed. "This is a school. That's why I'm here."

Uncle Fluster is my mother's twin brother. Just like my mom, his power falls into the low-temperature category. But unlike my mother, who can focus her freezing powers into an intense beam with her gaze, her brother radiates it from his entire body so its effects are mostly dissipated. Unfortunately, his mental power seems to dissipate in the same manner, leaving him almost constantly confused. That's where his name came from. When he was born, his parents named him Frost, but it didn't take long for it to evolve into Fluster. He was always trying to be a success at something, and my guess was that this ice cream truck was his latest attempt.

"So what's with the ice cream truck?" I asked.

"I bought it a few weeks ago to turn it into a coffee wagon, but—"

NAME: Fluster. **POWER:** An ability to cool the air around him.
LIMITATIONS: An inability to turn his power off. **CAREER:**
Except for his first job as a cheap form of air-conditioning at
a movie theater, Fluster's career has been chilly at best.
CLASSIFICATION: A constant case of cold confusion.

"But people didn't like their coffee frozen," I finished.

"That's right!" he said, astonished. "But then I found this metal cone"—he pointed up to indicate the ten-foot-high cone mounted atop the truck—"and I got the idea to go into the ice cream business."

"It certainly seems appropriate," I agreed.

"It's brilliant, isn't it?" he said with a sly wink. "I've found that if I stay inside the truck, my body chill keeps the interior the perfect temperature for producing ice cream. I've been experimenting for weeks to develop a whole range of interesting new flavors right here in my ice cream laboratory. In fact that's how I came up with the name of my business."

I looked where he pointed, and there was the name painted right on the side of the truck.

"The Creamatory?" I blurted out in disbelief.

"Isn't it perfect?" He beamed. "It's a combination of *ice cream* and *laboratory*."

"So it is," I agreed, not knowing what else to say.

"Now what can I get you?" he asked. "My treat."

I wasn't sure I wanted to be my uncle's first guinea pig. I decided to play it safe.

"Vanilla, please."

From the flustered look on his face, I knew I had thrown him a curveball.

"Umm, I don't have any vanilla."

"Chocolate?" I tried, with no success. "Neapolitan, fudge ripple, orange sherbert?"

Each time he shook his head.

"Well, what do you have?" I finally asked.

"I've just created a brand-new flavor I think you'll like." He lit up. "It's called moss."

"Moss ice cream?" I blurted out. "Who would want that?!"

The words weren't out of my mouth for two seconds before the Spore spoke up.

"I'll take one," he huffed breathlessly as he came forward to the window.

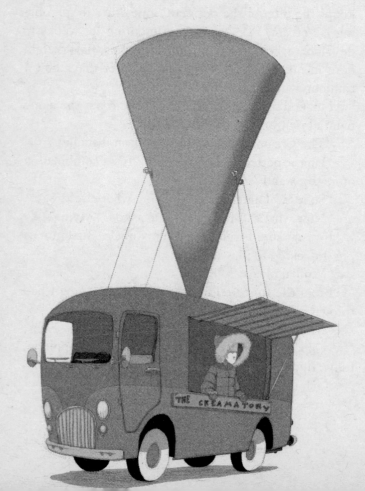

Uncle Fluster gave me a smug look as he scooped two dips of a greenish, speckled ice cream onto a cone and handed it to the eagerly waiting Spore.

"That'll be fifty cents," he said proudly.

The Spore dug a couple of quarters out of his pocket as he eagerly licked at the disgusting-looking cone.

"Who's next?" Uncle Fluster asked confidently.

My classmates immediately began backing away from the truck. I don't know if it was out of fear of my uncle's ice cream creations or because a group of five seedy-looking villains had just dropped out of the sky and were now hovering above Uncle Fluster's truck. I assumed they were villains because they looked really nasty. But the oddest thing of all was they appeared to have arrived here on a rainbow.

CHAPTER SIX

A Blast from the Past

Unlike a regular rainbow, this one was upside down and was carrying these villains as if they were sitting on a swing. As it lowered itself to the ground, its five passengers hopped off and surrounded my uncle's truck.

"That's right, little lemmings," said one of them. He had long, scraggly gray hair and lightning-bolt sunglasses. He pulled out a ukulele and began strumming it. "Just back away and do as I warn you. The Commune for Justice is here to inform you."

Although his verse was bad, the music was calming and I blissfully backed off along with my classmates. I also retrieved my copy of the *Li'l Hero's Handbook* to find out who the Commune for Justice was.

Hmm. Inactive hippies. So what were they doing here? I'd already figured out that the one with the ukulele must be Bliss. Meanwhile, the five villains had

TEAM NAME: The Commune for Justice. **MEMBERS:** Bliss, SkyDiamond, Aquarius, Rainbow Rider, and the Hammer. **PROFILE:** This Commune's idea of justice apparently meant rebelling against a society that expected them to bathe, get jobs, and take responsibility for their own actions. **CAREER HIGHLIGHT:** The Commune for Justice committed only one known theft—which was apparently all it took for them to realize that crime was work, too. **STATUS:** Inactive—as one would tend to expect.

turned back to Uncle Fluster's truck. We all stood and watched helplessly as they unleashed everything they had.

One woman started wrapping the ice cream truck in multiple rainbow bands. She apparently had the ability to manipulate rainbows and make them solid. However she did it, she had Uncle Fluster trapped inside.

"Good work, Rainbow Rider," said the other woman. "Now let him sample the power of Aquarius!"

Aquarius focused her attention on the truck, and Uncle Fluster looked down in alarm.

"Hey, where's this leak coming from?" he shouted as I saw a whirling cascade of water begin to churn around him.

"We're here for two reasons, capitalist," shouted the woman named Aquarius. "One is for your profits, so toss them out to us."

"But I haven't made any profits," protested my uncle as the water swished around him. "Business has been awful!"

"Profits are for the people, man. Don't disrespect it." Bliss said in an oddly relaxed manner. "You owe the people their share. We're just here to collect it." He turned to the biggest member of his team, who so far had just stood there silently. "Hammer, show him how society gets its share."

The Hammer began swinging his fist against the side of Uncle Fluster's truck as if it were . . . well, a hammer.

Uncle Fluster covered his ears as the pounding got louder and louder.

"Stop it! Stop it!" he began to holler. "I'll give you everything I've earned so far."

A few seconds later, the fifty cents he had made from selling a moss ice cream cone to the Spore came clinking onto the road. The Hammer paused as Bliss stepped forward and examined the two quarters lying on the ground.

"This is it?" he said with undisguised disgust. "We've got a trip planned, and it's not in our head. But if we're gonna take it, we gotta have bread."

"I don't have any bread," my uncle insisted, "but you might like one of my newest flavors—yeast!"

"Don't toy with us, proprietor," Aquarius shouted as she prepared to unleash a new torrent of water.

"Stay away from him!" I shouted, breaking free of my blissful trance. The entire Commune for Justice turned and stared at me. But before they could say anything, a loud noise from the sky distracted them.

"Step back, kids!" I heard someone shout. "The League of Ultimate Goodness is here to save the day!"

I looked up, and to my complete surprise, it was the Crimson Creampuff hurtling toward the ground. I dodged out of the way just in time as he landed with a soft, mushy thud right where I had been standing. Glancing up, I could see the Heliocopter he had fallen from. The League of Ultimate Goodness had indeed come to our rescue—or at least their idea of a rescue.

"You have one chance to surrender peacefully," the

53

Crimson Creampuff intoned as he got to his feet, "or face the might of the League of Ultimate Goodness."

"Us in the slammer? Show him, Hammer," Bliss answered with a lazy strum on his ukulele.

The Hammer lunged forward and buried his fist deep in the Crimson Creampuff's stomach. But instead of doing any serious damage, his fist sank into the hero's mushy midsection. Yanking his fist free, he punched again with similar result.

"Ha-ha-ha," the hero laughed, "no one can penetrate the awesome power of the Crimson Creampuff!"

In one sense he was right. No one could take a thrashing like he could. The problem was that he had no idea how to fight back, so basically he just stood there getting beat up as the rest of the villains joined in the pummeling. Before long, though, the Helio-copter bearing the rest of the league members had landed, and the Crimson Creampuff was joined by his comrades.

"Git yer filthy paws off the Creampuff!"

I turned to see Whistlin' Dixie leading a charge of three other members of the league. In addition to the siren of south Superopolis (who could whistle anything in perfect tune), I also recognized Major Bummer, named for his ability to depress anyone near him rather than for his enormous rear end; Spaghetti Man, who could fire long strands of spaghetti from his fingertips; and the Human Compass, who could always tell you which direction was north. Individually they were no threat to villains, but together . . . well, they still

NAME: Crimson Creampuff, The. **POWER:** Has a body the consistency of a creampuff. **LIMITATIONS:** Has a body the consistency of a creampuff. **CAREER:** Fired from his first job at a bakery when it was discovered he didn't actually have a creamy center, he went on to form the squishy core of the League of Ultimate Goodness. **CLASSIFICATION:** World's greatest punching bag.

weren't much of a threat. You see, the League of Ultimate Goodness was really the backup team for the Amazing Indestructo. And he had basically hand-picked them with one thought in mind: to make him look awesome in comparison.

"I'll restrain the fiend who's attacking the Crimson Creampuff," declared Spaghetti Man as he struck a heroic pose, pointed his fingers, and produced multiple strands of pasta that wrapped themselves around the Hammer loop after loop. Before the villain knew what had happened he found himself almost completely encased in ropes of spaghetti. Of course, the coils were only as strong as wet spaghetti, so a second later he had broken free to continue pounding the Crimson Creampuff.

In the meantime, Whistlin' Dixie unlatched her handy lasso and let it whistle through the air to land directly on Rainbow Rider. Pulling the rope tight, she began hauling the hippie toward her to the accompaniment of a perfectly whistled version of "Git Along, Little Dogies." The rainbow bands encircling Uncle Fluster's truck vanished almost immediately when Rainbow Rider's attention was diverted.

"The truck is free! It's just slightly north by northwest of us," shouted the Human Compass, as if this information was even the least bit useful to anyone.

Bliss began running for the truck. Before he could get very far, though, he ran smack into Major Bummer and fell to the ground.

"You've ruined my afternoon," grumped the Major.

"I had an appointment to have my back waxed and now I'll have to reschedule."

"Don't be down, feeling crappy," Bliss said soothingly from where he sat. "You deserve to be more happy."

"I'll show you my happy side," Major Bummer said as he turned and sat on top of the startled hippie, practically crushing him with his enormous behind.

Bliss's power (apparently the ability to make people feel happy and mellow) had had no effect. Of course, it might have just meant that the Major was happiest when he was depressed.

"SkyDiamond, baby, you bashful flower" Bliss's muffled voice cried out from beneath Major Bummer. "Now's the time to unleash your power."

Then I noticed the fifth member of the gang, who had been standing on the sideline. At Bliss's command, he threw off his big floppy hat and the poncho that was covering him, revealing a body made up of multiple glassy facets. I gasped as the sunlight hit one of them and six more SkyDiamonds appeared from nowhere. A second later they all moved to join in the attack.

As impossible as it may have seemed, the League of Ultimate Goodness had actually been winning for a moment. But now, with six additional copies of SkyDiamond joining the fight, things had turned in the favor of the crooks. The league needed help.

"Junior Leaguers!" I hollered. "Let's get 'em!"

Whatever trance my team had been placed in by Bliss, it vanished at the sound of my voice, and they dove into battle. Stench was there first, picking up one of the SkyDiamond duplicates and hurling it against two others. Tadpole's tongue, meanwhile, snaked out and wrapped itself around the legs of another duplicate, pulling them out from under him. I glanced over and saw Halogen Boy taking a drink of apple juice from his sippy cup. I knew that he would soon be illuminating himself to an extreme magnitude of brightness to blind our attackers. Usually, this was a good thing, but in this case it was the worst possible idea. I didn't know how many copies of himself SkyDiamond was able to create, but I sensed that it was light that allowed him to do it. And Hal was about to give him oodles of it.

"Plasma Girl!" I yelled. "Cover SkyDiamond—the original one!"

She knew immediately what I was worried about and ran right for the multifaceted hippie. As Halogen Boy began to grow brighter, a grin began to appear on SkyDiamond's face. It was quickly obscured as Plasma Girl turned to goo and flung herself onto the villain, spreading herself over him like a thick coating of frosting. His copies all vanished.

The battle swung back in favor of the League of Ultimate Goodness. But just when I thought we were about to finally wrap things up, an enormous funnel cloud appeared out of thin air. As its winds whipped around, it settled toward the ground, knocking everyone over who was near it. Then suddenly the winds came to a halt and the funnel cloud vanished, revealing a lone figure.

"Cyclotron," I whispered to myself. What was Meteor Boy's now-villainous former teammate doing here?

"Must I do everything myself?" Cyclotron said to the members of the Commune for Justice who were within earshot. "Even without that loathsome Amazing Indestructo, this league of incompetents is making fools of you."

The hippies took full advantage of the confusion his appearance caused. Free of Dixie's lasso, Rainbow Rider cast an enormous rainbow that arced up to the

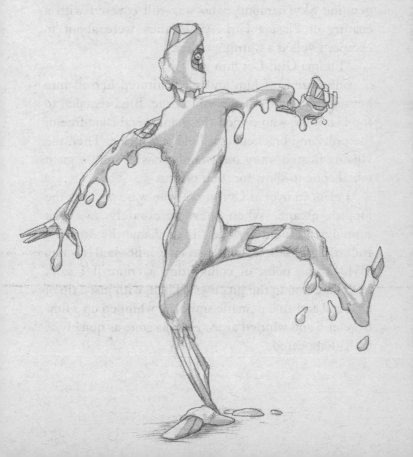

top of Uncle Fluster's ice cream truck. She glided up it and came to a stop atop the truck.

"Hammer!" shouted Aquarius. "Rescue Bliss!"

Reluctantly turning his attention from the Crimson Creampuff, the Hammer charged toward Major Bummer. Being if nothing else a realist, Major Bummer saw that he wouldn't be able to withstand the oncoming attack. So he calmly stood up and stepped to the side.

Bliss and the rest of his gang scurried up the rainbow until they were all standing next to the giant cone atop the Creamatory. The last to join them was the genuine SkyDiamond, who was still covered with a coating of Plasma Girl. Afraid they were about to escape, I yelled a warning to her.

"Plasma Girl! Let him go!"

She oozed off him and reconstituted herself into her normal shape. At the same time, Bliss signaled to the Hammer, who ripped the giant metal cone free of the bolts and brackets that held it in place. Then the villains floated away on a rainbow with only a giant metal cone to show for their efforts.

I glanced over at Cyclotron, who was watching the hippies escape. When they were safely away, he turned and caught my eye. "It's a shame the Amazing Indestructo didn't show his face," he said to me. "What's the point of committing a crime if I can't humiliate him in the process?" Then, with just a tip of his head and an enigmatic smile, he whipped up a funnel cloud and whirled away. He was gone as quickly as he had appeared.

The members of the League of Ultimate Goodness were suddenly left with no more villains to battle.

"We did it," shouted the Crimson Creampuff, breaking the uncomfortable silence. "We saved the day without any help from AI."

"An *al dente* victory, indeed!" agreed Spaghetti Man.

"It marks a new direction for all of us," proclaimed the Human Compass.

"Are you crazy?" I felt the need to speak up. "They got away!"

"Along with my giant ice cream cone," pointed out Uncle Fluster.

Major Bummer just sighed and rolled his eyes, while Whistlin' Dixie watched the receding villains, a look of concern on her face that I couldn't help but share.

CHAPTER SEVEN

A Word from Our Sponsor

When I finally got home, I walked in to find my dad stuffing a Maximizer brand Superdoodler into his mouth.

"How wuf skul, son?" he asked with his mouth full of snack cake.

"It was fine," I fibbed. "On the way home, though, Cyclotron and a group of really old hippies tried to rob Uncle Fluster's new ice cream truck. The League of Ultimate Goodness showed up to save the day. So of course the crooks got away."

"Oh, no." My dad swallowed the last of his mouthful. "He should have called on the New New Crusaders for help!"

"I don't think he even knows you exist," I replied. "After all, you only formed the group a few days ago."

"But we've had all this great press," my father insisted, holding up yesterday's edition of *The Hero Herald*. The headline blared: AMAZING INDESTRUCTO SAVES CITY. Below the headline in teensy-weensy type it added: With Help from Unidentified Heroes.

My dad seemed oblivious to the fact that his team was not only barely mentioned but also entirely unidentified. Personally, I thought this was a good thing since I couldn't believe what my dad was calling his team. It made them sound like a team of super stutterers. I decided to make my case.

"But no one knows your team's name," I tried to gently point out without hurting his feelings. "Maybe you should change it to something shorter and punchier."

"No, no, no," my dad said. "The name is just fine. What we really need is an endorsement deal. With someone behind us who can promote us there's no reason the New New Crusaders can't become the most famous team of superheroes in all Superopolis!"

As is often the case with my father, when he gets excited he tends to lose control of his power. The newspaper in his hands erupted in flames.

"My headline!" he shrieked, dropping the paper to the floor and attempting to stomp out the flames with his feet. Just then my mother arrived home with an armload of Mighty Mart shopping bags. Without blinking an eye or setting down the groceries, she focused her gaze on the burning heap of paper and froze it solid, extinguishing the flames in an instant.

"Thanks, honey," my dad said as he retrieved his

charred newspaper, now encased in a chunk of ice.

My mom was just coming home from her job at Corpsicle Coolant Corporation. She makes a lot of money there, which is a good thing, since my dad recently went back to being a superhero. It's hard to make money doing that without a corporate sponsor of some kind.

"Any progress today?" she asked as she began putting away the groceries.

"Windbag and I tried pitching our team to the board of directors at Fizzle Pharmaceuticals," he replied. "We thought we'd be the perfect representatives for their line of youth-enhancing vitamins, but they said we were too old."

"But they are made for people way older than you," I pointed out as I helped my mom unpack the groceries.

"That's what we told them," my father said with a shrug. "They said they only use heroes in their late teens and twenties to make people in their forties and older think that the pills will make them look and feel that age."

"Is anyone in the world honest?" I said to no one in particular.

"That's not the worst part," Dad continued. "They actually did end up offering us a sponsorship."

"Oh, dear," my mother said. "What was it for?"

"Their new line of adult diapers for over-the-hill heroes." He sighed in humiliation. "They've designed them to look like they're part of a hero's costume."

64

Mom and I glanced at each other across an uncomfortable silence. Neither of us knew what to say, so Mom just plunged ahead.

"I think you need to come up with some new ways to get your team some publicity," she suggested. "It's not an overnight process. Little by little the team's reputation will grow."

"I guess you're right." He sighed.

"And how was school, OB?" she asked, grateful to switch the subject.

Dad had asked me the same thing (but with his mouth full) and I had purposely avoided the question. Now with Mom home, I felt a little safer answering it.

"Principal Doppelganger moved the science fair from the spring all the way up to next week," I told her out of the corner of my mouth and in the softest voice possible. It wasn't enough, though. I could tell by the way my dad's ears perked up that he had heard what I'd said.

"What about the bake sale?" He jumped into the conversation. "Are they moving the bake sale, too?"

I knew this was coming. My dad *loves* the annual bake sale. Don't ask me why. Despite the fact that he uses the heat from his hands to cook most of our meals, I've never thought that he actually enjoys cooking. But for some reason he always looked forward to baking a cake for the school's annual fund-raiser. The problem is that he's not very good at baking and he almost always leaves the kitchen looking like a giant cupcake had exploded.

"Why are they having it so early?" my mother asked, glancing nervously at my father. Mom knew exactly who would be cleaning up the mess.

"They're turning it into a big deal this year to tie in to the unveiling of Crispo's new work," I explained. "They're even going to have celebrity judges for our projects."

"Celebrities?" My father lit up. "This is it!"

"What's it, Thermo?" my mom asked.

"That's how we'll get publicity. The New New Crusaders will participate in the bake sale. Don't you see? The place will be crawling with reporters."

"But they'll be focused on Crispo's new project," my mom pointed out. "Why would they pay any attention to the fact that your team baked a cake for the sale?"

"We're not going to bake just one cake . . . ," my dad said with a look of sly satisfaction on his face.

Mom and I glanced at each other nervously.

" . . . we're going to bake thousands!"

From that moment on there was no reasoning with him. He had focused on this cake-baking scheme and nothing would distract him from it. As Mom and I ate dinner, he began mapping out on paper his master plan for the coming week. When I made the mistake of telling him he should put it into a pie chart, he decided that he would also add thousands of pies to his program. Finally I decided to go to bed before I made the situation worse.

Emptying my pockets, I retrieved the chunk of

66

rock and removed the newspaper article it was wrapped in. Could this possibly be a piece of the rare prodigium meteorite mentioned in the clipping? I studied it closely for a minute and then set it next to the Oomphlifier on my nightstand. Examining the article once again, I looked at the photo. There was still one person pictured there who I wasn't familiar with. Getting out my copy of the *Li'l Hero's Handbook*, I turned to the "I's" in the "People" section.

Iconoclast, The Id (one of a trio of villains that included the Ego and the SuperEgo), Idle Eyes, Illusionist, Inflato, Inkblot . . . ah, here it was . . . InvisiBoy.

Vanished entirely? What was the deal with these kids? Meteor Boy was destroyed, Funnel Boy turned into a villain, and InvisiBoy vanished. And then there was Coach Inflato, who was just excessively annoying. Nothing seems to have gone well for any of them.

As I crawled into bed, my dad knocked on the door. I think he was really coming in to borrow my calculator to figure out how much he was going to need for ingredients, but when he saw me getting into bed he at least paused to say good night.

"Hey, hero," he said. "Going to bed already?"

"It's almost midnight," I pointed out.

"So it is," he said, glancing at my clock. "Hey, what's this?"

Picking up the chunk of rock I had found today, my dad weighed it in his hand.

"I found it wrapped up in this newspaper article," I

NAME: InvisiBoy. **POWER:** The ability to vanish entirely.
LIMITATIONS: Appears to lack any physical ability while invisible.
CAREER: A fearless daredevil throughout his teen years, his endeavors became increasingly risky, leading to an inevitable result.
CLASSIFICATION: Vanished entirely.

said. "But there's no date on it. Do you know when this happened?"

"Meteor Boy," he replied. "I do remember this event. The papers were full of news about Meteor Boy that weekend, and then that Sunday was the day he disappeared. I remember it because it was the same weekend I asked the Gemini Twins out for a date."

"Both of them?" I asked skeptically.

"Of course," he replied. "After all, they were inseparable then—literally. None of my friends thought I stood a chance since I was just sixteen, and they were both eighteen, but succeed I did! If you're lucky, you'll inherit my natural ability to attract the opposite sex."

As Dad elbowed me in the side, I tried to refocus the conversation.

"So that would have to have been twenty-five years ago," I said, doing the math. "Do you remember the date?"

"I'll never forget that date," he began to sigh, and then caught himself as I scowled at him. "Oh, you mean the day date. Of course. My date was on Saturday, October sixteenth. And Meteor Boy disappeared the next day, Sunday the seventeenth."

October seventeenth, I thought. The twenty-fifth anniversary of that event was coming up this Thursday—the exact same day as our science fair.

CHAPTER EIGHT

In Search of Meteor Boy

I woke up Saturday morning, and for the first time in my life did not get out of bed to rush downstairs to watch *The Amazing Adventures of the Amazing Indestructo* (*and the League of Ultimate Goodness*) on TV. I also woke up in my underwear, having abandoned the Amazing Indestructo pajamas that I had worn religiously since I was a little kid. I was determined to never put another dime in AI's pocket.

Getting out of bed, I was unaccustomed to the morning chill in the air so I quickly pulled on a pair of jeans and a white T-shirt. This was my normal "costume." After all, what else would a kid named Ordinary Boy wear?

When I came down for breakfast the kitchen was already a disaster area. There was no sign of Dad, but he was clearly up and about. The kitchen was filled

70

with stacks of cake pans, pie tins, cupcake trays, you name it.

"Morning, OB," I heard my mom say from behind one of the stacks. "How did you sleep?"

"Fine, thanks," I responded, looking around for her. Her head finally popped up above a stack of bread loaf pans. She had been bent over, getting the orange juice out of the refrigerator. As she poured me a glass and then gave it a good chill, I had to admit she was doing a good job of pretending that there was nothing odd going on in the kitchen. I moved a ring cake pan from one of the chairs so I could sit down. "So should I even ask what's happening here?"

My mom managed to hold the calm look on her face for a few more seconds and then it dropped like icicles off an awning.

"Your father is going around to all the houses in the neighborhood and borrowing every baking pan he can

get his hot little hands on." She started to seethe.

It's funny. My mom is one of the coolest people I know—and I don't just mean that literally. She's the living definition of calm, cool reason. In fact, the only person I've ever seen make her lose her cool is my father. To be honest, I kind of think that's one of the things she likes about him—not that I would ever tell her that!

In a sudden burst of frustration, she pushed a stack of pie tins onto the floor and sat down next to me at the table.

"Feel better?" I asked.

"Yes." She sighed as she let the tension flow out of her. "When he gets one of his crazy ideas I guess it's just best to get out of his way."

"That was my plan," I confided. "I have to get together with Melonhead later today, but this morning I'm meeting up with my team. I figure I might as well give them whatever help I can before I have to deal with my own unfortunate situation."

"Well, that's nice of you," my mother said, now back to her normally calm self.

"And I also wanted to do some research on Meteor Boy."

"Why Meteor Boy?" she asked. "That's a twenty-five-year-old event."

"I know," I admitted. "But I found out that Meteor Boy and his friends called themselves the Junior Leaguers. What do you suppose the chances of that are?"

"I don't think that's so strange," my mom replied.

"After all, twenty-five years ago the League of Ultimate Goodness was the most popular team, just like they are today. Those kids were probably modeling themselves after the league in the same way you and your team did."

"I guess that makes sense," I admitted.

Just then I heard an incredible metallic racket as a stack of cake tins tumbled through our kitchen door followed immediately by my father.

"I think I just about have enough," he announced as if we were as excited by his project as he was.

"That's my cue," my mother said as she stood up from the table. "I don't have any work to do at the office, but I'm going there to see what I can find anyway. I'll be back by dinner, assuming I can get into the kitchen."

"But honey . . . ," my father started to protest as she slipped out the door without another word. Then he turned his attention to me.

"Say, OB. You like to bake, don't you?" he said with that won't-this-be-fun look on his face that I had stopped buying into by the time I was three.

"Gee, Dad, I would," I lied. "But I have to plan my science fair project."

I backed out of the kitchen until I had cleared the doorway and then turned to bolt into the family room. There, out of sheer force of habit, I turned on the TV. I was just in time for the conclusion of *The Amazing Adventures of the Amazing Indestructo* (*and the League of Ultimate Goodness*), and what I saw just about made me choke. AI was on the screen making a live speech. Behind him was a huge banner that read: IN SEARCH OF METEOR BOY. Dumbfounded, I sank to the couch as his words thudded against my eardrums.

" . . . and that ultimate fantasy of every boy to fight crime alongside me, the Amazing Indestructo, will soon come true for one lucky winner. To go with the launch of our brand-new line of Meteor Boy action figures and toys, one lucky kid will win the chance to fight crime every week with me here on *The Amazing Adventures of the Amazing Indestructo*," AI boomed in his biggest superhero voice.

An off-camera voice whispered something to AI, who apparently thought he was finished.

"And the League of Ultimate Goodness," he finally added after a befuddled pause and in a far more lackluster tone.

I was already beginning to boil. AI had obviously decided to change his strategy about keeping Meteor Boy hush-hush, and was now preparing to exploit his long-gone sidekick for all he was worth. An announcer came on after AI.

"That's right, boys. Today only we will be holding auditions for the coveted role of Meteor Boy. One child will be selected to portray Meteor Boy both onscreen and at public promotional appearances. So streak like a meteor to the offices of Indestructo Industries by noon today for your chance to battle the forces of evil alongside the Amazing Indestructo himself."

I got up from the couch as outrage coursed through me. The announcer continued in a faster, quieter voice.

"MembersofScreenActorsEquityoranyotherunionareexcluded.Theroleof MeteorBoyisanon-payingrole;however,thewinnerwillbecontractuallyobligatedto appearwhereverandwheneverrequiredbyIndestructoIndustriesoritssubsidiariesor licensees.TheWinnerwillberesponsibleforbuyingandmaintaininghisownMeteor Boycostume. CostumewillbeavailableforpurchasethroughIndestructoIndustries. GirlsmayauditionaswellbutwillnotbechosenasMeteorBoyisaboy. IndestructoIndustriesisanequalopportunityemployer. MeteorBoyisaregistered trademarkofIndestructoIndustries."

AI had gone too far. And now he was going to answer for it.

CHAPTER NINE

The March of Science

Of course, *how* I was going to make the Amazing Indestructo, the most powerful hero in all Superopolis, answer for his actions was an entirely different question. I was so focused on it that I barely even noticed when the phone rang. My dad picked it up, then poked his head into the TV room.

"Some kid named Melonhead just called to cancel your meeting this afternoon," he informed me. "Well, actually he said he had to canthel it, but I'm sure he meant *cancel*. He said he could meet at the same time tomorrow, though."

Perfect, I thought. *Now I could use that time to deal with AI*. I bolted out of the house and headed for the tree house headquarters of the Junior Leaguers, situated in Stench's backyard.

I had only gotten about a block from home when I

heard a familiar tinkling bell coming up behind me. I turned around to find Uncle Fluster pulling up alongside me in his truck.

"Hi, OB," he greeted me brightly. "Can I give you a ride anywhere? I'm just on my way to Windbag's junkyard to get myself a new cone for the top of my truck. That's where I got the one that was stolen yesterday."

"Sure, Uncle Fluster!" I said as I hopped into the cab. "That's where I'm heading, too."

"Ahh," he responded, "there must be a meeting of the Junior Leaguers taking place this morning!"

"Very important business!" I said with every attempt at seriousness. But I couldn't hold it and we both started laughing. "Speaking of which, how's your business been?"

"The Creamatory? Not good," he admitted with a look of concern. "But I think I know the reason."

"It couldn't be the name, could it?" I asked, trying to raise just one of the possible problems.

"No, of course not! I think people haven't had a chance to see the full range of original flavors that I've come up with," he replied. "So I've printed up menus to distribute around town. Here, take a look."

He handed me a folded flyer and I opened it up. The list of flavors was truly staggering but not in a good way. There was mustard, broccoli, new car, fish and chips, bacon, mouthwash, and—one that really left me scratching my head—doorknob. There were dozens more, all similar to the extent that you would never see me trying a sample of any of them.

"Have you ever thought of doing at least a few flavors that people actually know?" I asked.

"Ha!" he replied. "No one ever became successful by doing the same old thing. It's the people who try new ideas that come out ahead."

Actually I could have named hundreds of people who had become successful by giving people exactly what they wanted, but Uncle Fluster's truck had just pulled up in front of Stench's yard.

"Well, I hope it all works out!" I said as I hurried to get out of the chilly truck. "And thanks for the ride!"

I headed toward one of the clear pathways between the stacks of junk, but I had only gone a few feet when I ran into Windbag.

"Hey, O Boy. How goes it?" he asked in his usual jovial manner. "I was just getting ready to head over to your house. Thermo has called an emergency meeting of the New New Crusaders. Any idea what it's about?"

"I'm not sure," I fibbed. Windbag should hear about the cake-baking scheme from the source. "But my uncle Fluster just dropped me off. I think he's looking for another one of those cones for his truck."

"Excellent!" Windbag let out a blast of air that nearly knocked me to the ground. "I knew if I held on to them long enough I'd find a customer—even if it did take twenty years."

As I glanced around the enormous collection of miscellaneous junk cluttering up Stench's backyard, I suddenly understood why there was so much of it. Windbag apparently felt compelled to buy anything

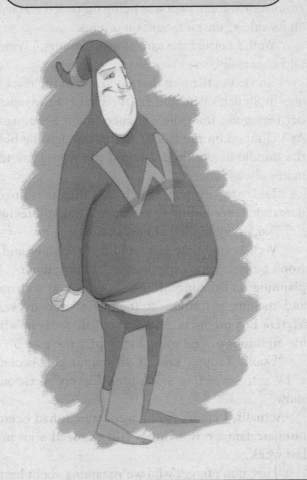

NAME: Windbag. **POWER:** Able to produce hurricane gusts of wind with his breath. **LIMITATIONS:** Gets winded easily. **CAREER:** A member of the New Crusaders when younger, Windbag currently owns a junkyard, pending the outcome of complaints filed by neighbors. **CLASSIFICATION:** His bluster is worse than his bite.

that anyone brought him. Even now, a huge above-ground swimming pool was being unloaded and leaned on its side against a mountain of junk.

"Well, I better take care of my customer," Windbag said cheerfully.

I hurried to the tree that sat in one of the few clearings in Stench's yard and grabbed hold of the rope ladder that hung from the entrance to our headquarters. As I climbed up the ladder and in through the hole in the middle of the floor, I found the rest of my teammates already there.

"Did any of you watch AI this morning?" I demanded, not hiding the outrage I was still feeling.

"No," they replied almost in unison.

"Well I caught the last minute of the show and you won't believe what's happening," I blurted out. "AI is planning on bringing Meteor Boy back as a character and making a fortune at the same time by selling Meteor Boy products. And worst of all, today he's holding auditions to find some kid to play the part."

"Cool!" Tadpole said. "Can you imagine becoming a TV star *and* acting alongside AI every week on his show?"

Actually, I could. And a week ago, it had been my ultimate fantasy. But things had changed a lot in the last week.

"Hey, don't forget who we're talking about here," I reminded them. "We all know what a jerk the Amazing Indestructo is."

"But it doesn't make sense for him to do this,"

Stench pointed out.

"Stench is right," Plasma Girl agreed. "AI has spent the last twenty-five years hiding the fact that Meteor Boy ever existed. Why change strategies now by creating all this attention?"

"I don't know," I admitted, "but somebody has got to stop him. We can't let him get away with exploiting Meteor Boy—a kid just like us who would still be here today if it hadn't been for AI."

Everybody looked at me sympathetically, but nobody chimed in. Instead, they all just glanced nervously from one to the other.

"We all agree that the Amazing Indestructo is a creep," Plasma Girl finally spoke for the group. "But Meteor Boy has been gone for over two decades. There's nothing we can do for him."

"We all have science fair projects to get done, too." Stench shrugged guiltily.

"And some of us haven't even come up with a project yet," Tadpole admitted.

"Maybe I'm just obsessing about this because I haven't had a science project to focus on," I agreed with a resigned toss of my hand. "Melonhead is just impossible to deal with so I haven't even been thinking about it."

"So help Stench and Tadpole with theirs," Plasma Girl suggested. "Little Miss Bubbles and I have already gotten ours worked out."

"It's a stupid project," Tadpole whispered in my ear.

81

"I heard that," she scowled. "It is not stupid. It's all about using various fruit juices to measure the acidity levels in tea."

"See what I mean?" Tadpole pretended to whisper to me. Plasma Girl just glared at us.

"What about you, Hal?" I quickly asked in order to change the subject. "What are you and Cannonball planning on doing?"

"He wants to do something with static electricity . . ." Hal shuddered involuntarily.

"And?" I urged him on.

". . . and use me as the experiment."

We all tried to look supportive.

"Don't worry," I finally said, trying to sound encouraging. "We won't let him get away with anything mean."

"At least you have a project," Tadpole butted in. "Me and Stench can't come up with anything."

"Just look for an everyday thing you're interested in and then figure out the science behind it," I suggested.

"Like what?" Stench asked, clearly frustrated.

"People use scientific principles all the time without even realizing it," I said. "Take for instance when you ride in a car. You always put on a seat belt, right? There's a very good scientific reason that you do."

I went over to the refrigerator that Stench's dad had been nice enough to outfit our headquarters with and got myself an egg. On the way back, I picked up a toy cart that was lying in the general mess of toys on the floor.

"Here," I said, placing the egg inside the cart. "Watch what happens when I roll the cart toward the entrance to our headquarters."

There was a raised lip of wood running all around the trapdoor's opening that had been put in place specifically to prevent things from rolling out of the treehouse. Everyone watched intently as I gave the cart a push. With plenty of force it went rolling toward the open trapdoor and the lip of wood. When the cart hit the lip, it came to a sudden halt. But the egg did not. It continued on, flying right from the cart and out through the trapdoor.

"See?" I said proudly. "That's why we wear seat belts. It's called the first law of motion."

But before I could explain how an object in motion tends to stay in motion, we heard a shout from down below.

"I'm gonna murder you little twerps!"

I jerked around and peered through the trapdoor. Down on the ground was Stench's annoying older brother, Fuzz Boy. My egg experiment was all over his head.

CHAPTER TEN

Open Call

I would have felt guilty about smacking Fuzz Boy with an egg if I hadn't also noticed what he was carrying. He had dropped most of them, but he was still holding three or four water balloons which he had obviously been about to pelt us with. And they weren't normal water balloons, either. These balloons were covered in hair. You see, Fuzz Boy's power is the ability to grow hair on whatever he touches—on anything from a billiard ball to . . . well . . . a water balloon. What's really disgusting about his hair-covered water balloons, though, is when they hit you, they not only leave you soaked, but covered with hair clippings.

All of us watched with horror as Fuzz Boy got back on his feet in a rage. With the handful of surviving hair balloons cradled in one arm, he began using the other to pull himself back up the ladder. It was the dumbest thing he could have done. As his head emerged into our clubhouse, Stench, with only a fraction of the force he was capable of mustering, slammed the trapdoor shut and then yanked it back open.

None of us could resist watching Fuzz Boy lose control of his water balloons and fall straight to the ground, squealing and clawing at the air the entire way. He landed at exactly the same moment as the balloons, which burst all around him, covering him in a shower of wet hair.

Soaked and hairy, he got to his feet and began cursing at us. But he was out of ammunition and had no choice but to stalk off and find more.

"Did you happen to notice that despite the fact that he weighs a lot more than the balloons, they all hit the ground at the same time he did?" I pointed out. "The science of falling objects could make an interesting project, too."

"Umm, that's really great, O Boy," Stench said. "Whatever that means. But we have to get out of here while we have the chance. When Fuzz gets this mad, there's no telling what he might try."

None of us were going to argue as one by one we climbed down the ladder.

"What do we do now?" Hal asked nervously as we assembled on the ground.

"I know where Fuzz Boy would never think to look for us," I proposed.

"Where would that be?" Plasma Girl asked suspiciously.

"Why Indestructo Industries, of course," I turned to depart without even looking at them. "We're going to make a call on the Amazing Indestructo."

"Here we go again," Tadpole said as he rolled his eyes.

"Unless of course you want to wait for Fuzz Boy to return," I shouted over my shoulder. Seconds later the rest of my teammates had caught up with me.

It didn't take long to get to the entrance of AI's corporate headquarters, and I led us right up the main sidewalk, beneath the enormous AI statue that stood before the building, and into the lobby. I wasn't at all surprised to see that we weren't the only ones to show up here today. There were kids everywhere.

"What is going on here?" Plasma Girl asked in disbelief.

"These," I announced with a wave of my hand, "are the potential Meteor Boys of tomorrow."

I may have exaggerated the case, since there were dozens of girls, at least ten men ranging in ages from twenty to eighty, two dogs, and even one goat. Although I think the goat may have wandered in by mistake. But mostly there were boys of every shape, size, and color. And every one of them was determined to be the new Meteor Boy. I was equally determined that they would not be.

"Stench"—I tipped my head to him—"if you wouldn't mind."

A look of embarrassment spread across his face as I took a deep breath and held it. Plasma Girl, Hal, and

Tadpole did likewise. There was so much noise in the lobby that I don't know if Stench's contribution was silent or noisy. But as soon as I saw the horrific expressions on the faces of wannabe Meteor Boys right around him, I knew it had been deadly.

Screams erupted in the area surrounding Stench and began spreading slowly outward like a vague rumor. The slowness at which it traveled only confirmed its hideous strength. Soon, kids who hadn't even caught a whiff of it yet were being shoved from the building by those who had and were trying to escape. The doors on opposite sides of the lobby were flung open as the evacuation of the building turned into a stampede. In a matter of moments it was over, and the five of us were left by ourselves in the lobby. Stench reached for the aerosol cans that were attached to the sides of his pants legs and grabbed one in each hand. He immediately began spraying the deodorizer all around him. With a sense of relief, we all gasped for breath.

Even where he had sprayed, we could still smell what he had dealt, and it wasn't pretty. His deodorizer was powerful, though, and the lobby was soon habitable again.

"Lock the doors on that side," I instructed Tadpole. "I'll get them over here."

"Now that we've gotten rid of everyone, what's the plan?" Stench asked, still a little abashed by the reaction so many people had had to him.

"The plan is that if no one auditions to play the

part, maybe we can kill this whole tasteless idea," I announced.

"But that will only work if you get rid of every possible contestant," Tadpole said.

"Who else is there?" I responded.

"Thuffering Thethame! It'th thtinkier out here than it ith in the bathroom."

The smug look fell off my face like a car off a cliff as I turned around to see Melonhead stroll out of the lobby bathroom.

"Tho where'th everyone elthe?" he asked with surprise. "Don't tell me I thcared them off! I mean, I know they didn't have a chanth, but theriouthly, they thould have at leatht tried."

"This is why we couldn't meet today?!" I pointed at him accusingly. "So you could try out for Meteor Boy?!"

He rolled his eyes and let out an exasperated sigh.

"Of courth, thilly. I wath thimply trying to thpare your feelingth," he explained amid an explosion of melon seeds. "Being powerleth, of courth, I knew you didn't thtand a chanth of being chothen ath Meteor Boy."

"And you do?!!" I shouted as my temper got the better of me. I couldn't help it. I get enough pity from people I like. To get it splattered at me in a stream of watermelon seeds from Melonhead was more than I could handle. "Your head looks like a watermelon!!"

"Pith poth," he said, dismissing my statement of fact. "I can't help it if I'm a thoo-in for the part."

"What's a thoo-in?" Hal asked.

My plan was falling apart. Letting Melonhead play Meteor Boy would be the ultimate insult to his memory.

"I've got to figure out how to prevent this," I said to myself, glancing nervously at the elevator bank where a car had just arrived. As the doors parted, out rolled a living legend.

"Bee Lady!" I heard Plasma Girl gasp in excitement.

We had run into the Bee Lady the last time we were at Indestructo Industries, less than a week earlier. She seemed to be in charge of product development for the Amazing Indestructo. In her day, though, she had been one of the founding members of the League of Ultimate Goodness and the first true female superhero. At least that's what the history books said about her. And the pictures always showed a young, slim woman in a yellow-and-black-striped leotard, unlike this picture of her in the *Li'l Hero's Handbook*.

That's odd, I thought. The book had a typo. They had mistakenly deleted "Ultimate" from the league's name. I had a sudden memory of having heard the team referred to that way once before, but I couldn't think when, so I shook the thought from my head.

Unfortunately, the years had not been kind to the Bee Lady. This was evident the second her scooter cart puttered out of the elevator, straining under the weight it carried. Now, she *may* have weighed under three hundred pounds, barely, but the problem was she still dressed in the same leotard that she had worn when

NAME: Bee Lady, The. **POWER:** The ability to control bees.
LIMITATIONS: The Bee Lady has overcome every limitation society has placed on her. Unfortunately this also extends to her diet.
CAREER: One of the original members of the League of Goodness.
CLASSIFICATION: As the first professional female superhero, the Bee Lady put the sting on crime, as well as on the male egos of her day.

she was young. It wasn't a pretty sight. And she spoke with a rasp that could only have come from a lifetime of unfiltered cigarettes.

"Hiya, kids," she greeted us with a smile as she put an unlit cigarette in her mouth. "Are you all here for the Meteor Boy tryouts?"

Then it hit me. The only way to avoid the disaster of Melonhead playing Meteor Boy was for someone else to win the part.

"Just me." I raised my hand to the complete surprise of my friends.

"Hmm." She gave me a considering look. "Yeah, I can see it," she added with a wink.

"I'm audithioning, too." Melonhead butted in, knocking me away from the Bee Lady.

"You're kidding me, right, kid?" she rasped.

"Yeth, it'th thilly, ithn't it?" He smirked his seedy smirk. "That they'd even make me go through the ektherthize when the rethultth are already obviouth."

"They sure are." She coughed in agreement, but not in the way I think Melonhead meant. "So what about the rest of you?"

Plasma Girl had been standing there all atwitter ever since the Bee Lady had emerged from the elevator.

"Oh, Bee Lady," she answered bashfully, "we're just here to give our friend O Boy some encouragement. Have I mentioned what an honor it is to meet you?"

"That's nice, sweetie," she replied as if she had gotten sick of hearing statements like that over thirty years ago. "How would you and your friends who aren't trying out like to come with me to the eighth floor to help with some test marketing?"

"We'd be honored," she answered for the whole team.

"Wait a minute," Tadpole interjected. "You don't expect us to test a bunch of girly toys, do you?"

Stench nodded his head. Hal might have also, but he was busy warily watching two bees that had begun hovering around his sippy cup.

"Don't worry, boys," she hacked. "I think you'll like it. Just let me have a quick puff out in the parking lot and then we'll head up."

She put her foot to the accelerator and proceeded to putter her cart smack into one of the doors we had locked. Amid her muttering curses about a clean air act, my friends went to Bee Lady's aid, unlocking the door and escorting her out to the parking lot. I was about to assist, too, but then I heard a piercing whistle behind me. I turned to find Whistlin' Dixie standing in the doorway of the elevator with a clipboard in her hand.

"Howdy, li'l buckaroos," she announced. "Sure'n if ah can't say ah weren't expectin' more contestants, but that don't make no nevermind. The Meteor Boy auditions are ready to begin."

CHAPTER ELEVEN

The Makings of a Hero

"Ah sure as shootin' was expectin' more li'l hopefuls than this!" Whistlin' Dixie commented as she looked once more around the deserted lobby. "Ah was plum sure we'd get ourselfs hunerts a contestants."

"I think I thcared them away," Melonhead said with a spatter of melon juice. "I thuppothe it'th pretty eathy to thee why."

For the first time, Dixie took a close look at Melonhead and her eyes widened in alarm. Glancing back at me, a look of relief broke across her face.

"Say thar, li'l feller, ain't you the boy that AI rescued from the clutches o' that thar evil Perfesser Brain-Drain jes the other day?"

"Yes, ma'am," I responded politely, deciding not to point out that she herself had had to sweet-talk AI into flying my dad out to Professor Brain-Drain's blimp where I was being held captive.

"A' course we all know who deserves the credit," she said with a wink.

Whistlin' Dixie whistled pleasantly to herself as the elevator climbed its way to the top floor of Indestructo Industries headquarters.

"Who's judging the contest?" I asked Dixie, secretly hoping that it might be her. I had the sense that she might not be anywhere near as inept as most of the members of the league.

"Thar'll be three judges," she answered, "Major Bummer, Mannequin, and yers truly."

I was happy that she would be one of the judges, but the other two worried me. Major Bummer always seemed so depressed; you could never tell which way he would swing on any issue. Mannequin I didn't know that much about. Sure, I knew she was a member of the league, but she rarely fought alongside the team. In fact the only time she ever appeared with them was at events and photo opportunities, where she always stood alongside AI, helping him look good.

And that was something she was great at! After all, she was Superopolis's most successful supermodel. Of course all models are technically "super" since this is Superopolis, but of them all, none was more famous than Mannequin. In case you're wondering, she got her name from her ability to remove her arms, hands, legs, and head as needed. It can be an unnerving (and in many ways useless) sort of power, but she knew how

NAME: Mannequin. **POWER:** The ability to detach her arms, hands, feet, legs, and head. **LIMITATIONS:** A tendency to scatter herself across too many projects at once. **CAREER:** Superopolis's most successful supermodel, and member of the League of Ultimate Goodness. **CLASSIFICATION:** She's fabulous and she knows it.

to make the most of it. Her judging ability, however, was an open question.

Then the elevator came to a stop, jolting me from my thoughts. The doors opened, and Whistlin' Dixie escorted us out and then into a large room. Waiting for us were Major Bummer and Mannequin.

"Since you two youngsters'll be our only contestants," Dixie began, "let's start by gettin' yer names."

"I'm Melonhead," Melonhead splattered.

"My name is Ordinary Boy."

"Zis eez eet?" Mannequin said with obvious disgust. "I vas told zat I vould be choosing from zee cream of zee crop of Zuperopolis youth."

"I wasn't expecting anything better," grumped Major Bummer.

"You never do," shot back Mannequin.

"Now, now, y'all," said Whistlin' Dixie, "let's give 'em a chance. Mannequin, why don't ya get the ball rollin'."

"Very vell," she said snootily. "Let us begin."

She looked from me to Melonhead, and I noticed her nostrils flare in alarm. Her eyes quickly returned to me.

"You," she said, indicating me. "Zhere eez nussing zhat eez more important zan how von enterz a room. Leave and zen return, showing me how you vould do it."

Turning, I headed for the door, planning my strategy as I went. Stepping out of the room, I paused for dramatic effect, then swung the door back open.

Standing straight, chest out, shoulders back, I stuck my nose in the air as I made a beeline straight for Mannequin. I strode slowly but confidently, tilting my head disdainfully one way and then the other as if on a fashion runway. Until I got to Mannequin—where my eyes stopped searching as if I had finally found someone worthy. I extended my right hand, palm up. When she presented her own right hand to me, palm down, I knew I had succeeded. Of course it was a little freaky that she had actually removed her right hand from her wrist and was handing it to me with her left, but I knew that if I flinched, I could ruin everything. So, as if it were the most normal thing in the world, I grasped her disembodied hand gently and gave it a gentlemanly kiss. As she took her hand back from me, she was at first silent. A little nervous, I looked up expectantly.

"Charming!" she finally said as if she were expelling the entire contents of her lungs in one deep, throaty breath. "Abzolutely charming."

Smiling, I stepped back, taking my place alongside Melonhead. "Your turn," I whispered smugly.

Taking my bait he turned and marched toward the door without even waiting to see if he was going to be asked to do the same thing. It was exactly what I counted on. No sooner had the door slammed shut than it reopened and Melonhead walked suavely back into the room—well, at least his version of suavely. I think he was trying to re-create my side-to-side dismissive tilt of the head, but since he had no neck, it looked more like half an orange twisting itself on a juicer.

Continuing on, in a manner not dissimilar to an egg leading a marching band, he proudly came to a stop before Mannequin. With an aghast look on her face she tentatively stretched out her hand, this time still attached to her wrist. With all the subtlety of a chainsaw, Melonhead grabbed it, pulling it loose from her wrist. He planted a big, juicy, slobbery, seed-filled kiss on it before handing it back. As with me, she was silent at first. But that was where the similarity ended.

"Zis child eez disgusting!" she hollered as her left hand held up her right, coated in melon juice and seeds.

Before either of the other judges could respond, she stood up from the table and stormed out of the room, holding her sticky right hand as far from her body as she could.

"Well, now," Whistlin' Dixie finally commented, "Ah'm sure'n she'll be jes fine after havin' a chance to rinse her hand. In the meantime, let's keep things a-movin'. Major, you go next."

"If I must." He sighed, shifting his enormous rear end on the seat of his groaning folding chair. "My question will be the same to both of you. What is the most depressing aspect of your life? You go first, Casabahead."

"It'th Melonhead, thir. Firtht, let me jutht thay that there'th nothing more deprething than being a thtep ahead of one'th peerth. You're rethented ath a rethult of it and alwayth made to wear your thuperiority ath if it were thome kind of a curth—"

98

"That's enough," Major Bummer interrupted. "I see where you're headed. Rather than waste time I could otherwise use contemplating my own unfulfilled promise, let me hear the response of the other contestant."

I had no idea what Major Bummer was hoping to hear for an answer. That's one of the problems with depressive, paranoid schizophrenics. They're sometimes difficult to read accurately. Lacking any surety, I decided to go with that old faithful—tell the truth.

"I have no superpower in a society where one's superpower defines who you are. I sometimes find that depressing."

Major Bummer stared at me cryptically for a moment before commenting. "Thanks for keeping it short, kid."

Just then, Mannequin strode back into the room in the same manner as I had for my demonstration. Her right hand was once again attached, as well as cleaned of watermelon juice and seeds. She took her seat at the table as Whistlin' Dixie asked a question of her own.

"Well now, ah sure as shootin' can see why you two li'l cowpokes would like to take on the hee-roic role of Meteor Boy," she began. "But ah'm wonderin' if y'all understan' what you might be gettin' yerselves inta. So answer this: Tell me everthing y'all know about Meteor Boy."

There was an audible gasp from Major Bummer and Mannequin.

"You go first, Melonhead."

From the atypical silence that followed Dixie's

NAME: Major Bummer. **POWER:** The ability to depress anyone around him. **LIMITATIONS:** They're never as depressed as he is himself. **CAREER:** After rapid promotions out of one army unit and into another, he finally retired from the military to join the League of Ultimate Goodness. **CLASSIFICATION:** Nobody's idea of a good time.

question, I could tell that Melonhead was stumped. And why wouldn't he be? Prior to a week ago, I had never heard of Meteor Boy either. The Amazing Indestructo had done a thorough job of covering up the existence of his ill-fated sidekick. As far as Melonhead knew, Meteor Boy was a brand-new made-up character.

"Thertainly," he finally replied. "Meteor Boy, ath hith name implieth, hath all the powerth of a meteor."

Whistlin' Dixie nodded for him to continue.

"He can fly through thpathe, trailing a glowing tail of ithe and thnow behind him."

"That's a comet, not a meteor, seed brain," I whispered.

"I meant to thay, that he can thend out pulthes of energy to thtun hith foeth," he corrected, clearly becoming flustered.

"Ain't that what a pulsar does?" Dixie asked him, saving me the trouble.

"Egthactly." Melonhead laughed nervously. "I wath jutht tethting you. We all know that Meteor Boy ith . . . yeah that'th it . . . , he'th a robot conthtructed by alienth who are big fanth of the Amathing Indethtructo, and they've thent him to Thuperopolith to aid AI in hith never-ending battle againtht villainy."

He looked hopefully at Whistlin' Dixie, but she betrayed none of her thoughts.

"And now yer answer, Ordinary Boy."

"Meteor Boy was a kid just like me who thought it would be incredible to fight crime alongside the greatest hero of them all."

I could have said more, but I didn't. From the kind smile on Whistlin' Dixie's face, I could tell I had said just enough.

"Well, pardners." She turned to Mannequin and Major Bummer. "I think ah'm ready to cast ma vote. Mannequin, ah reckon' you should go first."

"Zat eez so," she agreed. "I have no need to zhink long on my decizion. I cast my vote for zee handsome young man vith zee charming manners."

As she noticed Melonhead stepping eagerly forward, she quickly added, "Not zee disgusting melon child," she clarified. "Zee Ordinary Boy."

To maintain my classy image, I did not turn to Melonhead and gloat.

"One vote fer Ordinary Boy," Dixie recorded. "And you, Major?"

"Well, Ordinary Boy obviously has a fundamental understanding of who he is and doesn't appear to be anything but honest with himself. The other kid, however, is clearly delusional and has constructed a world for himself that bears no resemblance to reality. I have no choice but to cast my vote for Cantalopehead."

"Thank you, thir, Mithter Major, for thothe kind wordth," Melonhead gushed. "You've alwayth been my favorite member of the League of Ultimate Goodneth."

"Well, durn it if we don't have ourselves a tie," Whistlin' Dixie announced as she pointedly glared at Melonhead. "Ah guess it's all come down to yers truly."

Sensing his error, Melonhead quickly tried to make amends.

"Did I menthion that you're altho my favorite member of the League of Ultimate Goodneth, Mith Dikthie?"

"Save yer panderin', kid," she replied. "I already made up ma mind. Fer his courtesy, honesty, and respectful thinkin'—and not to mention jes lookin' more the part—ma vote goes to Ordinary Boy."

Melonhead was halfway up in the air with a *yippee* already forming in his mouth before he realized that it wasn't his name that had been called. As he came back to the ground in a state of shock, I sincerely thanked each of the judges.

"But"—Whistlin' Dixie gave a resigned sigh—"the rules also say we need ourselves a runner-up if the winner ain't able to carry out his new duties as Meteor Boy. So ah have no choice but to declare that our runner-up is none other than Melonhead."

This time he jumped into the air and let the "yippee" fully escape from his lips along with a shower of seeds.

"And now ah'm durn proud to introduce our new Meteor Boy to the greatest hero ever," Dixie announced as she gestured behind me.

I spun around and found myself facing none other than the Amazing Indestructo himself.

CHAPTER TWELVE

A Mess of Motives

"YOU!" The Amazing Indestructo looked at me with alarm.

I guess I should consider it a compliment that he remembered me. I mean, I know it had only been a few days since we had met in Professor Brain-Drain's lair, but I had pegged AI as the type of guy who only showed signs of recognizing someone when he passed by a mirror.

Of course I had no problem recognizing AI but I also instantly identified the man standing next to him—the Tycoon. The Tycoon's power was making money, and he had helped the Amazing Indestructo make mountains of it.

"It's a pleasure to meet you again," I lied as I stuck out my hand to AI. "And I'd like to thank you once more for saving my life this past week, as well as for the honor of being chosen as the new Meteor Boy."

"That's right." I watched him visibly hem and haw. "You know all about the original Meteor Boy."

Did I ever. Right in front of me, the Amazing Indestructo had crumpled like an empty potato chip bag while Professor Brain-Drain humiliated him over the fate of Meteor Boy and AI's involvement in it.

"Don't worry about it." The Tycoon elbowed AI. "Professor Brain-Drain's certainly not able to hold *that* over your head any longer."

"I suppose you're right." AI sighed nervously.

"Of course I'm right," the Tycoon insisted. "Just like I'm right that now is the perfect time to reintroduce Meteor Boy. The ten collector cards I released by mistake have shown there's a huge demand for a character the same age as your fans. Those cards are already worth a fortune, and word is building fast."

It suddenly occurred to me that the release of Meteor Boy collector cards had not been an accident. The Tycoon had known exactly what he was doing. His next words confirmed it.

"We've been missing out for years on the income that can be generated by products based on an appealing character other kids can relate to. The time to reintroduce your sidekick is now."

"You mean he wathn't a robot thent here by ekthtraterrethtrialth?"

The Amazing Indestructo's eyes widened in astonishment as he suddenly noticed Melonhead standing beside me splattering seeds in every possible direction.

It was the perfect distraction from his embarrassment at seeing me.

"Of course not . . . er . . . son?" he said as his confidence returned. "The real story of Meteor Boy has gone untold for far too long."

"And now we have the perfect young man to play the part." The Tycoon swept his hand in my direction, unaware that I was stiffening my resolve despite his flattery. "He's perfect for the part, and he'll look even better once he's wearing this."

The Amazing Indestructo whipped out a costume on a hanger from behind his back. It was fantastic! It was deep red with shimmering streaks of gold raining over it like a shower of meteors. It came with a matching gold belt and boots and goggles containing a mirrorlike reddish-gold glass. It looked just like the outfit Meteor Boy was wearing in his collector card picture.

"Go ahead, kid." AI laughed as he saw the look of awe spread across my face. "Try it on. We'll deduct its cost from your first paycheck."

"But first sign this," the Tycoon said as he pulled a sheet of paper from his coat pocket and shoved it in my face. "It will confirm you as the winner of the Meteor Boy role."

And legally hand over all my rights to Indestructo Industries, I suspected. What should I do? I had changed my strategy and tried out for the part in order to prevent AI from doing anything insulting to Meteor Boy's memory. But by signing this contract, I would be committed to doing anything they asked of me. The Meteor Boy costume again caught my eye. I looked down at the jeans and T-shirt which had been my wardrobe for most of my life, and . . . All right, fine. I admit it. My resolve crumbled like potato chips on a casserole. I took the piece of paper from the Tycoon, signed it, and shoved it back in his hands. Then I took the costume from AI and headed for a corner of the room where a screen was standing.

Once I was behind the screen, I was out of my jeans and shirt instantly. Pulling on the tight spandex costume, I began to feel like a real superhero for the first time in my life. But despite my excitement, I couldn't help but overhear the conversation taking place on the other side of the screen.

"Excellent choice!" AI complimented his teammates.

"And he's jes' cute enough to sell a whole heap o' posters to an admirin' crop o' preteen fillies," Whistlin' Dixie added.

Well, that was a disturbing thought. Maybe I shouldn't have been listening in.

"Let's also not forget, sir, that this boy owes his life

to you," added Major Bummer.

"Thet's right!" Dixie added. "Jes' think o' the PR, boss. 'The Amazin' In-dee-struc-to saves boy an' then makes him his sidekick.' The press'll go loony fer it!"

"Zat eez not all," I heard Mannequin speak up. "Are you avare of vhat zis boy's power eez?"

Suddenly, even as I was buckling Meteor Boy's gold belt around my waist, I felt my stomach lurch. Would the exposure of my weakness mess up my chance to be a hero? Mannequin had voted for me. I couldn't imagine she'd do anything to sink me now. Of course I should have realized that someone else would beat her to it.

"He doethn't have any thort of thuperpower at all," Melonhead volunteered in the most malicious way possible. "He'th ordinary!"

He had gone right for my most vulnerable spot. Well . . . maybe my second most vulnerable spot. But Mannequin ignored Melonhead's comment and continued.

"Zee annoying child eez correct. It eez a vonderful opportunity. He eez a boy vizout a power."

"That's good?" asked AI.

"Of course," she replied. "It's really very zimple. Zee contrast between zee boy and you vill be startling. For instance, I never let myzelf be zeen with anyvone as beautiful as myzelf. As a result, I look even more beguiling."

If Major Bummer and Whistlin' Dixie were as insulted by this statement as they should have been, I had no way of knowing it from behind my screen. And AI, the person who Mannequin was seen with most of all, clearly didn't get the slam.

"Oh, of course," AI said in a way that told me he had no idea what she was talking about. "But explain for the benefit of the others."

I could practically hear Mannequin rolling her eyes, which wasn't that odd considering her power.

"It eez like zis," she explained. "Zee kid has got no power. Zero. Zilch. Zo vhen he appears next to Zuperopolis's greatest hero—"

"Me! Right?" AI graciously contributed to the discussion.

"Yah, yah. You, darling. Who else?" Mannequin continued, sounding a little exasperated. "As I vas saying. Vhen he appears alongside you, heez powerlessness vill only serve to emphasize your own amazing abilities all zee more."

"I zee—I mean see," mulled the Amazing Indestructo, finally getting her gist.

"And that's not the only benefit," added the Tycoon. "Since he signed our contract, he'll have to remain silent about any potentially . . . embarrassing . . . incidents he may have seen."

"That's right." AI's tone brightened. "No matter what he saw or heard in Brain-Drain's lair, as an employee he's subject to the same gag rule that applies to everyone who works for Indestructo Industries."

Major Bummer started making some gagging noises that I doubt very much were genuine. But I paid no attention. The cynical discussion I had just over-heard had made me realize once again how ridiculous it was for me to think that I could have even a make-believe career as a hero.

I stopped as I was about to put on my gold boots. Who was I fooling? Indestructo Industries was just going to use me. I looked at myself once more in the costume, and then began to take it off.

I had come here to prevent AI from finding his new Meteor Boy, only to convince myself that I would be the best person to play the part. But as I put my own clothes back on, I suddenly realized there was another way to ruin AI's plans. With as much pride as I could muster, I stepped out from behind the screen dressed as . . . Ordinary Boy.

"What's with the costume?" AI asked in surprise. "Or the lack of it, I mean."

"I can't help you exploit the memory of Meteor Boy," I informed him as I shoved the costume into his hands. "And you should be ashamed of yourself, try-ing to make money off a kid you did nothing to pro-tect."

I could see AI's eyes begin to well up and sensed a self-berating about to start. The Tycoon quickly inter-vened.

"But it's too late," he said matter-of-factly. "You've signed a contract. You'll have to do everything the job calls for."

"Really? Take a look at my signature," I responded. The Tycoon unrolled the contract in his hands. His eyes scanned to the bottom and then bulged with frustration.

"What's wrong?" Major Bummer asked. "We all saw him sign it."

"He signed it 'Meteor Boy,'" the Tycoon erupted, "not his own name."

Without waiting for a response, I headed for the door. When I reached it, I turned and found everyone staring after me dumbfounded.

"So you want to have a new sidekick with lots of kid appeal fighting alongside you?" I asked AI accusingly. "Well, you got it, because this makes the runner-up the new Meteor Boy—and your new partner."

All I heard as the door swung shut was Melonhead's solitary, excited, "Yippee!"

CHAPTER THIRTEEN

What's the Buzz?

I had initially feared that letting Melonhead play
Meteor Boy would be a disaster—it just took me a little while to realize the disaster would be for AI, not for
Meteor Boy's memory. With a satisfied smile on my
face, I pushed the button for the eighth floor to join up
with my team. When the car stopped, the doors
opened to reveal every kid's fantasy—an entire floor
filled with Amazing Indestructo toys and products.

There was everything from existing items like the
AI Pedal-o-Copter, which I had wanted desperately
until the mounting lawsuits caused it to be taken off
the market, to the inconceivable, like the Professor
Brain-Drain Home Uranium Enrichment Kit, which
had apparently been planned and then dropped before
it ever got out the door. Hearing voices drifting down
the hallway, I made my way past a display of AI action

figures that showcased the evolution of his costume from his earliest psychedelic version all the way up to his current model.

I soon found the Bee Lady. She was sitting in a room, holding a clipboard and jotting down notes as bees buzzed about her head. I poked my head in the doorway and saw that she was watching all four of my teammates through a one-way mirror. They were inside a soundproof room, playing with various items. A hidden microphone was broadcasting their comments. I arrived just as Plasma Girl began arguing with Tadpole over what looked to be a pair of upside-down toilet plungers strapped to his back. Tadpole insisted the device was perfectly safe and proceeded to punch the buttons on a handheld control. He instantly shot to the ceiling where the plunger ends stuck fast, leaving him dangling helplessly. I laughed out loud, which made the Bee Lady notice me.

"Hey there, honey," she rasped. "All done with the audition?"

"Yes," I said, "but then I got in a fight with AI."

"Ha! Good for you, kiddo." She laughed. "Anyone with a spine, or a mind of his own, eventually gets in a fight with him."

"But *you* work for him!" I reminded her.

"I work *with* him," she corrected. "He knows better than to argue with me. I do what I want down here in product development, and he's happy with the profits so he leaves me alone."

"What are you working on now?" I asked.

"It's a rush job. We're going nuts getting stuff ready for the Meteor Boy launch."

I had figured as much. Stench was holding something that looked like a ray gun with METEOR BLASTER painted on it. As he pulled the trigger, a quarter-size ball shot out of the barrel toward Halogen Boy. Then suddenly, midway through its trajectory, the ball erupted in flames. When it hit Hal his cape briefly caught on fire. He and Stench quickly patted it out.

"It's clever the way we got it to erupt in flames," she half muttered to herself, "but I just don't think it will pass safety testing."

"I hope not!" I said in alarm. "And what's that thing?" I pointed to what looked like a catapult the size of a coffee table. It said METEOR LAUNCHER on the side. "Isn't that a little big and dangerous for a toy?"

"That's just a prototype, honey," the Bee Lady informed me. "We build it big to make sure it works, then make a small version for manufacturing."

Tadpole had somehow gotten down from the ceiling and was now shoving candy into his mouth.

"What's Tadpole eating?"

"You mean the kid with the tongue?" she asked, looking up from her clipboard.

We both watched as Tadpole used his tongue to begin stretching out a wad of whatever it was he had just begun chewing. He had anchored one end in his mouth while his tongue pulled and pulled at the sticky-looking substance. We both watched in amazement as he stretched the candy nearly ten feet.

"We're calling it Meteor Taffy," she explained.

"What does Meteor Boy have to do with taffy?" I asked.

"Nothing," she admitted. "But we have truckloads of leftover Amazing Indestructo Indestructible Taffy."

"I tried that once! It was awful! You could barely chew it."

"Exactly," she agreed. "The candy division made it too indestructible. So the Tycoon figured he'd use this opportunity to unload some more of it."

"That figures," I said, just as Tadpole let go of the ten-foot-long stretch of taffy. It snapped back, wrapping itself and his tongue around his head. As Tadpole wrestled with the wad of taffy Plasma Girl was examining a miniature kitchen range.

"What's that?" I asked.

"That's the Meteor Boy Atomic Oven."

"I doubt many boys are going to want an oven," I informed her. "Even if you slap the word *Atomic* on it."

"It's not for boys," she replied. "It's for girls. In addition to the usual stuff we can always get boys to buy, the plan is to make Meteor Boy appealing to girls, too."

I amused myself by imagining Melonhead's appeal to girls.

"So what is Plasma Girl making in the oven?"

"She thinks it's a cake."

"What do you mean, she *thinks* it's a cake?"

"She put a cake into the oven," the Bee Lady explained between puffs on an inhaler she had just pulled out of her purse, "but then the kid with the tongue replaced it with a Meteor Boy action figure."

We both turned to watch as Plasma Girl donned an oven mitt and opened the door. As she retrieved the melted hunk of plastic she began hollering.

"Tadpole, you are such a creep!" Her voice blasted through the speakers.

"That girl has spunk," the Bee Lady said. "Is she your girlfriend?"

"No!" I whipped my head around and glared at her before turning back to watch Plasma Girl battering Tadpole with what looked like a giant inflatable pickle. Unfortunately for him, he still had his tongue—and Meteor Boy Taffy—wrapped around his head. He could barely see to defend himself. But it was hard to feel sorry for him.

"If these are the kinds of toys you're going to produce, maybe you should also sell Meteor Boy life insurance," I suggested jokingly.

"Don't laugh," she replied. "We thought about it. But AI himself nixed it as being in bad taste."

"Well, that's gotta be a first," I replied.

"It would have been a reminder that the original

Meteor Boy needed it himself . . . thanks to AI's failure to save him," she pointed out.

Then it dawned on me. The Bee Lady was one of the original members of the League of Ultimate Goodness. Maybe she had been there the day Meteor Boy vanished!

"Had you already joined forces with the Amazing Indestructo at the time he was working with Meteor Boy?"

"We had just merged our operation with his," she responded. "The entire league was there that day."

A million questions about Meteor Boy instantly came to mind, but only one popped out of my mouth.

"What was he like?"

She was silent for a long time as we both watched Stench stroll over and, despite its weight, effortlessly pick up the coffee-table-sized prototype of the Meteor Launcher catapult.

"He was a great kid," the Bee Lady said with a kindly smile. "When I met him, I was sick and tired of fighting crime, but I didn't know what else to do. I had all this pressure on me to keep at it, because of my status as the first female hero. But Meteor Boy made me realize that the decision was mine to make."

"And what was your decision?" I asked.

"For over twenty years I had used my talent to make weapons and gadgets for the league," she informed me with a wheeze, "but what I really wanted to create was toys. Meteor Boy convinced me that I could and even encouraged me to work for AI in his new company. Don't get me wrong. AI is a jerk, but the job is great. If Meteor Boy was here, I'd tell him it was the best advice I'd ever gotten.

"In fact, here's the first toy I ever created," she said, reaching up to a shelf and grabbing a small tube no more than ten inches long. "In honor of him, I called it the Meteor Collide-a-scope. Go ahead. Try it."

I brought the toy to my eye and looked into it. Flaming meteors appeared suspended in the air, and then I realized that the tube could be turned. As I did so, the meteors began hurtling toward me. Instinctively, I jerked my head back from the tube.

"Now, that's the reaction I was expecting!" The Bee Lady laughed and coughed simultaneously. "The only person who ever looked into it without flinching the first time was Meteor Boy. He sure was something."

We both paused and watched silently as Hal picked up a Meteor Boy Bowling Ball (with flames on it, naturally) and loaded it onto the catapult.

"It's fitting that you're going to be playing the

role." She turned and smiled at me. "And I have one item in particular that you're going to love."

Before I could correct her, she lifted an object that made me gasp. It was the size of a small, flat backpack, and it was made of a shiny, gold metal. It had a single strange opening at its base.

"Like it?" She smiled. "It's one of a kind."

"It's beautiful," I said, "but what is it?"

"Well, if you're going to play the part of Meteor Boy, we have to have a way to make you fly."

I was so stunned by what she was saying, I never even noticed as Stench cranked back the arm of the Meteor Launcher. He had it aimed safely away from anyone. But he didn't account for a blinded Tadpole attempting to escape from Plasma Girl's inflatable pickle. He ran smack into the Meteor Launcher, which

lurched around until it was facing in the opposite direction—right at the one-way mirror that the Bee Lady and I were standing behind.

"But I'm not going to play Meteor Boy," I blurted out. "Melonhead is."

"No, no, no!" she said suddenly agitated. "That would be a disaster."

She began hacking like crazy and bent down to set the flying device on the floor while she caught her breath. It was lucky she had. Just then a bowling ball came crashing through the mirror. If she hadn't been ducking, the bowling ball could very well have knocked her head off, but instead it whacked the beehive smack out of her beehive hairdo. I only had a second to look up and see Stench, Hal, and Plasma Girl looking wide-eyed at me through the broken mirror.

"It wasn't my fault," Stench started to protest, "it was the Meteor Launcher—"

Normally, I would have rushed to help the Bee Lady, but unfortunately, it just wasn't going to be possible. A swarm of bees had begun rising from the battered beehive which now lay on the floor. The Bee Lady was too dazed by her near decapitation to control the little buzzers. They were angry and looking for payback.

"Umm, guys," I said, my eyes focused on the gathering, buzzing cloud, "I've got a lot to tell you. But for now . . . RUN!"

CHAPTER FOURTEEN

Cake-tastrophe

Luckily for Tadpole, Plasma Girl didn't hold a grudge. As Stench, Hal, and I ran, she grabbed the still-blinded Tadpole by the arm and dragged him along with her. I knew we couldn't wait for an elevator, so I headed for the fire exit. Of course it was locked.

"Stench!" I hollered.

With barely a grunt, he shoved his shoulder against the door, and I heard the bolt snap. This is one of the benefits of having the strongest kid in Superopolis on your team. He, Hal, and I rushed through the door and held it open until Plasma Girl pulled Tadpole in behind her. I slammed it shut just as the front wave of the bee attack reached us. I heard dozens of them smacking into the door.

"Man," I gasped in relief, "only AI would keep the fire escapes locked in his building. Someone ought to report him."

"Maybe he does it so that he can look like an even bigger hero saving everybody if there's a fire," Hal said. He was probably right.

It was then that I noticed I was still holding the Bee Lady's Meteor Collide-a-scope. Thanks to the bees, there was no going back to return it now.

"Cld smbdy hlp me?" I heard Tadpole's muffled voice. Between his tongue and the taffy there was little of his actual head to be seen. I shoved the Collide-a-scope into the waistband of my jeans and, with my teammates, gathered around him to begin removing the taffy.

"Crfl, tht's my tng," he screeched once or twice. In a remarkably short time, though, we had him disentangled and most of the taffy off his face. Then we began the walk down eight flights of stairs. Everyone was silent at first, and then Plasma Girl asked the question on all of their minds.

"So what happened up there? Did you win the part?"

I told them the whole story of my audition and my *very* brief career as Meteor Boy as we walked down. When I told them how Melonhead ended up with the part, they all thought it was hysterical.

"It serves AI right," Tadpole said, laughing. "Nobody is going to buy any toys that he uses Melonhead to promote."

"Besides," added Plasma Girl, "those toys are all retreads of other things. The Meteor Boy Atomic Oven is identical to the Whistlin' Dixie Cow Patty Oven-on-the-Range Range Oven—right down to the same ten watt baking light."

"That's hardly atomic-level power," Stench pointed out. "That catapult sure packs a wallop, though."

"Hey you guys." I stopped and turned to Tadpole and Stench. "Why don't you do a science fair project on how balls move through the air? You already demonstrated it with the Meteor Launcher back there."

"I don't think they'll allow us to throw bowling balls at people," Stench said.

"Not bowling balls," I corrected. "Dodgeballs."

"That's it," Tadpole's face lit up. "We'll use science to beat that creep Cannonball and his team!"

When we finally reached the bottom floor, we pushed open the fire door to emerge into the crisp fall afternoon. We walked back to our neighborhood, discussing the Meteor Boy mystery as well as our various science fair headaches. I spent a couple more hours with Stench and Tadpole, helping them to develop their project, and then headed for home as the sun began to sink toward the tops of the Carbunkle Mountains.

I hadn't even gotten to the door of my house before my mom came running out to meet me.

"Don't go inside, OB," she warned. "Your father has gone crazy."

"What's happening?" I asked.

"It's the cakes . . . every kind of cake you can possibly imagine. And there are hundreds of them. He and his team have taken over the kitchen," she said, her fingers on her temples.

Like I said, my mom is the picture of cool, calm reason, except when it comes to my dad. He seems to have a unique ability to push her over the edge.

"I have to go look," I insisted, eager to see the level to which my father had taken this latest mania.

"Oh, fine," she said. "But don't be long. Then you and I will take a walk to Dinky Dogs for dinner."

"Excellent!" I loved Dinky Dogs—but almost never got to go there for dinner.

I ran around to the back door to see what was driving my mother out of her home. The answer was obvious. The New New Crusaders had not only taken over the kitchen but also the dining room, family room,

and living room. Everywhere I looked I saw cakes: layer cakes on top of the refrigerator, ring cakes stacked up on the dining room table, sheet cakes spread out all over the living room sofa. There was even something that looked like a tiered wedding cake sitting on the toilet seat in the downstairs bathroom. And amid these cakes, my dad and his team were busy making more.

The Levitator was mixing up cake batter in about a dozen mixers that he had going all at once. The fact that the batter was splattering all over the kitchen didn't seem to be a concern. The Big Bouncer was busily pouring the batter into a wide array of cake pans that he had scattered all around him. He then handed them to my father who had a pan balanced on each of his hands, supplying just enough heat to bake the cakes quickly without burning them. From there they

went to Windbag, who cooled them with a strong burst of his breath before frosting them.

If you didn't consider the enormous mess they were creating, it was a fairly impressive assembly-line setup.

"Hey, OB," the Levitator greeted me. "What do you think of our little operation?"

"It's something," I answered. "Are you almost done?"

"Just starting," he replied as he turned a mixer on too high and chocolate batter splattered everywhere.

"Yeah," the Big Bouncer added, "today we've been doing cakes. Tomorrow is pie day. Monday is cupcakes. And Tuesday will be cookies. We haven't decided what to make on Wednesday."

"Maybe you should think about using that as cleanup day," I suggested helpfully.

"Oh, I'm sure your mother won't mind," my dad piped up, proving how clueless he could be when it came to understanding women.

"You might want to rethink that idea," I offered. "I'd hate to lose my father so young."

This time he got it, as the realization crept across his face.

"Maybe you're right about Wednesday," he admitted meekly. "By the way, where is Snowflake?" He looked around as if just noticing her absence.

"Mom's taking me to Dinky Dogs," I said happily. "So although you're driving her crazy, I'm at least getting a good meal out of the situation."

"Glad we could help." Windbag gave me a wink.

I still had the Meteor Collide-a-scope tucked in my waistband, so I ran up to my bedroom and set it on my nightstand next to the Oomphlifier and the rock I had found at school the other day. Then I hurtled down the steps and back out the door, where I found my mother taking deep, cleansing breaths as she waited.

"Ready, Mom?" I asked.

"Yes," she answered, her calm now restored. "Let's take a walk."

It was a pleasant early evening, the sun just beginning to set, as we walked the six blocks to Dinky Dogs. But what should have been an enjoyable outing was ruined the second we walked into the restaurant. Don't ask me why I was even surprised. Plastered all over the windows and walls were signs announcing that starting next Friday, all Dinky Dog Dinky Meals would come with a free Meteor Boy figure. COLLECT ALL SIX! the posters screamed.

"Do you see this?" I asked my mom in disgust. "This is what AI is up to now."

Thinking about AI again almost ruined my appetite—but I still ordered a Dinky Dozen for my dinner. In case you're wondering, Dinky Dogs are tiny hot dogs, each in their own miniature bun. My mom ordered a Slinky Dinky Salad. As we sat down to eat our meals, she saw that my mind had drifted off again.

"Okay, OB," she finally asked, "what are you thinking about now?"

"I've just thought of something strange," I said, as

DINKY DOGS

With over twenty locations scattered throughout Superopolis, Dinky Dogs is the city's most successful fast-food operation. The ingredients that go into their hot dogs are a closely guarded secret. The fact that they're triple-ground ensures that they remain a mystery. Perhaps the chain's greatest success has been its ability to sell ever smaller hot dogs without ever decreasing their prices.

I popped an entire Dinky Dog in my mouth. "Who are Meteor Boy's parents?"

My mom's face went blank as she poured a packet of dressing onto her salad. "I don't know," she admitted. "Now that I think about it, no one ever came forward and reported him missing."

"Doesn't that seem strange?" I asked.

"It does," my mother agreed. "But what do you suppose it means?"

"It makes me wonder if Meteor Boy really disappeared after all."

"How could that possibly be?" my mom asked. "Where has he been all this time?"

"Think about it," I said. "Why would his parents never have come forward? Maybe they never really lost him."

"But why keep his existence a secret?"

"I don't know," I admitted with a shrug as I stuffed the last Dinky Dog in my mouth. "Maybe there was a reason to keep him hidden. Maybe he would be in danger if people knew he was still alive. Or—or maybe I'm just grasping at straws." I shook my head in frustration.

"So seek out the truth," she said matter-of-factly as she took one more bite of her salad and then set it aside.

I stood up from the table, lost in thought as my mom emptied our tray in the nearest garbage can. I barely noticed as she guided me from the restaurant with a hand on my shoulder. We walked several blocks in silence.

"If Meteor Boy survived," I finally spoke up just a

129

block from home, "and went into hiding, he'd be an adult now, wouldn't he?"

"I suppose he would," she said. "That doesn't exactly narrow things down, but I have no doubt you'll—hey, *stop that!*"

I immediately looked in the same direction as my mom and noticed that Uncle Fluster's ice cream truck was parked in front of our house. But that wasn't what Mom was yelling about. No, the cause of her irritation was the five seedy hippies—the same ones from yesterday—who now had Uncle Fluster trapped on top of his ice cream truck.

CHAPTER FIFTEEN

Hippies on Ice

My mom went into action instantly. Focusing her gaze on the rainbow that arced from the ground up into the air above Uncle Fluster's truck, she froze it solid in under a second. The Hammer was standing atop it holding both the cone he had just ripped from its brackets and my uncle. Right behind him, Rainbow Rider slipped on her now icy band and crashed into him. Both of them, along with my uncle and the cone, came sliding down the frozen rainbow in a mass of tangled arms and legs.

Uncle Fluster wasted no time getting to his feet, grabbing one end of his cone, and making a run for it. Unfortunately, he was stopped almost immediately by SkyDiamond and Bliss. It was now dark, so there was only one SkyDiamond, but then he pulled a flashlight from his belt and turned it on himself. Suddenly there were half a dozen other SkyDiamonds all closing in on my uncle. Meanwhile, the Hammer and Rainbow Rider were back on their feet, and, along with Aquarius, turned to take on my mom.

"Hammer," Aquarius shouted. "The hydrant!"

Mom and I both turned our attention to the hydrant on the street corner as the Hammer lumbered over and swung his arm against it, knocking it loose from its metal bolts. A gush of water shot into the air and Aquarius instantly directed it toward my mom. She obviously had no idea who she was up against!

Before the mass of water gained even a yard, my mom had frozen it into a solid block. The look of shock on Aquarius's face told me she had met her match. As the Hammer ran up to smash it, Rainbow Rider unleashed her power on us, wrapping both Mom and I in rainbows and then lifting us into the air.

"Prepare yourself for a drop, OB," Mom warned me, turning her gaze on the multiple colored bands. As each one froze solid, she gave it a kick, smashing it into a million colorful pieces. When she struck the one holding me, I dropped onto our lawn in a crouch and then pounced on Rainbow Rider. Grabbing her by the ankles, I yanked them out from under her, and she came crashing down amid her shattered rainbows.

I was just getting back on my feet when I heard my mother holler.

"OB! Duck!" she said. I didn't stop to ask why, and as the side of my face hit the turf I felt the woosh of the Hammer's fist passing an inch from my cheek. I rolled away before it came crushing down on me again. But there was no need to worry. As I got to my feet a couple yards away, I saw that he was still holding his fist in the air—which I guess makes sense considering my mother had frozen him solid. I knew he would thaw quickly, though, so I decided to make the best of it and ran to help Uncle Fluster.

"That ice chick, man, is just too intense," I heard Bliss say as he strummed on his ukulele. "We need to mount a new defense."

"She's no chick," I hollered. "She's my mom."

My temper got the best of me as I lunged at the laid-back, long-haired louse. It had cost me the element of surprise, though, and I was grabbed by a half dozen SkyDiamonds.

"Easy there, little dude," said one of them. "Violence isn't the answer."

"Unless it's to get something *you* want," I pointed

out as I struggled helplessly.

"We call that the fight against oppression," he clarified. "And you should know—"

He suddenly froze solid in mid-sentence. In fact, so did all the SkyDiamonds. I struggled out of their now icy grasps just in time to see my mom coming toward me. But I also saw someone else behind her.

"Mom! Duck!" I yelled.

She followed my instructions instantly. As she dropped to the ground, the Hammer's fist swung right over her head. Unfortunately for the six frozen SkyDiamonds, the Hammer smashed into them, shattering them into pieces.

The original SkyDiamond, who was still standing by Bliss and Uncle Fluster, had a look on his face that I can only describe as freaked-out.

"Oh, man, this trip's turned bad," he shouted, his eyes wide with shock. "Let's get out of here."

Then, without warning, a cyclone appeared from nowhere right in the middle of our yard. It wasn't hard to guess where it had come from.

"Must I do everything?" Cyclotron said as the funnel cloud rose up to reveal him standing in our yard. "Can't you take on even a single hero?"

As my mom began to pick herself up from the ground, the rattled members of the Commune for Justice ran toward Cyclotron. Bliss stopped and looked down at the ten-foot-tall metal cone lying in our yard.

"Hmm, we can't forget our souvenir," he said. "Hammer, baby, bring it here."

The Hammer lumbered over and easily picked up the heavy cone. A moment later, a tornado rose up around all the villains and carried them away. Mom tried to freeze the funnel cloud, but it was moving too fast.

As my mother, Uncle Fluster, and I watched it recede down our street, who should step out on our front porch but my dad. He had Mom's frilliest apron tied around his waist and was holding a chiffon layer cake in his hands. Standing behind him were the other three members of the New New Crusaders.

"What was all that noise?" he asked cluelessly.

"That was Mom single-handedly fighting off a gang of supervillains," I said, practically bursting with pride.

"Oh, no," he said in despair, "we missed another opportunity to show our stuff!"

"Well, at least the cakes are safe," my mother commented dryly. Of course, a moment later, Dad's chiffon cake erupted in flames as his frustration got the better of him. As I trudged up the stairs to my room, I barely paid attention as his teammates consoled him. I was too baffled as to why these villains had once again tried to rob my uncle.

As I flopped onto my bed, I thought back on what had happened. What were the hippies after? Both times they had gotten nothing but those useless metal cones. Unless that was what they were after in the first place? But that didn't make sense. They were just giant metal cones.

Hmm. Cones. The second I said the word, it instinctively made me think about my science fair proj-

ect. Tomorrow I would be meeting with Melonhead. I had to admit I had no idea how we were going to come up with a clever experiment for something as impossible as time travel. But somehow, the idea of cones was sticking in my brain.

Without even thinking about it, I reached for the Collide-a-scope and absentmindedly brought it up to my eye. I had to admit, the Bee Lady had designed a very clever thing. Wondering whether I could make the meteors fly backward, I tried twisting the tube the opposite direction. To my complete surprise, the entire top half of the Collide-a-scope came loose in my hands.

I was about to try to reattach the piece when I noticed the corner of a white piece of paper sticking out from it. I grabbed it and began pulling. It was more than just a scrap of paper. As more and more of it emerged, I realized it was an envelope.

Finding a letter hidden inside a twenty-five-year-old toy was strange enough, but it couldn't possibly compare to the shock I got when I saw what was written on the outside. In an elegant flowing script it said: *Please deliver to the leader of the League of Goodness. Many thanks!* It was signed: *Meteor Boy.*

CHAPTER SIXTEEN

Time and Again

I barely slept that night. Instead, I obsessed about what appeared to be a letter from Meteor Boy himself. For twenty-five years this message had remained hidden inside the Bee Lady's Collide-a-scope. I ran my hands over the envelope. I was dying to open it, but it wasn't addressed to me. Despite everything, I wasn't going to open somebody else's mail, even if that someone else was—apparently—the Amazing Indestructo.

By morning, I had shoved that unpleasant thought aside for the moment and turned to another pressing matter. Today I was supposed to meet with Melonhead to work on our project. I quickly got dressed, slipping the letter from Meteor Boy into my pocket. I also grabbed the chunk of rock. At some point I needed to determine whether it was actually prodigium or not.

I had only been to Melonhead's house once before, for his sixth birthday party. All the kids in the neighborhood had been forced to attend. He spent the party telling us how much smarter he was than any of us, belittling the presents we had brought him, and covering us all in seeds and melon juice. Oddly, by the end of the party he was convinced he had made dozens of new friends.

At his door, I rang the bell. A moment later it opened and I found myself being stared at by Melonhead's father, Argus, and most of his dozens of eyes. Of course, you shouldn't get the wrong impression when I say *eyes*. I don't mean normal eyes. After all, Argus's head looked more like a potato. And the eyes looked like what you'd expect to find on a potato. I assumed he could see out of them since I couldn't detect anything I would call normal eyes.

"Hello, Ordinary Boy," he said jovially enough for a guy with a potato head. "I hear you're the lucky one who got paired with my boy. It's a guaranteed A, you know, and I'm sure you haven't seen many of those."

Well, it was clear where Melonhead had gotten his charming manners. Not that it made it easier knowing I was considered an idiot, solely because I had no superpower. It was hard to get too insulted, though, hearing it coming from an enormous spud.

"Yes, sir," I replied. "Can you tell me where to find him?"

"He's in the cellar." Argus chuckled softly as he let

NAME: Melonhead. **POWER:** The ability to fire a barrage of watermelon seeds from his mouth. **LIMITATIONS:** Watermelon seeds are rarely lethal. **CAREER:** Assumes Superopolis will recognize his brilliance any day now. **CLASSIFICATION:** A swelled head could just be the result of too much juice retention.

me in. "Be careful not to trip on any roots."

I found Melonhead in a corner of the basement playing with a huge collection of Amazing Indestructo toys. He was wearing his Meteor Boy costume. Conveniently, its red color hid most of the juice stains. The seeds stuck here and there even looked a little like shooting meteors.

"Nice costume, Melonhead," I said.

"Ithn't it amathing? I have to go back thith afternoon and pick up a thpethial devithe they have for me."

I thought of the gadget the Bee Lady had said would be able to make me fly, and a tinge of regret stabbed at me.

"Now don't be thoar," he spattered as he caught the look on my face. "I beat you fair and thquare."

"Of course you did," I said, rolling my eyes—and putting the issue behind me. "And now are you going to show me the amazing time machine we're going to win the science fair with?"

"Abtholutely." He stood up. "It'th going to knock your thockth off!"

He led me over to the center of the basement and pointed to an object sitting all by itself on a worktable. I looked at it and then back to Melonhead to make certain he was serious. I could tell by the eager look on his face that he was. I looked back down at the object again and then once more at him. He was panting like a dog expecting a snack treat.

"It's a potato," I finally said as calmly as possible.

"It'th a potato time mathine," he corrected. It did

141

appear to have some wires running out of it.

"It's a *potato*," I repeated a little more insistently.

"It'th thenthathional, ithn't it?" he asserted. "It wath my father'th thuggethtion."

Somehow, I didn't doubt that.

"I thought you were building a time machine?" I said accusingly.

"It ith," he insisted. "It keepth perfect time."

"That would make it a *clock*," I pointed out, "not a time machine."

"I doubt the judgeth will be thuch thticklerth," he pooh-poohed.

"I doubt you'll live long enough to find out," I said, finally losing my temper and lunging for his throat. Of course, it's impossible to get your hands around someone's neck when it's as thick as a watermelon, and we just ended up tumbling to the floor and rolling around. The door opened upstairs and a voice carried down into the basement.

"You kids play quietly," his father's voice boomed jovially. "Remember, I've got eyes in the back of my head!"

Then the door closed again blocking off his chuckling. My efforts to pummel Melonhead were fruitless (no pun intended), so I finally rolled off the spluttering moron.

"You're thertifiably inthane," he spattered with an eruption of seeds. "You didn't think I wath theriouthly going to conthtruct a time mathine, did you? It'th not even pothible."

142

"I thought you were a genius," I said sarcastically.

"Thome thingth are even beyond my abilitieth." He brushed himself off as he got to his feet. "It'th impothible to travel through time!"

"No, it's not." I shook my head. "We're traveling through time right now."

"How tho?" he asked.

"At this moment you're right here," I pointed to where he was standing. "And now, five seconds later, you're still here."

"Tho what? I never moved."

"You didn't move in space, but you did move in time," I pointed out.

"I didn't move an inth," he sputtered in protest. "You're crathy!"

"Oh, you moved, all right," I insisted, "but unlike moving left or right or forward or backward, you have no control on moving through time. It carries you ahead whether you want it to or not."

"Tho how can you pothibly change it?" he spat.

"I'm not sure, but let's think about it," I said as I grabbed a sheet of paper and a pen. "Let's draw a line that represents space.

"And another that represents time.

"The point where the space line and the time line meet represents now. Moving upward on the time line represents moving forward through time. Of course, the area below the space line represents the past."

"But ther'th no way to aktheth it," Melonhead smugly pointed out.

"You may be right," I admitted as I pondered the matter, "but first let's think about how movement forward in time works. What happens when you drop a rock into a pool?"

"It thinks," Melonhead answered.

"Rocks can't think," I pointed out just to irritate him.

"Thinks! Not thinks!" he sputtered with a frustration I was enjoying way too much. "It thinks to the bottom of the pool."

"Oh, sinks!" I said as if I had just realized what he was trying to say. "Well, you're right. But that's not what I meant. What happens to the surface of the water?"

"Rippleth thtart thpreading out from where it hit the water."

"Right," I agreed. "Now let's mark it on our time line. One second up the time line from where the rock hits the ripple is here.

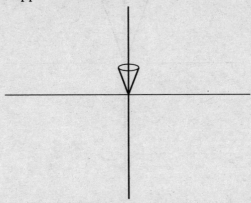

"The second after that, it's now here.

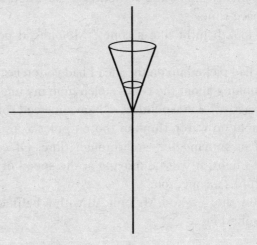

"And by the third second, the ripple has reached this point.

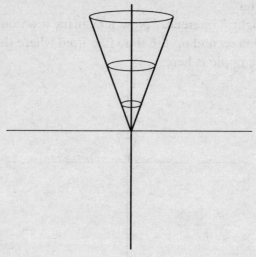

"So what looks like a widening circle in regular space actually looks like something else when spread over space-time."

"It lookth jutht like a cone," Melonhead pointed out.

He had picked up on the idea I had gotten last night after thinking about the cones stolen from my uncle.

"Exactly," I responded. "Now, instead of just movement on water, think of those ripples as the light around us moving forward through time. Of course, since it's light, it will be moving at the speed of light. But it forms a cone, too."

"How tho?" asked Melonhead with a baffled look on his round face.

146

"Well, nothing can move faster than the speed of light," I responded, "so all possible futures must occur within the area of a light cone. Basically, your entire future can be represented by the shape of a cone."

Melonhead stared at me blankly. "It lookth thort of like an upthide-down dunth cap," he finally responded.

It was too easy, so I just let it pass.

"But what about the patht?" he continued.

"That would also look like a cone," I said. "Like this."

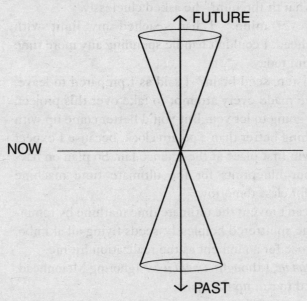

"But there'th thtill no way to aktheth it," he replied smugly.

"That may be true," I acknowledged, "but we're going to have to get a lot closer than your spud clock if we're going to have any chance of impressing the judges at the science fair."

"What'th wrong with my clock?" he demanded.

"How long did it take you to build?"

Melonhead paused. "About twenty-thikth min-uteth," he finally admitted.

"Exactly!" I pointed out. "So I think we're going to need to put a little more time into the project—no pun intended."

"What'th the pun?" he asked cluelessly.

"Never mind." I had reached my limit with Melonhead. I couldn't handle spending any more time with him today.

"Listen, seed brain," I said as I prepared to leave, "you've made every attempt to take over this project, so I'm going to let you. But you'd better come up with something better than a potato clock, because I expect us to win first place at the science fair. So plan on hav-ing your blueprints for the ultimate time machine ready for class tomorrow."

"I can't invent the ultimate time mathine by tomor-row," he spluttered helplessly, seeds flying all akimbo.

I froze for a moment as the realization hit me.

Ultimate, I thought. *Could it be?* Ignoring Melonhead, I turned to run up the stairs.

"But what about our project?" I heard him holler-ing behind me.

"Leaving so soon?" Melonhead's dad appeared as I

came up from the root cellar. "Are you able to find your own way home?"

I spun around to glare at him, but couldn't figure out which of his dozens of eyes to focus on. In exasperation I just nodded and slipped out the door as quickly as I could. Once outside, I took out my copy of the *Li'l Hero's Handbook*. Flipping through the pages, I came to the entry on the League of Ultimate Goodness. I had read the entry dozens of times before, and, as I thought, it discussed only the league as I knew it today, complete with all its useless members. It said nothing about the team's original founders—the members who'd made up the team twenty-five years ago.

Tentatively, I turned back a page and found an entry I had never noticed before. It said simply: the League of Goodness. And there they were, the original five founding members: the Bee Lady; Zephyr; the Animator; MagnoBox; and the leader of the group, Lord Pincushion.

I pulled the letter from my pocket, and sure enough, it said "Please deliver to the leader of the League of Goodness." There was no *ultimate*. The Amazing Indestructo was not the intended recipient of this letter. I quickly looked up Lord Pincushion and found his address—number one, Needlepoint Hill.

It took me about an hour to reach the hill and its thousand stairs. The thought of climbing them was a bit upsetting, but I knew it would never stop a true hero. So I sucked it up and started my ascent. As I climbed, I thought through what I knew of the original

NEEDLEPOINT HILL

Of the many odd geologic formations found throughout Superopolis, none is odder than Needlepoint Hill. Once an active volcano, it has long been extinct. Perched on its peak is Pinprick Manor, one of the finest homes in all of Superopolis, and definitely the one with the best views. It can only be reached by climbing the thousand or so stairs that wrap their way around the hill up to its top. It is also the only home in Superopolis never to have been bothered by door-to-door salesmen.

league. I had already met one of the five founding members, the Bee Lady. I was also aware that Zephyr had died quite a few years back. The remaining three members had retired. They occasionally reappeared as characters in the AI comic books, but as far as I knew, no one ever saw them in person anymore.

The first couple hundred steps went fine, but they were so steep that it didn't take long for me to get winded. I distracted myself by thinking how annoyed I was going to be if it turned out nobody was at home. A full two hours later, with a weary huff and a puff, I took the final step onto a very short sidewalk that led right to the front door. A sign at the entrance read PINPRICK MANOR. As I caught my breath, I nervously reached up to ring the doorbell. For a few minutes there was no response. Then, just as I was thinking I had made the climb for nothing, the door slowly creaked open. I let out a gasp at the well-dressed, elderly man in the doorway. After all, he had a sword stuck right through his middle.

CHAPTER SEVENTEEN

Tea with Two

I have to admit that seeing someone with a sword run through his stomach was a bit disturbing. But as I looked closer I noticed that he also had a machete wedged into his shoulder . . . knitting needles protruding from his thigh . . . a butcher knife sticking out of his chest . . . and a fork neatly jabbed into the center of his forehead. In fact there were sharp objects of every shape and kind stuck into every part of his body. It wasn't difficult to figure out who I was facing.

"Lord Pincushion?"

"Yes?" he replied with a piercing gaze, seeming not the least bit pleased at having a guest.

"My name is Ordinary Boy."

He wrinkled his nose a bit but said nothing.

"I've come to see you regarding a very important matter."

NAME: Lord Pincushion. **POWER:** Pierced throughout with an array of weaponry always at his disposal. **LIMITATIONS:** Doesn't handle blunt objects very well. **CAREER:** Founder and leader of Superopolis's first and greatest team, the League of Goodness. **CLASSIFICATION:** Incredibly sharp, but often prickly.

"Important to you, possibly," he said sharply, "but I doubt very much that it is important to me. Good day."

"I'm very sorry," I apologized swiftly as the door began to close, "but I have a letter for you."

The door paused just before it was about to click shut.

"It's from Meteor Boy."

The door instantly opened. Lord Pincushion reappeared, a look of astonishment on his face.

"Is this a joke?" he asked.

"No, sir," I replied nervously. "It's addressed to you. See?"

I fished the letter from my pocket and held it up. Some of the longer implements sticking out of him clanged and clattered against one another as he leaned forward to examine the envelope. Standing back up, he stared as if he were reappraising me. Almost instantly, his eyes widened in surprise.

"I think I do see!" Lord Pincushion replied as he looked me over silently, if a bit skeptically, for a moment. "Now the only question is how could it possibly be true?" Then the prickly expression on his face relaxed and slipped away.

"My apologies for my rudeness," he continued as he swung the door wide open for me. "We seldom have visitors anymore, and I'm afraid my manners have gotten rusty. It would be my sincere pleasure to have you join us for afternoon tea."

We? Us? I thought as I followed him into the foyer.

But then all questions were silenced by my first sight of the interior of Lord Pincushion's home.

"Welcome to Pinprick Manor," he said with pointed pride.

It was spectacular. I was in a huge, grand hallway that stretched off at least fifty feet both to the right and left. In front of me were two enormous staircases on either side of the foyer, each sweeping up and around a central gallery. Everywhere I looked there were beautiful paintings, decorative vases, knickknacks of every kind, and rows upon rows of suits of armor that, appropriately enough, were stuck through with a number of swords.

"We Pincushions have had a long yet somewhat perforated history," my host mentioned as he caught me studying the armor.

"Your home is extraordinary," I said, honestly impressed.

"Why thank you, my boy," he replied, seeming genuinely touched. "If you would come with me, I will show you to the east garden where we prefer to take our afternoon tea."

I turned to the right and politely followed Lord Pincushion at a safe distance, since his back was as covered with sharp objects as his front. He led me down one of the long hallways. A series of high, narrow windows on my right cast bright rectangles of daylight on the wall on my left. Every few feet there stood more suits of armor, some stuck through with weapons, others not. Finally, Lord Pincushion halted at the end of the hall before a large door.

"Welcome to the east garden," he said proudly.

I'm sure I must have gasped. It was a garden, all right. But it was a garden *inside* the house. Well, kind of. The room was inside the house, with four enormous arched windows, two on the east wall and two on the south wall—except there was no glass in them. They were completely open to the outside. The room was also full of expensive-looking furniture, yet the floor of the room was a thick lawn. And then there was the full-grown oak tree in the center of the room. Even with a forty-foot ceiling, it looked like the top branches were scraping against it. Lord Pincushion saw the dumbfounded look on my face.

"Let me explain," he said with a chuckle. "As you may have noticed, the house itself covers the entire summit of Needlepoint Hill. There was no land left on which to construct a garden. So instead, we created a garden inside the house."

It made sense, I guess, in an odd sort of way. But then I realized he had once again said "we." It was possible that he was referring to himself in the plural, but somehow I doubted it. Then I noticed another man of about the same age sitting at an oval table set for tea. He was wearing big round glasses with heavy black frames and had a railroad conductor's hat perched on his head.

"Oh, goody, goody!" He clapped his hands as his face lit up with excitement. "Do we have a guest for tea?"

"We do," Lord Pincushion responded formally. "Ordinary Boy, I would like to introduce you to another of the founding members of the League of Goodness—the Animator."

"I'm honored," I said as I shook the Animator's hand.

"Oh, no," he shushed me. "The honor is mine. Have a seat. Have a seat."

Lord Pincushion moved to a stool at the opposite side of the table from the Animator. With an entire set of kitchen cutlery sticking out of him in every direction, he required a seat without arms or a back. I took a more traditional chair in between my two hosts. I almost shot back up, however, when the right arm of my chair suddenly moved, producing a cloth napkin. The left arm proceeded to assist the right by spreading it out on my lap.

"Sorry," the Animator said sheepishly, "I should have warned you in advance."

"What an incredible power," I said, awestruck.

"Not everyone thinks so," he said with a mischievous gleam in his eye as he made a candelabrum pull out a match and light its own candles.

"He means the Amazing Indestructo," Lord Pincushion informed me. "From the moment AI joined us, he began trying to oust the Animator because his power so overshadowed AI's own."

I couldn't help but ask the question that was gnawing at me.

"Why did you let AI into your group in the first place?"

NAME: Animator, The. **POWER:** The incredible ability to bring inanimate objects to life. **LIMITATIONS:** No power over animate objects. **CAREER:** Despite taking his amazing power quite lightly, the Animator has nevertheless used it to dramatic effect numerous times throughout his career with the League of Goodness. **CLASSIFICATION:** A fully animated personality in every respect.

"Oh, my, my. That's a very bittersweet story," the Animator said as he picked up a small bell and gave it a gentle ring. "We really had no choice."

"He's correct, I'm afraid." Lord Pincushion sighed. "The sad fact of the matter is that, at the time, the league was flat broke. Things were different then. There were no sponsorship deals or television plays or product placement or any of the things that make it financially feasible for a hero today to devote himself to fighting crime."

"How did heroes support themselves, then?" I asked. The door from the hallway slowly creaked open.

"It was a simpler time, my dear boy," Lord Pincushion pointed out. "Independent heroes had always been able to make a modest living. The people they saved usually showed their gratitude with either a few dollars or a chicken or something."

Despite my fascination, my attention was distracted by the suit of armor that had just entered the garden, carrying a large tray.

"Of course, in my situation," he continued, "there was a family fortune to back up my crime-fighting ambitions."

"His family was loaded," the Animator said with a wink as the suit of armor clankily made its way to the table.

When it reached us, I could see that the suit was empty. It bent slightly and set the tray on the table. In addition to a tea service, the tray held a deep pan on a rack with an open flame under it. There was also a bowl filled with chunks of bread.

With only a nod from the Animator, the service pieces began moving from the tray to the tabletop all of their own accord. One teacup came over right in front of me, rolling its saucer in front of it. When the saucer came to a rest flat on the table, the cup jumped into it. The teapot came next and began filling my cup.

"Anyway," Lord Pincushion continued, "I had just inherited the family title and fortune, and it gave me a unique opportunity to fight crime without having to worry about supporting myself. So I did something no one else had ever done before. I created a superhero team—the League of Goodness. At the time, there was a villain named the Red Menace. I'm sure you don't remember him. But he had Superopolis in his grip and no one could overcome him. So I assembled a group of talented heroes whose powers would complement each other, and together we took him on."

"And you provided the first real opportunity for a female hero," I added. "My friend Plasma Girl idolizes the Bee Lady."

"Indeed!" Lord Pincushion smiled appreciatively. "The Bee Lady was a real spitfire in her youth. There were even more barriers to equality then than there are now, and I was determined to bring down at least one of them."

The sugar bowl and creamer went from cup to cup, offering themselves to each of us as Lord Pincushion continued with his story.

"And we were successful. The Red Menace was

defeated, and the League of Goodness reigned at the top of the superhero game for the next twenty years. Unfortunately, I paid so little attention to anything other than our missions that I hadn't realized how we were rushing headlong toward financial collapse. I had always assumed there would be plenty of money to finance the team, but I hadn't taken into account how expensive crime fighting could be. Fondue?"

"Huh?" I said.

"Would you like some fondue? It's really quite delicious," Lord Pincushion said, extending his left arm to me. In between a gardening shear, a straight razor, and a series of skewers, I saw three long slender forks. Both Pincushion and the Animator helped themselves to one, so I took the third for myself. It had two very sharp prongs.

"But when people found out, surely they helped you," I said. I watched my hosts use their forks to each spear a hunk of the bread.

"I assumed they would, too," Pincushion agreed as he dipped the bread into the pot sitting atop the flame. When he retrieved it, it was coated with melted cheese. "My fortune was gone with the exception of this house. In order to keep functioning I either had to sell it or find money somewhere else."

"What did you do?" I asked, reaching out with my fork to spear my own chunk of bread.

"Why, we decided to hold a telethon, of course," the Animator replied as if it were the most sensible idea in the world.

"Yes," Lord Pincushion said. "We naively assumed that the good citizens of Superopolis would come forward to help us."

"Did they?" I asked, as I retrieved my fork from the bubbling cheese mixture and moved it toward my mouth.

"No." My host shook his head sadly. "They barely contributed enough to pay for the rental of the TV studio. The old custom of people giving a little something back for the help they were given was long gone. I was just about ready to close down the league when I met Meteor Boy. He saved us from financial collapse."

I know it looked to my hosts as if I had burned my mouth on the hot cheese I had just stuffed in my face, but it wasn't the fondue that had startled me.

"Meteor Boy saved the League of Goodness?!" I blurted out.

"Why of course, kiddo!" The Animator nodded.

"He was an incredibly talented young man," Lord Pincushion agreed as he set down his fork and extended his hand to me.

I knew what he wanted. I fished out the letter I had come to deliver. He accepted it with a sad sort of smile on his face.

"He was destined to be quite a hero," he continued. He retrieved a letter opener from the general vicinity of his pancreas and used it to slit open the envelope.

Both the Animator and I watched Lord Pincushion remove the letter and scan it briefly. His eyes went wide with amazement.

"After all, his abilities must have been exceptional," he added after a brief pause. "How else could he have known that you would be delivering this letter to me on this very date?"

CHAPTER EIGHTEEN

A Message from Meteor Boy

I sat at the table utterly speechless as both Lord Pincushion and the Animator regarded me with odd expressions. Finally, I found my voice.

"He mentions me?" I blurted out in disbelief. "By name?"

"Indeed he does," Lord Pincushion confirmed. "And today's date."

"But that's impossible!" I sputtered. "It would mean . . ."

I couldn't even say it. What it meant was any number of things, none of which made any sense.

"May I see the letter?" I asked.

Lord Pincushion returned his gaze to the letter in his hand and then looked back up at me.

"Sadly, I'm afraid not," he said as he folded the letter, slipped it into a pocket in his jacket, and then stabbed the letter opener through not only it but his chest as well. "He specifically tells me not to let you see it. He said you would understand."

"What?!" I nearly shouted in exasperation. "That doesn't make any sense! I don't understand anything!"

I really thought I might start crying I was so frustrated, but I was determined not to do that in front of these legendary heroes. They could tell I was upset, though.

"Please don't think harshly of me," Lord Pincushion said. "Twenty-five years ago, Meteor Boy came along and assisted me in a way that I can never repay. Despite his own doubts about the advice he provided, I can only confirm that he did me a tremendous service. At the time, however, I don't think I was adequately appreciative, and I never did get a chance to thank him properly. So, if for no other reason, I feel I owe it to him to honor his wishes by not revealing the contents of his letter."

"I understand," I said. And in fact I did. I got up from my chair, sensing it was time for me to leave. But there was still a question I felt I had to ask.

"Can you at least tell me how Meteor Boy saved the league?"

"That, my dear boy, is a story I feel I must tell you," he responded graciously as he rose from his seat, the sharp objects sticking out of him pointing me toward the garden's exit. "We met Meteor Boy shortly after our disastrous telethon. In fact it was he who introduced us to the Amazing Indestructo."

"Was he already Superopolis's 'greatest' hero?" I said, barely hiding my sarcasm as I preceded my two hosts through the door and into the grand hallway.

"He was calling himself that," Lord Pincushion said dismissively as he followed me through, "but he had only just gotten started. Still, there was much to be impressed by."

"He was quite young and very handsome in those days," the Animator added.

"Did he offer to help?" I asked.

"In a way," Lord Pincushion replied. "What he offered was to take over the league in exchange for a lump sum of cash and ongoing royalty payments. My only other choice was bankruptcy, so I accepted his offer. The contract I signed, however, took away any control I had of the group."

"He's big on having people sign contracts," I agreed.

"Indeed." Lord Pincushion nodded as the three of us made our way back to the main entrance. "He began making changes immediately. He went out and made huge endorsement deals capitalizing on the league's good name, bringing in enormous sums of cash. Soon after, he pushed us to the background."

"Is that when he added 'ultimate' to your name?" I asked.

"Exactly," Lord Pincushion affirmed sadly. "Never has there been a man so cravenly devoted to adjectives."

"That's when he began to replace us with heroes who couldn't possibly show him up," added the Animator.

"A trend that hasn't changed in twenty-five years," I confirmed as we finally reached the front door.

"Quite. The sad fact was that the public actually preferred the new incompetent League of 'Ultimate' Goodness." Lord Pincushion sighed. "I guess because it made them feel that anyone, no matter how average, could be a successful superhero."

"But we were ready for retirement anyway," the Animator said with a shrug.

"The money that has rolled in over the years from that imbecile's enterprises has completely replenished my family fortune," Lord Pincushion said. "It was Meteor Boy that made it all possible."

There, he had gone and done it. He had brought up the subject that was gnawing at me, but that he wouldn't (or couldn't?) tell me about. I was once again completely frustrated. Without thinking, I shoved my hand in my pocket and felt the chunk of rock I had grabbed from my bedstand that morning.

"Maybe you can help explain what this is?" I asked as I retrieved the rock from my pocket.

"Good heavens!" Lord Pincushion's eyes went wide with surprise. "A piece of prodigium! My boy, do you know how rare this object is? It may be the only sample left in existence."

"There was a much larger piece," I corrected him. "Meteor Boy and his friends prevented the theft of an entire meteorite of prodigium from the science museum."

"Only temporarily," the Animator shook his head

sadly. "Professor Brain-Drain eventually got his hands on that meteorite."

"Indeed," agreed Lord Pincushion. "He was in the process of using it for some foul purpose when Meteor Boy intervened."

"What kind of purpose?" I asked.

"No one knows." The Animator shrugged. "He had converted the enormous water tower in Telomere Park into a device of some kind, but we were never able to determine its purpose. The prodigium appeared to play a key part in its operation, however."

"What happened to the meteorite?" I asked, already sensing the answer.

"Meteor Boy snatched it, preventing Brain-Drain's nefarious plot," Lord Pincushion said as his head bowed solemnly. "It vanished along with him."

The two elderly gentlemen stood silently for a moment. Finally, I turned to reach for the door. Lord Pincushion put his hand on my shoulder.

"There's an easier way," he said, leading me to a large wooden panel in the foyer, where he pushed a hidden switch. The panel slid open to reveal an elevator.

"We never use the stairs. But they're great for keeping away unwanted visitors," the Animator informed me as I stepped into the car and then turned back to look at these two great heroes.

"There are strange forces at work," Lord Pincushion added soberly.

"In case you hadn't already figured that out from the twenty-five-year-old letter that mentions you," the

Animator said with a mischievous smile and a twinkle in his eyes.

"Exactly," Lord Pincushion said as he shot his former teammate an annoyed look. "There are events taking shape, and your involvement in them is not merely coincidence. You're an intelligent boy, and I know what a rarity that is. Think things through. Your instincts will serve you well."

"Thank you," I said, despite my monumental confusion. I gave the legendary heroes a halfhearted smile as I pushed the ground floor button in the elevator and the doors slid closed. There were other buttons I could have chosen, and I was more than a little curious about what other floors I might find here in Needlepoint Hill, but for now it was time for me to get home.

When I got there, I walked in to find my mom and dad in the kitchen. There was frosting splattered everywhere, including all over them, and they were both laughing.

"Oh!" my mother said when she saw me. "I was just icing your father's cakes," she rushed to explain. She then turned and poured a liquid glaze over a nearby ring cake and froze it in place with a single quick stare. "See?" she nodded, as if for additional proof. Dad, meanwhile, started wiping up the frosting.

One minute Mom's furious at him, the next everything seems fine. I'll never understand parents. It's just nice to see that Mom had gotten over being mad.

"Are you okay, Dad?" I asked. He finally seemed himself again.

"I'm fine," he nodded. "In fact I'm better than fine. I know I've been a little crazy lately. I just want you both to understand how important it is for the New New Crusaders to make a splash next week."

"Are you certain you'll get the attention you're looking for just by baking all this stuff?" I asked skeptically, glancing at the hundreds of pies and cakes around the house.

"What do you mean?" my father asked.

"I mean that you guys are looking for attention, but you're just baking regular stuff. I know you're making hundreds, but they're still just normal pies and cakes."

"What else can we do?" he asked as he absentmindedly picked up a cupcake.

"I don't know," I replied, "but it needs to be something big."

"Hmm," my father pondered. "Something big."

I know my dad well enough to know that he's a literal thinker, so it shouldn't have come as a surprise to me that "big" is exactly what he came up with.

"I've got it," he announced proudly. "We won't keep making hundreds of ordinary pies and cakes. We'll just make one. The biggest cake that anyone's ever seen!"

I saw him getting that crazy look in his eyes again, and my mom saw it, too. I knew I had to find a way to shift this idiotic idea out of our home.

"I've got the perfect solution," I said.

"What is it, OB?" my dad asked.

"Stench's dad just got an enormous aboveground

swimming pool in his junkyard. It must be twenty feet across. You could use it to make your enormous cake!"

"That's it!" he cried as the cupcake in his hand instantly burnt to a charcoal lump.

My mother still looked horrified. I hurried on to the part of my idea that would save their marriage.

"But you'll have to make the cake over there. The pool is too big to fit anywhere here."

"That's no problem." My father waved his red-hot hand dismissively. "Windbag will love this idea. He won't mind us shifting operations over to his place."

I could practically hear my mother's sigh of relief. She mouthed "thank you" in my direction. I returned a wink and a smile and then turned to head upstairs to my room. On the way I helped myself to a bunch of cupcakes. Amid all this chaos, I doubted either of them would pay attention to my entirely non-nutritious dinner.

The things I had learned today had my brain going a mile a minute—although that possibly could have been the sugar. But no amount of pastry-induced hyperactivity could distract me from the inescapable conclusion I had come to. Meteor Boy was alive and well.

CHAPTER NINETEEN

Suspicion

The facts spoke for themselves. First of all, Meteor Boy's parents had never come forward to report him missing. Second, Meteor Boy had left a message about me—a *recent* message. Finally, my gut instinct said Meteor Boy was alive. Okay, so maybe that's not a fact, but in a way it was the strongest evidence. And Lord Pincushion had told me to trust my instincts.

When I came down into the kitchen on Monday morning for breakfast, I found Windbag and Uncle Fluster sitting at the table along with Mom and Dad. The room was already developing a chill.

"Those two attacks were just a coincidence," my father insisted as he slapped Fluster on the back, leaving a handprint where he evaporated a layer of frost. "But if it makes you feel better, you can hang out with the New New Crusaders today. We can use an extra hand with the project we have planned."

As he said this, he gave Windbag a conspiratorial wink. Stench's dad chuckled, clearly having heard and liked my dad's giant-cake idea.

"I guess then I could also replace the cone on top of my truck." Fluster shrugged. "Do you have any more?"

"You bet," said Windbag. "I have one more, and you're welcome to have it."

"I don't think it's a coincidence," I said aloud, and they all turned and noticed me for the first time. "I think those hippies will be after Uncle Fluster again."

This sent another wave of panic through my uncle. My dad looked thoughtful.

"Is that so?" he mused. "In that case, the New New Crusaders are going to have to be there waiting for them."

"But these guys are really dangerous," I insisted.

"No need to worry," said my father. "We haven't lost a fight yet."

"You've only had one fight so far," I felt compelled to point out.

"Exactly!" he said proudly. "A perfect record. We'll use Fluster to lure these criminals to their defeat."

As I left the house, I told myself that the NNC should have no problem handling the Commune for Justice. At least that's what I wanted to believe.

At school Miss Marble wasted no time getting us into pairs to work on the science fair.

"By the end of today, I expect all of you to not only

know exactly what your projects are but how you're going to have them ready by Thursday," she said sternly. "Now get to work."

Reluctantly, I pulled my desk up alongside Melonhead's. He rolled his eyes in annoyance.

"So what have you come up with since yesterday?" I asked.

"My time mathine ith perfect jutht ath it ith," he insisted indignantly.

"Only if everybody else's projects spontaneously combust," I responded.

For the next two hours we continued to argue back and forth about the project, accomplishing nothing. Finally, as lunch approached, I got him to admit that his potato was not really a time machine.

"Okay, tho it'th a clock," he sputtered. "You tell me how we tranthform it into a time mathine if you're tho thmart."

"Well . . . ," I pondered the problem. An idea began to form. "Let's think about it this way," I said. "Remember how yesterday I talked about how time moves forward at an unchanging rate and there's nothing we can do to stop it?"

Melonhead listened to me intently, his head nodding in agreement—at least to the extent that the neckless wonder was able to nod.

"Maybe that's just how it appears to us." Melonhead stared at me blankly. "Maybe time behaves differently in different places."

"That'th impothible," he spluttered.

"Is it?" I asked. "There are other forces that appear to be constant but really aren't."

"Like what?"

"How about gravity?" I said.

"The thing that maketh you fall down?"

"Exactly. Think about it for a second," I said. "Like time, gravity appears to be an unchanging force. But gravity *can* change as you move away from its source. If you travel into space, our planet's gravitational force no longer has as powerful a hold on you. Don't get me wrong. Gravity is still a force. But it shows that it isn't a *constant* force. In some places it's weaker and other places it's stronger. For instance, near a spinning black hole, gravity is so strong that it can alter the direction of light."

"Tho what doeth that mean?" Melonhead responded, totally confused.

"Maybe a strong enough gravitational force can also alter the direction of time."

"Tho all we have to do ith fikth my potato clock tho it can increath the forth of gravity," he proposed confidently.

"I doubt your potato is technologically advanced enough for that," I answered cheerfully. "But, like a black hole, if we could somehow get an object to spin fast enough—say at near the speed of light—we possibly could increase gravity enough to also affect the movement of time."

"How about thomething like thith?" Melonhead said, reaching into his lunch bag and pulling out a tall, cylindrical package.

"What's that?" I asked, genuinely curious as I noticed a picture of the Amazing Indestructo on the can.

"They're potato chipth," Melonhead informed me. "I found thith at Indethtructo Induthtrieth."

"But how could potato chips fit in a tall can like this?"

"They're all identical," he insisted. "They're thtacked."

"No two potato chips are alike. That's impossible."

"No it'th not. Here, look."

Melonhead opened the can and shook out a few of the chips. They didn't really look like potato chips, but they *were* identical. Hesitantly I reached for one and took a small bite. It didn't taste awful, but it certainly wasn't a potato chip. It was like some strange alternate-reality version of a potato chip. I looked again at the label on the can.

"'The Amazing Indestructo's Amazing Pseudo-Chips: Each One as Perfect as Him!'" I read aloud. "But I've never seen these for sale anywhere."

"I think it'th thomething new that he hathn't put on thale yet."

Just then the bell for lunch rang and Melonhead grabbed back his can, emptied the remaining chips into his hand, and shoved the can back at me.

"Tho here you go," he said. "I've done my part by finding thith thylinder. Now you need to figure out how to make it thpin at the thpeed of light."

"That will be tricky," I replied.

"Well, it really doethn't matter," Melonhead said. "Printhipal Doppelganger thaid we were guaranteed to win jutht by attempting a time mathine."

"What?!" I said, thinking I had misheard him.

"That'th what he thaid when he took me out of clath the other day," Melonhead informed me. "After all, he wath the one who thuggethted the thubject in the firtht plathe."

With that he got up and went to lunch. I stared blankly at the potato chip can and then stuffed it into my book bag. All my thoughts had shifted to Principal Doppelganger. Why had he given Melonhead the idea for our project? I needed to meet up with my teammates. I had an awful lot to tell them.

"Doppelganger picked your science fair project?" Tadpole asked in disbelief as we walked to the cafeteria.

"That's really strange," Plasma Girl said.

"I've got other news, too," I informed them.

I began by relating my strange visit to Pinprick Manor. The early history of the League of Goodness fascinated them, but it was the letter that really got their attention.

"A letter from Meteor Boy, and it was addressed to you?" Halogen Boy asked with wide-eyed amazement.

"Not to me," I corrected him. "It was addressed to Lord Pincushion. But according to him, Meteor Boy mentioned me by name in the letter."

"But how could that be possible?" Plasma Girl asked for probably the third time in less than a minute.

"It isn't possible." Tadpole snorted dismissively. "Someone's messing with you."

"It's improbable, not impossible," I corrected him. "And I don't think Lord Pincushion or the Animator would have any reason to lie."

"Maybe the Bee Lady is behind this," Stench interjected. "She could have put that letter in the Collide-a-scope."

"Don't you dare say anything bad about the Bee Lady," Plasma Girl responded angrily.

"I agree, she didn't do it," I cut in quickly to head off an argument, "which leads me to the unmistakable conclusion that Meteor Boy himself left that message where he knew I would find it."

"But he vanished twenty-five years ago," Stench protested. "He had no way of knowing you were even going to exist now!"

"That's true," I agreed, "*if* he planted the message twenty-five years ago. But *not* if he just planted it recently!"

"But he's dead," Hal pointed out, saying what all of us believed but had never said aloud. "And has been for twenty-five years."

"Is he?" I posed the question I had already answered for myself the night before.

"Is who dead?" a voice suddenly asked from behind me.

We all looked up to find Principal Doppelganger hovering over us. I stared at him for a moment without answering, searching his blank face for an answer to some unknown question still stuck in the back of my mind.

"Professor Brain-Drain," I finally answered. "We were talking about his destruction last week in the flames of Mount Reliable. We were wondering if he really is dead."

"Of course," Principal Doppelganger replied. "Who else would you have been talking about?"

With that, he turned, whipping his cape around, and strolled away, leaving us all standing there with our mouths hanging open.

"He's up to something," Hal said, voicing a thought we all shared.

"I agree," I said. "I just wish I knew what."

The five of us turned in the opposite direction and headed for the cafeteria. On the way there, who should we see coming from the opposite direction, but Coach Inflato. I stopped in my tracks and turned to watch him as he passed by us.

"Wait for me," I said. "I need to talk to the coach."

My teammates watched in surprise as I sprinted after Coach Inflato. By the time I caught up to him, he had gone into the gymnasium and was headed for the door of his office.

"Coach!" I hollered as I ran to catch up to him. "I have a question I'm hoping you can answer."

He turned and regarded me with annoyance.

"I knew you'd eventually come and ask me this," he said.

He did? Why did everyone seem to be a step ahead of me lately? I came to a stop but didn't know what to say.

"There's no point, kid," he continued. "You don't have a power and so there's no way you're ever going to be a decent athlete."

"What—?!" I started to say, caught completely off guard.

"Deal with it, kid," he continued. "Not everyone has athletic ability. Only a few of us are gifted enough to be spectacular athletes."

I knew he meant himself and it made me furious.

"I'm not a bad athlete," I exploded. "And I didn't even come to ask you about that, and never would, because I think you're a lousy athlete."

He looked stunned that a student would speak to him like that. I was pretty stunned, too. But before he could reprimand me, I blurted out the question I had come to ask.

"I want to know about Meteor Boy!"

He reared back in alarm, his face tightening up. He opened his mouth to respond, but all that came out was a blast of air as he shot violently backward, ricocheting around the corners of the gymnasium. When he settled to the ground, he got back on his feet and rushed to get into his office. His flimsy hand grabbed my arm and pulled me along with him.

"Meteor Boy ruined the lives of my friends Funnel Boy and InvisiBoy," he said bitterly. "And he robbed me of my rightful role as the Amazing Indestructo's sidekick."

I didn't even know what to say, I was so shocked by what he was revealing.

"Where did you hear about Meteor Boy?" he said with as much insistence as an empty balloon could manage. "He was supposed to be forgotten."

"Everyone is going to know about Meteor Boy, very, very soon," I informed him, freeing myself from his feeble, rubbery grip. "Professor Brain-Drain may have destroyed him, but the Amazing Indestructo is intent on re-creating him."

The look of despair that spread across his deflated face almost made me feel sorry for him—until he spoke.

"Professor Brain-Drain didn't destroy Meteor Boy," Inflato said as he dropped his head into his hands. "I did."

CHAPTER TWENTY

Old Heroes Never Die

My teammates were as shocked as I had been by our gym teacher's confession.

"Coach Inflato was responsible for Meteor Boy's death?" Tadpole blurted out.

"That's what he told me," I confirmed. "But he wouldn't tell me *why* he thinks that."

"Maybe dodgeball was involved," Hal said softly.

"But I thought AI was responsible," Stench pointed out, ignoring Hal.

"That's right," agreed Plasma Girl. "At least AI sure seems to think it's true."

"Could they both have been responsible?" asked Tadpole.

"Anything is possible," I answered with a shrug. "Of course the problem is that we only know what people are willing to tell us. And even that information is twenty-five years old."

"Maybe we can use Melonhead's time machine," Tadpole snorted. "Is it working yet?"

"That won't be an option for quite a while," I responded. "But maybe there's another way to see what happened."

"How? There is no visual record," Stench said. "Is there?"

"Isn't there?" I mused. "After all, there's still one more living member of the original League of Goodness who we haven't spoken to yet."

"MagnoBox!" they all said practically in unison.

When school let out a few hours later, all five of us headed for the other side of town to the location listed in the *Li'l Hero's Handbook* as MagnoBox's address. We soon found ourselves standing at the front entrance of a boring but pleasant-enough looking building. The sign in front of it read: WESTING HOUSE RETIREMENT HOME. Below it in smaller letters it added: For Heroes Who Are Just too Tired to Fight Anymore.

I guess it shouldn't have come as a surprise to us that it was completely filled with old people. They were everywhere—in chairs, on sofas, in wheelchairs. It wasn't until Halogen Boy tugged on my sleeve and pointed him out that I realized there was even a guy floating a couple feet above our heads. He was a little puffy looking in his white leotard. The blue briefs he had on looked even puffier.

"Hello there, young'uns," he said. "Yer lookin' a mite out of place in here. Is there anything I can help you with? The name is Cumulonimbus."

"Thank you, sir," I replied as we all backed up slightly. "We're looking for a particular resident of the home."

"Certainly," he said. "Which one would that be?"

"MagnoBox," answered Stench. "We read that he might live here."

"Oh, he does. You can usually find him in the TV room." Cumulonimbus tilted his head in the appropriate direction as he bobbed a little from left to right with excitement. "He's one of our celebrity residents. Used to be a member of the League of Goodness, you know."

"We did know," Plasma Girl agreed politely.

I sensed a story coming on.

"MagnoBox won't tell you this himself . . . too modest, don't you know . . . but he was directly responsible for bringing down the Red Menace. Now *there* was a villain . . ."

The story had the potential to be a long one, but then in the midst of his excitement at having someone to talk to, something unfortunate happened to Cumulonimbus.

"Today's villains don't know the meaning of . . . Uh-oh . . ."

Suddenly, there was a loud clap that sounded like something else, but for politeness sake I'll say it was thunder. And then a downpour erupted from Cumulonimbus. We all backed farther away, grateful that none of us had been right under him. The way they began puffing up, I quickly realized his briefs were actually diapers. In fact, I'm sure they were the same brand my dad's team had been offered an endorsement deal on. But no matter how absorbent they were, they couldn't handle this big of a job.

"Oh, dear," Cumulonimbus blushed with embarrassment, "I used to have no problem at all controlling my power."

I felt really awful for him, but I didn't know what to do to help. As he floated off to get assistance, I led my teammates toward the TV room.

When we got there my heart fell. The dimly lit space appeared empty. My first fear was that

MagnoBox had gone to take a nap or something. The only thing in the room was an old-fashioned television set, and it wasn't even turned on. Then, I suddenly realized that the TV was sitting on top of a slightly stooped pair of shoulders, which in turn belonged to a body that was slumped in an easy chair. There was only one superhero I had ever heard of who had a TV for a head, and we had clearly found him.

I paused for a moment, looking at the darkened screen. Hesitantly, I reached over to touch one of the knobs.

"Excuse me. Mr. MagnoBox?"

Then, without warning, it suddenly lit up and a face appeared on the screen.

"Oh, my goodness, we're on the air!" he announced as he realized he had an audience. "What can I do for you, children? Comedy? Quiz shows? Cartoons? Do you kids know that Moo-Maid brand Milk Shakes Build Little Heroes' Muscles? And please. Call me MagnoBox."

"Thank you," I replied, as we all tried following his rapid-fire delivery. While it's a little hard to tell with someone whose face is on a screen, I got the sense that MagnoBox was quite old. His features were well-lined despite what looked like some heavy makeup and strategic lighting, but the eyes were still lively and intelligent.

"If we could, we'd very much like to ask you some questions about an event from twenty-five years ago—that is if you think you might be able to remember."

NAME: MagnoBox. **POWER:** The ability to broadcast real-time events occurring at any location. **LIMITATIONS:** Prone to commercial interruptions and reruns. **CAREER:** His ability to reveal the actions of criminals in the act helped make the League of Goodness unbeatable. **CLASSIFICATION:** MagnoBox is entertaining, informative, and a treasure trove of knowledge. He is seldom utilized these days.

"Child you wound me," he said melodramatically, "which is why I always keep Blitz Bandages on hand. You see, I've always had photographic memories, and I still have the ability to replay them all."

"You remember everything?" I asked, hoping I wasn't sounding too eager.

But MagnoBox picked up on it as he turned to me and the face on the screen raised a suspicious eyebrow.

"I sense a mystery over the airwaves," he said with a sly expression on his face. "Do tell what you're looking for, and if it's in my listings I will be happy to program it for rebroadcast."

"We've come to see you about Meteor Boy," I replied gravely. "Can you tell us what happened that day you all faced Professor Brain-Drain—the day Meteor Boy disappeared?"

"Ahh! A sad day, indeed. But I can do better than tell you, my boy." He smiled. "I'll show you."

MagnoBox's face vanished from the television screen and was replaced by an image that we all instantly recognized. It was set off in the distance, but there was no mistaking the water tower that sat atop Crater Hill in the center of Telomere Park. It was just as Lord Pincushion had stated.

The water tower looked different than it does today, but before I could pinpoint why, the image turned and we found ourselves looking directly into the face of Meteor Boy himself.

CHAPTER TWENTY-ONE

Rerun

It was Meteor Boy all right—in living black and white. For the first time, we were all seeing him as more than just an image on a collector card. This was a real person.

"Come on," he said, looking straight at us. "We have to stop Professor Brain-Drain."

Of course he was really looking right at MagnoBox almost twenty-five years earlier. I watched in fascination.

"We're right behind you," I heard MagnoBox's voice, only it was a much younger and richer voice than the one I had heard just moments ago. "Telomere Park is right ahead of us. And did you know that Dr. Telomere's Potato Chips are a key—and crunchy—part of a healthy hero's diet?"

The image turned slightly, and I saw that the heroes following Meteor Boy were actually moving quite fast, but only appeared slow in comparison to

189

TELOMERE PARK

Running north of Dr. Telomere's Potato Chip Factory, and alongside the impassable Carbunkle Mountains, Telomere Park contains over a thousand acres of land ranging from heavily forested nature preserves to beautifully manicured picnic and recreation areas. The most obvious feature of the park is the enormous water tower that sits atop Crater Hill in the center of the park, providing water to the enormous Telomere potato fields to the south. Though privately owned by the factory, the park is open for public use.

Meteor Boy's extraordinary speed. It was the entire League of Goodness. What amazed me was that they all appeared to be flying! The Animator had on a thick pair of aviator goggles in place of his regular glasses as he soared through the air with his arms extended like a bird. The Bee Lady was in the midst of a swarm of bees. Lord Pincushion was dressed just as I had seen him the previous day, in pinstripes and tails, but he also held a top hat tightly to his head. The numerous sharp objects sticking from his body were all bending back into the wind, giving him the look of an aerodynamic porcupine. Of course there was no sign of MagnoBox, since this was all from his point of view.

I had no idea how a group of heroes with no flying ability among them could be doing just that, but then the perspective changed. And there was Zephyr, gliding on air currents above the others and obviously commanding the winds to carry his teammates along. Then suddenly Meteor Boy whipped right by them again. The speed of the wind seemed like nothing compared to his power.

"Where's the Amazing Indestructo?" Meteor Boy asked as he slowed himself to coast alongside the league. "We're going to need his abilities against someone as powerful as Professor Brain-Drain."

"Apparently, this is something that he considers his sidekick's duty to handle," Lord Pincushion said sarcastically. "I believe he has an important meeting with an investor to attend."

"Look! There he is!" Meteor Boy announced.

"Who?" asked the Animator. "The Amazing Indestructo?"

"No," said the Bee Lady. "It's Professor Brain-Drain!"

MagnoBox's replay switched angles and focused on the Professor. The first thing I noticed was that he was standing next to a large lever mounted on the floor of a platform that surrounded the entire base of the tower. Arrows pointing in opposite directions were painted on the side of the tower on either side of the lever. Mounted between the two arrows was a digital counter, but it was too far away for me to make out the numbers on it.

Professor Brain-Drain looked quite a bit younger and still had hair on his head. Quite a bit of it, in fact. He actually had a big bushy head of hair. Resting atop his do was the familiar colander that he always wore.

Without any warning, the water tower began to spin—slowly at first, but it built up speed rapidly.

"You're all too late." I heard Professor Brain-Drain cackle as he grabbed the upright lever and pulled it all the way to the left. "My Tipler has begun turning and when it reaches full speed, Superopolis will be destroyed."

Well, if nothing else, Professor Brain-Drain's goals had remained remarkably consistent over all these years. But what was a Tipler? And what was it supposed to do? We all leaned toward the screen.

"What's happening?" I heard the MagnoBox of the past ask in surprise. More worrisome, the image on the screen began to get fuzzy.

Then the image vanished altogether, replaced completely by static and snow.

"Where's the picture?" I asked with a tone of panic in my voice. "Or even the sound?"

"I'm afraid that's all I was able to record," MagnoBox said as his own face reappeared on the screen. "Whatever that device was, it interfered with my reception. Of course, Electro-Bunny brand antennas provide crystal clear reception! Perhaps it was due to the stolen meteorite that Brain-Drain had mounted atop the tower. Meteor Boy was attempting to retrieve it when he vanished."

"Did he succeed?" Hal asked in a quiet voice.

"Well, let's take a look," MagnoBox said as we all simultaneously held our breaths. "As soon as he vanished in a blinding flash of light, the interference vanished as well."

The image of the water tower reappeared on Magno-Box's screen. The first thing I noticed was Professor Brain-Drain howling in furious despair. Obviously his plan, whatever it was, had been ruined. Then I noticed that the lever was now pulled to the right, and

the view was close enough to show what was flashing on the digital panel. It was the number twenty-five.

What could that mean? But I didn't have time to puzzle over the mystery. Instead, along with MagnoBox's own view, my gaze rose up and up and up to the top of the tower. There I focused on my first close-up view of the water tower. There was no sign of any meteorite, but what I did see sent an eerie shudder down my spine. Attached near the top of the cylinder was a wire structure with three ringed spokes. Each of the rings had a distinctive metal cone resting point down within them. I had no doubt whatsoever that they were identical to the cones now being stolen from my uncle Fluster.

CHAPTER TWENTY-TWO

Let 'Em Eat Cake

"It's the cones," I said. "They're the exact same ones my uncle has been using on top of his truck. That's what Cyclotron and the hippies have been after."

"The *same* cones!?" asked Stench. "How could they be?"

"My uncle got them from your dad," I said frantically. "In fact, your dad told me he's had them sitting in his junkyard for over twenty years."

"I'd believe that," Stench grudgingly admitted.

"But what use are they to anyone?" Plasma Girl insisted. "Professor Brain-Drain is dead, and whatever he invented was taken apart."

"The young lady is correct," MagnoBox's face appeared once again on his screen. "After apprehending Professor Brain-Drain, we dismantled his device and returned the water tower to its normal function.

Free-Lax will leave you functioning normally, too!"

"What did you do with the pieces?" I asked.

MagnoBox thought about it, and the expression on his face turned grave.

"We scattered them around to various junkyards throughout the city," he admitted. "I fear your suspicions may be on target."

"And if I'm right, it means that there is one more cone these crooks are still trying to get their hands on." I turned to Stench in a panic. "We have to get to your dad's junkyard."

We dashed from the Westing House Retirement Home. As we neared Windbag's junkyard, it wasn't hard to see that something big had happened. Three blocks before we got there we already noticed police cars, fire trucks, and even an ambulance heading in that direction. Without speaking, we all began to pick up our pace. By the time we neared his house, we were practically running. I also began to notice strange-looking chunks littering the ground as we got closer. I realized they were pieces of cake.

"Something has gone really wrong," I said.

As we reached Stench's yard it wasn't hard to see what had happened. My father had taken my advice to the extreme. He hadn't just used the swimming pool to create a single cake, as I had suggested. Dad used it to make multiple cakes which he and the rest of the team had stacked into a gigantic layer cake. My guess was that they had completed seven layers, each of them twenty feet across. Stacked up, they must have been over fifty feet tall. The only problem was that the New New Crusaders' seven-story cake had tumbled over.

My only question was: Where were the New New Crusaders? Then I caught sight of . . .

"Uncle Fluster!" I shouted to him as he wandered out into the middle of the road, looking dazed. "What's happened here? Where's my dad?"

"I tried to warn them," he rambled. "I tried to warn them, but they insisted it would be a piece of cake. Oh, I think I made a joke, ha-ha. Get it?"

"Is my dad okay?" I pressed him. I even grabbed him by the collar and began shaking him. Whatever the reason, he began to get more lucid.

"I was preparing to attach the cone to my truck," he said. "But the moment Windbag brought it out, those horrible hippies attacked. And then all the flashes went off."

I suddenly realized that there were reporters and photographers crawling all over the scene like maggots on . . . well, on an enormous cake.

"Where did *they* all come from?" I asked.

"Thermo invited them to record his team in action."

"Where is my dad?" I asked for what felt like the dozenth time.

"He's under the cake," Fluster responded. "So are the rest of the New New Crusaders. They had almost beaten those hippies, but then Cyclotron showed up and whipped up an enormous tornado around the cake and pushed it over on top of them. But don't worry, they're fine. Right now they're eating their way out from the center. That's what all the reporters are hanging around to photograph. They should be free in about fifteen minutes."

Clearly, he had no concept of how fast my dad could eat cake. Only seconds after Uncle Fluster said it, my dad suddenly erupted from beneath the house-sized heap of dessert. He looked a little dazed, as anyone would who had just eaten who knows how many pounds of cake. There were crumbs all over him ranging from speck sized to fist sized. His mouth was still stuffed and chewing, as well. But worst of all, the second his eyes began to focus, flashes started going off by the dozen. He had wanted publicity, and, much to my horror, publicity was what he was getting.

He wasn't upset, though. He clearly thought it was incredible. Brushing as many of the cake crumbs off himself as possible, he strode confidently forward to meet the press, followed closely by the rest of his team. Stench sighed with relief as his father appeared, blowing the crumbs off himself with one gust of his breath.

The New New Crusaders talked it up with the reporters, clearly enjoying the exposure, regardless of the situation. Meanwhile, I turned to Uncle Fluster.

"Did they get away with the cone?" I asked, already fearing the answer.

"Yes." He sighed. "And it was the last one. It's such a shame, because they were great for advertising my business."

I didn't bother pointing out to him that so far he had still sold only one ice cream cone. Instead, I turned to my teammates, who were focusing on the chunks of pastry littered all around us.

"It's nt bd," Tadpole mumbled as he shoved a huge hunk into his mouth.

"Maybe your dads should open a bakery," Plasma Girl agreed as she sampled a daintier-sized piece.

"How come there's no frosting?" Halogen Boy asked in disappointment.

"The frosting is going to be added tomorrow," I heard my father say from behind me. "Although, we may have to put that off for a day while we rebuild."

"Rebuild?" Stench said in alarm. He'd noticed how close this cake had come to crushing his house.

"Sure!" my dad replied. "Today we did seven layers. I think we can salvage a few of them, and tomorrow we should be able to bring the total to ten!"

"Cool!" Tadpole, Hal, and Plasma Girl all responded. No one else seemed to share my concern that all three of the giant metal cones were now in the hands of villains, but of course, we still had no idea what they were or what use they were to anyone.

"But I think that's enough for today," my father continued. "OB, let's go get your mom and celebrate the NNC's publicity coup."

I would hardly describe the past hour's events that way, but I waved good-bye to my teammates and turned to head home with my father. He was in a great mood despite the fact that his team had gotten beaten and then buried under tons of pastry.

"We're going to be the hit of the bake sale," he said confidently. "Everyone's going to come see our giant cake. And I owe the whole idea to you."

This disaster *had* been my idea, I realized. And my Dad was thrilled about it. So who was I to complain? He was unhurt and that was all that really mattered. The truth was I had problems of my own that I should be focusing on instead.

"I wish I could say the same about my science project." I sighed.

"That doesn't sound good," he said. "Tell me how it's going."

"Well, it's been hard making much progress with Melonhead," I admitted. "But I think I have an idea for a model of a working time machine. If I can get a cylinder to rotate at near the speed of light, in theory it could redirect the flow of time in such a way that you could pass either into the future or into the past. To make it work, though, there are three problems I still need to solve."

"What would those be?" my father said.

"First, I need a power source that could make the cylinder turn at nearly the speed of light."

"Is that difficult?" he asked.

"Very," I responded. "Second, I need a device to calibrate movement either into the past or into the future. There's no point having a time machine if you can't set it to travel to exactly the time you want."

"Of course," he agreed, as we reached our front porch.

"And finally, there's the issue of the light cones—the cone-shaped paths of light which contain all past and future possibilities. When the cylinder rotates at near light speed, the gravitational distortion will cause a warpage of space-time . . . but of course the problem is that these light cones, which represent past and future pathways of time, are invisible. In order to show that the machine is working, it needs to come attached with— Oh, my gosh!"

"What is it, OB?" my dad asked.

All of a sudden, it struck me. The spinning water tower, the cones, and everything else I saw in MagnoBox's replay finally all made sense.

"It has to come attached with cones that will visibly show the warping of space-time. Don't you see?! Professor Brain-Drain's device was a time machine—a *Time* Tipler! The water tower in Telomere Park was the cylinder, the lever set the direction of time either forward or backward, and the metal cones were the visible indicators that the cylinder had achieved a warpage of space-time. When the cones tipped far enough, travel through time became possible."

"But what about that speed-of-light business?" he reminded me. "You said that would take an awful lot of energy."

"Nearly the speed of light," I corrected as I pondered this mystery. And then I had it.

"The meteorite!" I shouted. "The prodigium meteorite on top of the tower was Professor Brain-Drain's power source—the meteorite that Meteor Boy stole from him at the very last second!"

And then I remembered the number I saw on the digital counter when MagnoBox showed me his rerun of the events of that day twenty-five years ago. The number was twenty-five. All of a sudden everything made sense, including the lever that had been switched to the forward position.

"Meteor Boy wasn't destroyed," I said as calmly as I could. "He was propelled into the future—twenty-five years into the future. By my calculation, he's due to arrive here in about seventy-two hours."

CHAPTER TWENTY-THREE

When Melons Fly

I put aside my shock that Professor Brain-Drain had apparently invented a time machine and that the device may have catapulted Meteor Boy into a future that was just three days away. I had a science experiment to work on, and the realization that I might be on the right track had me focused once again on the project.

Digging an old battery-powered phonograph from the attic, I took the tall potato chip can from my book bag, punched a hole in the bottom of it, and then attached it to the turntable. Flipping the switch, I soon had a revolving cylinder just like Professor Brain-Drain's, only on a much smaller scale.

For a moment I paused, pondering the incredible coincidence. Independently, I had devised a prototype for a time machine that was nearly identical to one invented twenty-five years earlier by Professor Brain-

Drain. A chill ran down my spine. Was it a good thing that I had been thinking along the same lines as the late, loathsome egghead of evil?

By Tuesday morning, I had managed to put that disturbing thought behind me. I gathered up my time machine prototype, and then, as an afterthought, the chunk of prodigium and the Oomphlifier from my nightstand. I shoved both of them in my pockets thinking either might provide a source of power for the device.

I met up with my friends at school and they immediately began asking about my spinning potato chip can. I had painted over it to save myself having to explain this strange product that AI was apparently going to be launching soon. I also refrained from mentioning my new theory on Meteor Boy's upcoming reappearance. It just sounded too far-fetched to believe. I needed more proof.

As the bell rang, Miss Marble dove right in.

"All right," she grumped. "You had all yesterday to work out what your projects are going to be. Now I want to hear about them. First I want an explanation of your subject and then a description of how you plan to demonstrate it. Let's start with Tadpole and Stench."

My two buddies looked helplessly at each other, arguing with their eyes over who should do the talking. Stench finally realized that he couldn't possibly do a worse job of describing their project than Tadpole, so he plunged ahead.

"We're studying the paths that objects take when they're launched into the air, and how gravity makes them come back down in specific ways."

"For our experiment," Tadpole interrupted, "we're going to fire off water-pressure bottle rockets."

"Dream on, kid." Miss Marble stopped him cold. "If you think I'm letting you launch weapons into the air, you're nuts."

"We have some other ideas," Stench added, elbowing Tadpole in the side.

"You better," concluded Miss Marble. "Okay, Cannonball, what have you and Halogen Boy come up with?"

Hal just sat sheepishly next to Cannonball, letting him do all the talking.

"Our project concerns static electricity and how it can be used to generate a magnetic field," the jerk answered smugly.

"And what kind of an experiment are you planning?" Miss Marble asked suspiciously, glancing over at Hal.

"Halogen Boy's power is going to represent an electric charge," Cannonball responded matter-of-factly. "And then we'll demonstrate the static electricity that occurs and its magnetic properties."

"So," said Miss Marble, "you've turned your partner into the experiment."

"Exactly," replied Cannonball, not the least bit ashamed of himself.

"And how do you feel about this, Hal?" Miss Marble asked.

With a brief, nervous glance at Cannonball, Hal

answered as he'd been instructed.

"Uh, it's fine," he said reluctantly.

"Hmm, we'll see," Miss Marble said. "But for now let's keep moving."

Team by team, Miss Marble continued to question us about our projects. Plasma Girl and Little Miss Bubbles were far along on their "tea party" experiment. Lobster Boy and Limber Lass were going to show how beakers of water could be used to make a xylophone. The Quake and Sparkplug, ever eager for destruction, were building a volcano. Meanwhile, Puddle Boy and the Spore had planted some peas in the hope of growing something by Thursday.

It wasn't until she called on me that I realized Melonhead wasn't there. His unexplained absence left me with the job of making my spinning can and his potato clock sound interesting. That turned out to be a task beyond my abilities. By the time I finished, I think Miss Marble had resigned herself to the inevitability of a science fair disaster.

"Well, I guess these projects are about as exciting as one can expect with only a few days to prepare," she said with a shrug. "Now break up into your teams and let's see what we can do to liven some of them up. I'll come by and review them one at a time."

The day dragged on as Miss Marble spent almost a half hour with each pair of my classmates. While all this was happening, I sat by myself and pondered the mystery of Meteor Boy. Would he really return in two days time? Or had he vanished in a flash of light because he had been destroyed? I had already determined that time travel wasn't necessarily impossible, just highly improbable. Perhaps the energy in a large chunk of prodigium could have provided all the power Professor Brain-Drain needed to operate his time machine.

I pulled out my copy of the *Li'l Hero's Handbook* to look it up.

My theory that the prodigium was the Professor's power source appeared to be accurate. I patted the chunk in my pocket, imagining what its value might be. (The book had said incalculable, but I can calculate pretty high!) As the afternoon flowed by, more pieces of the puzzle fell into place, and I felt like I was beginning to finally grasp the problems involved with developing a time machine. A little more time to myself was all I needed to . . .

"Greetingth, fellow thkolarths!"

I closed my eyes in frustration, reopening them to watch Melonhead make his triumphal entry as Meteor Boy.

"What's with the new costume?" Cannonball asked. "Are those melon seeds streaking across your chest?"

"Don't be thilly." Melonhead chuckled patiently. "Thith ith my new uniform for fighting crime alongthide the Amathing Indethtructo himthelf. From thith moment on you can call me Meteor Boy!"

And then, to the astonishment of all my classmates, Melonhead shot into the air. He hovered there for only a moment and then let himself settle back down to the ground.

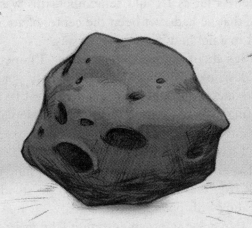

PRODIGIUM

A substance so rare that it may not even exist. None has been seen in Superopolis since the only known sample of it was stolen from the Museum of Science. If any does exist, however, its value would quite likely be incalculable. It's the amount of power compressed into the substance that makes the material so utterly unique.

"Wow!" the rest of my classmates said in amazement. A huge grin burst across Melonhead's face. With the exception of my teammates, the kids in my class mobbed Melonhead, each of them shouting "How did you do that?!"

"Thorry, guyth," he informed them in his most condescending manner, "I'm afraid that'th a thecret. I'm under contract to Indethtructo Induthtrieth, and I'm not allowed to thpeak about any company buthineth."

As the rest of my classmates protested and complained, Melonhead took his seat with a self-satisfied smile. As far as I could remember, this was the first time that he had ever been the center of attention—at least in a nonhumiliating sort of way.

"It's about time you showed up," I griped as I slid my desk over toward his. "We've only got a couple more days to get this thing figured out. I've built us a rotating cylinder. Now we need to develop a gauge to measure the movement of time."

"I have the perfect tholuthion," he said.

Eagerly he bent down to fish something out of his book bag. It was no surprise when he stood back up revealing—his potato clock.

"I've made improvmenth to it," he insisted.

"Can you control the tides with it now?" I asked sarcastically.

He looked at me blankly, not sure if I was joking, and then decided to plunge ahead.

"Thee? I've added another thet of handths to it."

"So?"

"Tho now it can meathure time both backward and forward."

I closed my eyes in frustration and counted to ten in an effort to calm myself down. When I opened them back up, Principal Doppelganger was standing in the front of the room. Miss Marble had just noticed him as well, and took a break from working with the Spore and Puddle Boy on their experiment.

"I'm here with exciting news, Miss Marble," he informed her.

"Exciting for you maybe," she huffed. "You're not the one who has to get nearly a dozen projects into some sort of a semicompetent state by Thursday."

"You'll do just fine," Principal Doppelganger said soothingly, apparently as intimidated by our teacher as we were. "I have some more news about the fair."

"And what would that be?" she asked.

"Oh, nothing to be worried about," he said. "Just the location of the fair. It will be taking place right in the center of Telomere Park—near the giant water tower, which also just happens to be the subject of Crispo's latest sculpture. Isn't that exciting?"

I would hardly have described the look on Miss Marble's face as excited, but my mouth dropped open in shock. Our science fair occurring twenty-five years to the day after Meteor Boy's disappearance, and at the exact location, could not be a coincidence. Could it?

CHAPTER TWENTY-FOUR

The Thubththtitute'th Thubththtitute

"I can't explain why," I told my teammates as we left school, "but something suspicious is going on at Telomere Park."

"You don't have to explain," Stench insisted. "We saw MagnoBox's broadcast. We know that was the site where Meteor Boy vanished."

"And we can tell that Cyclotron and those hippies are trying to reassemble Professor Brain-Drain's device," Plasma Girl added.

My teammates just didn't know what that device was, I reminded myself. But I would tell them—as soon as I was sure that I wasn't crazy for believing it.

We reached Telomere Park in about fifteen minutes and then made our way toward Crater Hill in the park's center. We arrived to find the water tower hidden beneath a shroud with a large platform built around it. A reviewing stand had been set up alongside it, and a large crowd was gathered in front of the platform. At first we couldn't see what was going on, but then the crowd parted enough to reveal . . .

"The Amazing Indestructo," we all groaned in unison. Sure enough, AI was standing on the platform that surrounded the tower.

"What's he doing here?" Plasma Girl said in disgust.

"And look who's with him," added Stench. "It's Mayor Whitewash!"

"That's not all. Melonhead is here, too!" I rolled my eyes in exasperation. "No wonder he left school so fast."

The annoying little creep was flying around above the crowd as if he were Meteor Boy himself. And then I saw the enormous banner hanging from the tower platform. It proclaimed: THE RETURN OF METEOR BOY! This was nothing more than a huge publicity gimmick to help build interest for AI's big launch of Meteor Boy products on Thursday. Once again, and certainly not for the last time, his lack of decency astounded me. I could barely concentrate as the mayor began to speak.

"I'd like to welcome all you VIPs to this special sneak preview! And a big welcome to our fine city council members as well," he added as he indicated the people in the reviewing stand. "It gives me great pleasure to be here today to help our fair city's number one hero, the Amazing Indestructo, celebrate that legendary young hero of the past—Meteor Boy!"

The crowd erupted into spontaneous applause . . . or at least I thought it was spontaneous until I noticed the giant flashing APPLAUSE signs mounted on either side of the platform. Melonhead flew in front of the banner, waving spastically to the crowd.

"Look at me, I'm Meteor Boy!" he kept repeating over and over—probably because it didn't require him to pronounce any *s*'s.

"Now many of the older heroes among us remember the original Meteor Boy," the mayor continued, "and the heroic sacrifice he made to save Superopolis, even as the Amazing Indestructo did everything in his power to shield the young tyke from danger."

Boy, was that a sugar-coated version of the truth! I thought. But then again, that was what Mayor Whitewash did best. And the crowd bought every word of it.

"Thank you, Mayor, for those kind words," AI said quickly, stepping in to take over. "I certainly appreciate you giving the crowd the famous Whitewash treatment when it comes to the story of the original Meteor Boy."

As my opinion of AI sank lower than I thought possible, Melonhead did something truly heroic himself . . . not that he intended to, mind you. But the result is what mattered. In the middle of AI's speech, while attempting to do what I think was meant to be a midair loop the loop, the aerodynamically challenged melon-shaped

moron smashed headlong into the main support beam of the platform holding the city council. It gave a sickening crack, and then before our very eyes, it collapsed with a thundering crunch of splintering timbers. The rest of the audience thought it was the planned end of the presentation and began to applaud wildly, even without the prompting of the APPLAUSE signs.

"Come on." I motioned my teammates toward the destruction. "People are going to need our help."

The Junior Leaguers swung into action like any good heroes would. Stench began lifting the beams of the scaffold out of the way, while Halogen Boy provided the light necessary for him and Tadpole to climb into the wreckage and look for people who might need rescuing. Plasma Girl reduced herself to a puddle of ooze and snuck into crevices that no one else would have been able to reach, directing Stench to clear the areas where people were trapped.

With the help of other heroes in the crowd, it didn't take my team long to get everyone freed. With no power of my own, I tried to just move among the victims and offer what help I could. Some were injured, with scrapes and bruises but nobody was seriously hurt. And then I stumbled upon the one exception—Melonhead.

Don't get me wrong, most of his physical injuries were minor, but his ego had been bruised beyond repair. The finishing touches of his humiliation were being applied by the Amazing Indestructo as I found them. AI had come down from the tower platform, but he wasn't bothering to help with the rescue. Instead, he was pulling off the flying device that had been attached to Melonhead's back. I actually felt sorry for the annoying, seed-splattering jerk.

"Look, kid," AI was saying, "it's going to cost me most of the initial profit on this deal just to pay the city council's hospital bills—not to mention what I'm going to have to contribute to their campaigns just to keep 'em happy after this little disaster!"

"Pleath, thir," Melonhead practically begged. "Jutht give me one more chanth."

"Sorry." AI shrugged as he slipped the jet pack under his arm. "But you can keep the costume if you want, since you already paid for it."

"But it doethn't fly anymore," Melonhead added helplessly.

"Them's the breaks," was all AI said as he turned to walk away. Unfortunately, that was the moment he spotted me.

"You!" he said, but this time not quite so accusingly. In fact, I got the sense that the wheels were already turning in his head. "You know you're still the perfect person to play this part."

"Why would I ever help you profit off the memory of Meteor Boy?" I responded matter-of-factly.

Without warning, AI burst into tears.

"I've felt so much guilt for all this time," he blubbered. "And I finally thought I had come up with a way to make it up to the kid by letting everybody know his story. But now everything has been ruined."

218

It was really embarrassing. Thank goodness Whistlin' Dixie came running up just as I thought AI was going to collapse onto his knees.

"Thar, thar." She wrapped her leather-fringed arms around him. "What's the matter with my big bucka-roo?"

"Our launch is going to be a complete disaster because he won't help us out," he wailed in despair, pointing an indestructible index finger right at me.

"Ev'rthin'll turn out jes' peachy," she promised him. "Stop yer frettin'. Ah'll handle this fer ya."

Dixie knelt down in front of me and took my hands in her own. She had never been anything but nice to me, so I felt compelled to listen to what she had to say.

"Ah know AI hasn't given ya any reason to trust him," she began.

"I'm still standing here," he pointed out, but we both ignored him.

"But this is 'bout more than jes' him," she contin-ued. "Meteor Boy is gone, and this is the only way he'll ever have a chance to be remembered."

I felt like telling her Meteor Boy was due back here in just forty-eight hours, but then thought better of it. It wasn't the type of thing that anyone would believe, plus I didn't want to look like a complete idiot on the chance I was wrong.

"I know," I fibbed, "but I hate the thought that AI is going to make money off Meteor Boy's memory."

"He signed a contract," AI began to protest. "I have it right here."

219

"Darlin'? Maybe ya should jes' go get yerself ready." She turned and motioned him away with a wag of her finger. "Ah'll whistle fer ya if ah need ya."

The Amazing Indestructo lumbered toward a door in the base of the platform that surrounded the water tower, and Dixie continued her perfect pitch.

"You and ah both hate that part," she admitted, "but facts are facts. It's the only way that li'l tyke is gonna get the recognition he deserves. Whether it's right or completely wrong, this is how he'll be known. Do ya want all Superopolis to remember him as the boy he was"—she paused before going in for the kill—"or as a flying watermelon?"

As I began to visibly waver, Whistlin' Dixie moved to cement the deal. She reached into her side saddle-bag and retrieved the costume I had tried on this past Saturday.

"Follow me, li'l cowpoke." She tipped her hat and flashed me a smile. "It's time to getcha dolled up."

I trailed after Whistlin' Dixie as she led me through the same door that AI had entered a few minutes earlier. To my surprise there was an entire makeup room set up beneath the stage. There were barber chairs and mirrors and sinks and . . . sure enough, the Amazing Indestructo was already seated in one of the chairs having his face powdered by none other than Mannequin.

"Dahling," she was tsk-tsking him, "your pores are a disaster! And vhy are your eyes zo poofy and red?"

"Uh, sinuses," he lied.

220

NAME: Whistlin' Dixie. **POWER:** Can whistle in perfect tune.
LIMITATIONS: Her power doesn't extend to singing or humming.
CAREER: Discovered in the chorus of the short-lived Amazing
Indestructo stage musical by Al himself, Dixie has proven herself indispens-
able to the League of Ultimate Goodness. **CLASSIFICATION:** Her
common sense keeps her perfectly in tune.

"Yah, zee indestructible guy has bad sinuses," she scoffed. "Tell me another von."

Dixie and I ignored him as she led me to a dressing room. Taking the costume from her, I went in and began changing my clothes. As on Saturday, the costume fit me perfectly. I discovered that it also had pockets, so I transferred the chunk of prodigium and the Oomphlifier from my jeans.

I emerged to find none other than the Bee Lady waiting for me, jet pack in hand.

"I always knew you were meant to wear this," she rasped. "Try it on, kiddo."

I accepted the amazing gift with a silently mouthed thank you. Slipping it on from behind, I realized that it had almost invisible straps. Whistlin' Dixie helped me fasten the straps across my chest in an X pattern. As they came to rest against my costume, they appeared to vanish.

"And here are the controls," the Bee Lady explained as she ran two fine adhesive wires along each of my arms and attached them to small devices she clipped to the inside of my sleeves. "There are switches that slide forward into the palms of your hands. You'll see how easy they are to operate the first time you try them."

"And now fer the final touch," Whistlin' Dixie said, handing me a pair of gold mirrored goggles.

I quickly slipped the goggles over my eyes and turned to face Dixie and the Bee Lady. I also caught the attention of the Amazing Indestructo.

"Wow!" he said. "He sure looks better for the part than the flying melon."

"Can I try out the jet pack?" I eagerly asked Dixie. "Can I?"

"Not yet, kiddo." She waved her finger. "After today's li'l fiasco, Ah think we gotta keep ya under wraps 'til Thursday. But hang 'round a mite 'til the mess out front is cleared up, and we'll let ya take a test spin. Fer now, jes' sit tight 'til ah give ya a holler."

I couldn't have been more disappointed, but I did as she instructed. I left the dressing room (since the last thing I wanted to do was be anywhere near AI) and walked back up onto the platform. The shroud covering the tower was right in front of me, and I was reminded of my original reason for coming here. Villains were plotting to hijack Crispo's new project, and someone had to warn the famous artist. Looking around to see that no one was watching, I ducked underneath the enormous sheet.

The first thing that struck me was how much the tower resembled the Tipler I had seen in MagnoBox's rebroadcast, complete with a floor-mounted lever and a digital number panel. The second thing was the realization that the three giant metal cones were already in place high above my head and the upper portion of the tower appeared to be rotating slowly. But the strangest thing of all was the fact that standing right in front of me was Professor Brain-Drain himself, looking very much alive.

CHAPTER TWENTY-FIVE

The Artistry of Evil

For someone who had been incinerated in the flames of an erupting volcano just last week, Professor Brain-Drain looked remarkably good. The funny thing was, he looked at me as if *I* was the one who had just returned from the dead.

"I wasn't expecting you for another forty-eight hours," he finally said. "And where, pray tell, is my meteorite?"

Then it dawned on me. Not only had he just confirmed my suspicions about Meteor Boy's fate—he thought that I *was* Meteor Boy! I decided to play along.

"Uh . . . that's right," I stuck my chest out. "I've come from the past to administer the justice that's been due you all this time."

I don't know if I didn't sound like Meteor Boy or if I just wasn't a very good actor, but Professor Brain-

Drain tilted his head and stared at me as if I was the phoniest phony he'd ever seen.

"Of course not. It's too early," he muttered to himself. "You're not Meteor Boy. But there is something very familiar about you."

I backed away as he approached me. Sniffing the air around me, he slowly raised one of his creaky arms, his finger moving toward me like a divining rod toward water.

"You're that boy who paid me a visit last week," he quickly deduced.

"And you're supposed to be dead," I pointed out. "I saw you and your blimp go up in flames."

"Yes, that's right," he admitted, "my beautiful blimp. Do you have any idea how long it takes to have a new one built? It will be months before my order is filled."

"But how did you survive?" I blurted out in frustration.

"I didn't," he replied enigmatically.

"Huh?!" I said, thinking I had misheard him.

"Rather, I should say my duplicate did not survive."

"What?!" I said in disbelief. "That doesn't make any sense!"

"Doesn't it?" he said. "Think about it. You're not a stupid boy."

And then it hit me. The last people to see Professor Brain-Drain before he went on his ill-fated blimp ride were me . . . and the Multiplier.

"The Multiplier made a duplicate of you," I said, barely believing what I was saying.

"Exactly," he said. "And what a discombobulating experience it was! The Multiplier was only able to accomplish it because of the power boost from the Oomphlifier. Without it, the best he could have done on his own would have been a duplicated liver or lung sac or something unpleasant like that. But with the power boost he was able to produce a full duplicate. By the way, I hope he doesn't still have the Oomphlifier. He's really far too dense to be trusted with it."

"He doesn't have it," I said, resisting the urge to touch the pocket that held it.

"Good, good," he answered pleasantly. "Anyway, I sent my new duplicate off on the blimp because things had begun to go awry, in large part thanks to you and your friends, and I sensed things could get even worse. By the way, did you think the duplicate was the real thing?"

"Yes," I admitted. "He was acting and talking just like you."

"Interesting," pondered the Professor. "I had no sense what he was up to. He was truly a wholly independent new entity. It's probably good he was destroyed, since he would have eventually come after me."

"Why would he have done that?" I asked, mystified.

"Because that's what I would have done," he replied matter-of-factly.

Whenever I began to think Professor Brain-Drain actually sounded somewhat sane and reasonable, he managed to come up with a statement that was truly twisted.

"But that's all in the past, now, isn't it?" he said as he absentmindedly licked his lips and edged closer. If I didn't change the subject fast, I got the distinct impression that my intelligence would soon be a thing of the past as well.

"What have you done with Crispo?" I demanded.

"Oh, he's perfectly fine." The Professor chuckled. "In fact, he's just about ready to make an appearance."

Then to my utter shock, Professor Brain-Drain slipped off his white lab coat and reached for another that had been draped over a chair. This one was covered in multicolored spatters of paint. Then he picked up what looked like a shower cap from a countertop and proceeded to slip it over the entire shiny, stainless steel colander that sat atop his head. I had never seen a picture of Crispo, but I found it hard to believe that in the past two decades, no one had seen through such a flimsy disguise.

"It's not possible," I said, dumbfounded. "You can't be Crispo."

"And why not?" he replied, clearly insulted.

"Crispo is a talented artist, while you're just an evil genius," I said, hoping it didn't sound as inane to him as it did to me.

"Thank you for the compliments." He chuckled. "Both of them. But I am, in fact, Crispo."

"That's impossible," I protested. "Crispo creates, while all you do is destroy."

"Even destruction can be creative," he stated. "I imagine. I invent. I destroy. They are all part of the

NAME: Crispo. **POWER:** An ability to create amazing works of art—also sometimes known as a talent. **LIMITATIONS:** His creations are usually limited only by budget. **CAREER:** After exhausting the subject of potato chips as art, Crispo has lately been focusing on huge, spectacular projects that encompass everything but subtlety. **CLASSIFICATION:** After earlier, harsher art historians mysteriously vanished, Crispo was declared Superopolis's greatest artist by a new crop of critics.

same process, and I pursue whichever strikes my fancy at a given moment."

"What about when they contradict each other?" I asked accusingly.

"Do you never hold contradictory thoughts in your head?" he responded with a sly grin. "Only the truly dim think one way and only one way, their minds never changing. And you, my boy, are not dim."

Once again he began moving toward me. Instinctively, I backed as close as I could to the base of the water tower.

"But why invent another identity?" I asked.

"I created the persona of Crispo a generation ago in preparation for this very moment. I've kept his reputation pure and unsullied so that no one would be suspicious as I prepared for a project I began over a quarter of a century ago and will finally complete this coming Thursday."

"I know it's a time machine," I revealed as I backed against the lower, stationary portion of the water tower's enormous main cylinder. It clanged dully as if it was hollow, and my hand reached back for what appeared to be a door handle. Just four feet above my head the upper portion of the cylinder continued to spin slowly.

"You're one hundred percent correct. Very good!" he complimented me. "I call it the Time Tipler! I'm testing its rotation right now. Can you also tell me how it works?"

"This," I said, pointing at the screen panel

mounted above a number pad, "indicates the number of years either forward or backward in time that the machine will send you. Whether it's forward or backward is determined by which direction this central lever is switched."

"That's right." He beamed. "In fact it still shows the number the machine was set on the last time it was used." The number on the screen was 25—the number of years that Meteor Boy was flung into the future.

"But a mistake occurred," the Professor continued. "I had set the Tipler with a different number. Somehow that number got changed. More important, the device is currently set for the future. It was supposed to have been set for the past." The Professor grabbed the large lever and slid it to the left with a loud clank. "That was another mistake that won't happen again."

"But it was a mistake that has prevented you from operating the machine since then," I said in a deliberate attempt to goad him. "You've had no power source."

"I soon will," he glowered back at me, "at exactly four thirty-five on Thursday, when Meteor Boy returns with the prodigium meteorite he stole from me."

"Why prodigium?" I asked. "Doesn't anything else work?"

"No other substance contains such an immense amount of energy," he scowled. "And prodigium is nearly impossible to find. So I've had to travel these twenty-five years the old-fashioned way in order to reclaim what is mine."

"You know, Meteor Boy would never have been able to steal your power source in the first place if you hadn't put it in such an exposed place, right on top of the Tipler," I cheerfully pointed out.

"That's true," he admitted. "But in this particular case it was necessary to mount the meteorite on top of the Tipler. Step aside and I'll show you why."

Reaching for the same handle I had backed up against, he lifted a latch, releasing a door in the side of the enormous central cylinder. Ushering me in, we entered a small chamber, which was empty except for some control panels and what looked like a microwave oven. There was an identical latch that would allow the room to be locked from the inside as well.

"The Tipler is really two devices in one. This smaller chamber can be operated in a completely contained area, utilizing only a small piece of prodigium placed here in the power conversion chamber." He opened the door of the ovenlike device. "This allows only the contents of this room to be transported through time. The problem, of course, is that once something is sent through time it can never get back, because the machine itself remains in the present."

"What use is that?" I asked as I instinctively squeezed the small rock of prodigium I carried in my pocket.

"Oh, you'll see in about forty-eight hours." The Professor chuckled menacingly. "But place a large piece of prodigium atop the Tipler on the outside, and—"

"And it can transport the entire surrounding area through time," I finished his sentence as a shiver coursed through my body.

"Yes, including the Tipler itself," the Professor explained. "But Meteor Boy grabbed my power source at precisely the moment the Tipler was activated, thrusting *him* forward in time, but leaving the Tipler behind."

"Which the League of Goodness then dismantled," I added.

"Exactly." Professor Brain-Drain nodded. "So instead of just waiting for my Tipler to arrive from the past along with Meteor Boy and my power source, I've had to reassemble it from its original parts."

"Which you've been having those hippies and Cyclotron round up for you," I concluded.

"Yes, Cyclotron offered his aid," the Professor confirmed, "for which I was grateful."

"You should be," I said. "Those hippies wouldn't have accomplished anything on their own."

"They are remarkably incompetent," the Professor agreed, "but they helped me on this project originally and are hoping it will be successful this time."

"Why?" I asked, actually quite curious.

"Twenty-five years ago, I promised to send them forward in time to a perfect utopia—in other words, some place where they could be as lazy and irresponsible as they wanted. Of course, I never bothered to tell them there is no such place." He chuckled.

"And now why are they helping you?" I asked.

"I've promised to send them back to the past," he said matter-of-factly, "which they now seem to remember as having been perfect in every way."

"People always seem to think the past was better than it actually was," I agreed.

"You're correct." He smirked evilly. "You *are* an intelligent lad." I realized there was nowhere in the chamber to hide. "And I think it's high time that I relieve you of some of the intelligence."

He lurched at me faster than I would have guessed a creaky old man could move, and got his bony grip around my neck. I saw a finger from his free hand moving toward my head.

Just as I was afraid I was going to be taking the express train to Idiotsville, we heard an announcement coming from the loudspeakers out on the platform. It was the voice of Mayor Whitewash.

"And now that we've gotten ambulances for those who need them, I'm pleased to return to our original program and present to you Superopolis's greatest artist, Crispo!"

"Curses!" Professor Brain-Drain spat as applause erupted from the crowd out front. "I must retain my image as Crispo for at least another two days. For now you'll just have to wait here."

He shoved me away from the door and adjusted the shower cap that covered the colander on his head, chuckling softly.

"When I return, I'll deal with you . . . and then all of Superopolis."

His chuckling got louder and louder as he slammed the door shut and I heard the outer lock fall into place, trapping me inside the Tipler. I began to panic. I didn't know how far, but clearly Professor Brain-Drain intended to transport a large portion of Superopolis into the past. To make matters worse, I was the only person who knew, and now I was his prisoner. I had to warn someone. I frantically looked around the interior of the cylinder. But it was empty except for the power conversion chamber.

Then it struck me. There was only one person I might be able to reach. It was a desperate act, but I realized it was my only chance. I fished the small chunk of prodigium from my pocket and hoped fever-ishly that the setting on the outside panel was still where the Professor had left it. I set the meteorite frag-ment in the power chamber and closed the door.

Almost immediately, the cylinder began to spin faster and faster until it became a blur. I knew that just outside this locked chamber, space-time was beginning to warp and the cones atop the tower were beginning to tip. I was about to travel back in time twenty-five years! I had to warn Meteor Boy.

CHAPTER TWENTY-SIX

Everything Old Is New Again

Suddenly the walls of the Time Tipler stopped spinning. I examined the chunk of prodigium I had placed in the power chamber and saw that it had been reduced to a mere pebble. I retrieved it and slipped it into my pocket. If Professor Brain-Drain had been correct, only the contents of this chamber had been transported. So I knew I must be standing inside an *earlier* Time Tipler. I reached for the handle, and the door opened without a problem. Hesitantly, I stepped outside the Tipler to find myself facing a completely deserted Telomere Park. No collapsed grandstand of city officials, no Amazing Indestructo, and no Professor Brain-Drain disguised as Crispo. I was definitely not in my own time.

Then I turned around and saw the exterior of the Time Tipler. It had no shroud covering it, and all three of its cones were securely in place. I had returned to a time forty-eight hours prior to Professor Brain-Drain's original plot.

It reminded me why I was here, and I took off in a run. I had to find Meteor Boy and warn him about what was going to happen. Sprinting across the park, it began to sink in what I had done. I was twenty-five years in the past. How would I get back home? But even if I'd had more time to think about my decision, I still would have had no choice. It was either send myself to the past, or let Professor Brain-Drain destroy my mind, my friends and family, and probably all Superopolis.

All these thoughts were passing through my head as I ran, which may explain why it took me a moment to remember what I had strapped to my back—Indestructo Industries' jet pack! I screeched to a halt and stretched my arms out before me. Just as the Bee Lady had said, the controls slid out from under my sleeves to fit snugly in my palms.

With an anticipation that practically made me dizzy, I curled my fingers into a fist until they came in contact with the switches. A fraction of a second later I was rocketing straight into the air, my teeth practically rattling in my mouth from the speed. All thoughts of my predicament, my mission, and even my lack of a power vanished in an instant. I was flying!

I got the feeling for the controls right away, almost

as if they were a part of me. I did loop the loops, corkscrews, and barrel rolls like an acrobat of the air. I even flew straight up for almost a quarter of a mile. When I turned to come back down, I saw all Superopolis stretched out before me. It was familiar, but not. There were landmarks I recognized: Needlepoint Hill, Mount Reliable and Lava Park, Dr. Telomere's Potato Chip Factory, even the Vertigo Building, looking much newer and shinier. But there were other things missing: the Cavalcade of Candy was nowhere to be seen; there was obviously no Indestructo Industries or giant statue of AI; and most jarring of all, my neighborhood was nothing more than a vast stretch of open farmland.

And it would stay that way unless I accomplished my mission. I put my excitement about the jet pack aside and returned to the ground. I had more important things to think about for now.

The sun was sinking toward the tops of the Carbunkle Mountains, and I knew within the hour it would start to get dark. I wasn't sure where to go exactly, so I headed straight for the Science Museum. If the newspaper clipping I'd found in the hidey-hole was right, that was where I would find Meteor Boy.

As I soared twenty or so feet above the rooftops, I saw something that made me screech to a halt right in midair. The museum was still several blocks away, but I circled back. Sure enough, there, down on the street, was none other than the Amazing Indestructo himself. He was dressed in his original "hip" psychedelic costume and appeared to be hiding behind a car, spying on someone. I hovered a few yards above him and watched with fascination.

He was closely watching three boys around my own age approaching the door of a house. They were holding boxes filled with small packets. Nervously, one of the boys reached up and rang the doorbell. Within moments, the door swung open, revealing a very tall woman wearing an enormous pair of glasses that magnified a large set of very crossed eyes. The eyes were so disconcerting it took me a moment to realize she also had a medium-sized beak. The boys were startled as well and just stood there with their mouths hanging open.

"Tell her about the product," I heard AI hiss, poking his head up from behind the car.

One of the boys got up his nerve and began to speak.

"Er, ma'am"—he looked up at her uneasily—"I'd like to tell you about this incredible new line of Amazing Indestructo flower seeds."

The woman's eyes widened even more. She didn't say a word, but she did pull up one of her knees as far as it would go. The boy who was giving the sales pitch was clearly flustered but continued to speak as the woman stood there, now on just one leg.

"These amazing seeds aren't available in stores, and the flowers they grow are indestructible."

"Indestructible *looking*," AI whispered loudly, already well aware of how to make a product claim vague enough to avoid lawsuits.

"Uh, yeah," the boy corrected himself, "they're indestructible looking."

"Do you have gardenia seeds?" the woman suddenly shrieked, to the surprise of everyone. The boy just stood there with his mouth hanging open.

"Tell her yes!" AI hissed loudly. "Even if you don't have any."

All three boys began frantically sifting through the packs of seeds in their boxes in an attempt to find gardenia seeds.

"I found some," one of them cried victoriously.

To the surprise of all three boys the woman dove her head into the box of seeds and began pecking at them like a jackhammer, all while still standing on just one leg. In a panic they dropped their boxes of seeds and scattered. One of them spun himself into a small tornado and took off across the lawn. Another spastically began flying about the yard like a popped balloon. Meanwhile, the third just vanished entirely. It was easy to see I had found three of the original Junior Leaguers: Funnel Boy, Inflato, and InvisiBoy.

"You forgot to collect the money!" AI started shouting frantically as he abandoned his hiding place behind the car.

I was about to descend from my position and ask them where I might find Meteor Boy, when a commotion farther down the street suddenly caught my attention.

A large crowd of people were coming right toward us. They were all shouting and pointing into the air.

Looking up, I saw a familiar sight: a rainbow in the form of a large balloon drifting overhead. It was moving so slowly, though, that the crowd on the ground was having no problem keeping up with it.

"Stop those hippies!" one of them yelled.

"The museum's been robbed!" shouted another.

"They've stolen the only prodigium meteorite in existence!" hollered another, confirming what I had already guessed.

I'm sure this crowd had begun as a handful of museum guards, but as it pursued the slow-moving balloon it had attracted reporters, photographers, curious bystanders, and eager heroes looking for a chance to show their stuff. But none of them could fly. And the one hero who *was* able to fly just stood there watching stupidly.

"AI! Stop those villains!" I finally shouted in annoyance. The Amazing Indestructo looked around in surprise and then up in the air. His eyes settled on me and practically bulged out of his head.

"What the . . . ?" he sputtered in surprise.

"They're getting away," I yelled at him. "Fly after them and get them. They've stolen a meteorite from the museum."

"I can't fly," he shouted back in frustration.

To my chagrin, I realized he was right. He hadn't yet gotten his jet pack.

"But obviously *you* can," he added with amazement and a hint of jealousy.

I hated to admit it, but he was right. This was up to me. For the first time in my life I was a hero with a power and I wasn't going to waste the chance.

The rainbow balloon was almost fifty yards past us at this point, but that was nothing for a kid with a jet pack. I curled my fingers until they touched the controls and blasted off toward it. I bridged the distance in seconds and found just who I expected lurking in the balloon—the Commune for Justice. Only these hippies were young and appeared even more in need of baths and haircuts than their future selves. They all looked up at me with utter surprise as I blasted over their heads and grabbed the prodigium meteorite right from the Hammer's hands.

I was back to where AI and his sidekicks were standing before the hippies even realized they'd been robbed. They reacted quickly, however. Rainbow Rider let her rainbow balloon sink close enough to the ground for the other hippies to jump out. They were after me in a flash. I tossed the meteorite to AI to safeguard, but I should have known better. He looked at it briefly, then at the oncoming villains, and, without even a hint of embarrassment, passed it over to Funnel Boy.

To his credit, Funnel Boy spun himself into a whirlwind and roared off like a tornado with the meteorite in hand. But he soon found himself trapped as six duplicate SkyDiamonds surrounded him from all sides. Before I could come to his aid, another group of heroes beat me to it.

"The League of Goodness!" I heard InvisiBoy say with awe.

I looked up just in time to see a much younger Lord Pincushion, the Animator, MagnoBox, and the Bee Lady swooping in on a gust of wind, courtesy of Zephyr, who in this time was still very much alive.

"SkyDiamond, Hammer," I heard Aquarius holler, "let's get out of here! It's the League of Goodness!"

Even as the heroes hit the ground, the Bee Lady directed a swarm of her little buzzers toward the bewildered SkyDiamond. Directing his six duplicates to handle the league, he grabbed the meteorite from Funnel Boy's hands and ran for it.

I blasted after the fleeing fleabag. Within seconds, I had again grabbed the meteorite from out of his hands. He quickly gave up and grabbed a line hanging from the balloon just as it lifted into the air.

I returned to the ground, the meteorite safely in my hands. InvisiBoy, Funnel Boy, and Inflato all came running up to me, waving their arms in excitement. The Amazing Indestructo was right behind them, followed by a bunch of photographers.

"Golly," said InvisiBoy, panting for breath, "that was amazing!"

"Now, now," said AI as he came up behind the kids. "Let's not forget who the amazing one is here."

He laughed as if he had meant it as a joke, but I knew he was really serious.

"Gee whillikers," added Inflato, as I made a mental note to teach these guys some less corny exclamations. "You fly almost as well as I do!"

I'm not sure I would describe Inflato's uncontrolled gyrations as flying, but I was secretly pleased that I had flown at least as well as Meteor Boy himself. And just as I was about to ask them where I could find the real Meteor Boy, Funnel Boy said something that caught me totally off guard.

"You must be new around here, kid. What's your name?"

What's my name? Even if I was only dressed as him, surely they recognized their friend's costume! My mouth dropped open, but no words came out.

"He must be new," added InvisiBoy. "No one with a power like that could have been around here long without us finding out about him!"

And then it hit me. In a state of shock, I answered their question with what I suddenly, yet undeniably, knew to be the truth.

"I—I'm Meteor Boy."

CHAPTER TWENTY-SEVEN

New Friends

"Meteor Boy." Inflato rolled the words around on his tongue. "That's almost as cool a name as mine."

"And what a great power," added Funnel Boy.

"And the name makes sense," agreed InvisiBoy. "After all, he just prevented a meteorite from being stolen."

Meteor Boy.

The reality of what they were saying had left me speechless.

"You kids were incredible," gushed a photographer. "Let me get a picture for *The Hero Herald*."

"And what an incredible save of this valuable object," added the Amazing Indestructo as he butted his way into the middle of the frame just as the photographer took our picture. "Thankfully I was here to ensure the success of the rescue operation."

"Stop trying to steal credit from the lad."

I turned around and saw Lord Pincushion approaching. The other four members of the League of Goodness were right behind him. "After all, if you're going to set yourself up as the leader of a team of children, it might not be a bad idea for you to act at least a trifle bit more mature than them." And then he noticed the meteorite for the first time. "Good heavens, what is this thing?"

"It's a prodigium meteorite," I explained as I lifted it up for him to study. "It's the only one in existence."

"I've never seen anything like it," Pincushion explained as he removed a small, sharp-headed hammer from an area near his appendix. With it, he chipped away a small chunk protruding from the meteorite. The small piece soon came loose and fell into his hand. "I'd very much like to know just what those unwashed ruffians were planning to do with this unusual material. This small piece should be enough for me to examine in search of an answer."

"I know what they wanted it for—" I started to say, but I got interrupted.

"We're retiring, Pincushion," Zephyr reminded him. "Leave it to the younger heroes to discover. This boy is obviously smart enough to handle this little mystery on his own."

"Clearly he is," the sharp-looking superhero responded.

Suddenly, the Amazing Indestructo stepped in front of me as if he were protecting me from Lord

Pincushion's pointy protrusions, and grabbed the meteorite from my hands.

"He's not on his own. This kid's on my team," AI insisted, as if I had no say in the matter. "We've already shown that we work great together. The proof is in this valuable object we just prevented from being stolen."

As if on cue, Bliss dropped from the air on a rainbow bungee cord right above our heads.

"Easy come, bro," he said with a giggle as he reached for the chunk of stone in the Amazing Indestructo's hands, "easy go." And then, as quickly as he had appeared, he ricocheted back into the air, taking the meteorite with him.

"Yes," offered Lord Pincushion dryly, "and what a smashing job you've done."

Flustered, AI pressed on. "I may just be getting started," he protested, "but soon I'll be Superopolis's greatest hero. And I'll have the greatest team as well. So whaddaya say, kid?"

"Is no one concerned that the meteorite has just been stolen from right in front of us?" I practically hollered in frustration.

"Frankly, no," huffed Zephyr, who stood there with a cranky look on his face.

"You'll have to pardon our rudeness," the Animator explained. "We were just on our way down to city hall to file bankruptcy papers. You see, our money has run out."

"Yes," confirmed Lord Pincushion. "And our attempts to gain some assistance from the 'good' citizens of Superopolis have led to naught."

"I saw your telethon the other night!" piped up Funnel Boy. "Zephyr's hand shadows were really keen!"

"Thank you, lad," he huffed with pride.

"It's a shame you were the only one who thought so," Lord Pincushion added pointedly.

"But what about the meteorite?" I asked, trying to get back to the subject at hand.

"Frankly, we're just not that concerned about a stolen rock." Zephyr shrugged.

"Don't get us wrong." MagnoBox hastily stepped in. "We came to your aid because you were in danger. See the full story tonight at eleven! But our days of putting ourselves at risk over stolen objects are past."

"Say, maybe you should join up with me!" the Amazing Indestructo suddenly blurted out. "I've got all sorts of great ideas on how to make the hero business pay for itself and more!"

"Such as selling seeds?" Lord Pincushion said in disgust as he used a fencing blade to spear one of the scattered packs blowing about the street.

"He doesn't sell them," pointed out InvisiBoy sullenly. "We do."

"Revolting," Pincushion exclaimed.

"Hey, the kids are part of a team I'm forming," AI protested. "They're just doing their share to help finance it. Besides, kids are cute. People buy more from them than they would from me."

"So I see," giggled the Animator, glancing back at the beak-faced woman who was just finishing off the inventory.

"I hate to say it, boss," the Bee Lady whispered to Lord Pincushion, "but the lunkhead may have a point. Having kids on the team could help sell stuff to other kids. I've been inventing devices for us for years. It might be fun to try making toys instead."

"Well, we're too late to file for bankruptcy today, anyway," he replied with a resigned sigh. "And now we have the whole weekend in front of us. I'll decide tonight whether I've whittled my self-respect down to the point where I might consider what you're suggesting."

Lord Pincushion signaled Zephyr, who whipped up a breeze strong enough to lift all five members of the league.

"Hey, can you do that for me, too?" asked the Amazing Indestructo. "I need some cool sort of way to get around town. I doubt the meteor kid is going to be able to carry me."

Lord Pincushion already had an adamant no forming on his lips when the Bee Lady piped in.

"Let's bring him along," she whispered. "I've got a device I've been dying to test that he would be perfect for."

"Very well," Lord Pincushion said with resignation.

Zephyr summoned a gust to lift up Superopolis's soon-to-be greatest hero. In a matter of seconds the winds had carried them all away, and I found myself alone with Funnel Boy, Inflato, and InvisiBoy.

"Did you hear that?" Inflato said excitedly. "They might make me a member of the League of Goodness!"

"They might make all of us members," Funnel Boy pointed out, "not just you."

"Aren't the three of you a team?" I asked.

"AI started with me and InvisiBoy," Funnel Boy explained. "He just added Inflated Head to the group earlier today."

"I can't help it if he thought you guys needed my help," Inflato protested.

InvisiBoy and Funnel Boy just rolled their eyes. Inflato was clearly as annoying to them as he would be to me in the future.

"So what does the Amazing Indestructo call you?"

"He's never really given us a team name," admitted InvisiBoy. "Although a couple of times he's called us the Ankle Biters."

"You guys need a real name," I decided. "Who do you respect more, AI or the League of Goodness?"

"Well, we all thought AI was pretty neat," said Funnel Boy.

"Until we got to know him," InvisiBoy interjected.

"That's a common reaction," I confirmed.

"Now I guess we'd say we respect the League of

Goodness more." InvisiBoy shrugged.

"So call yourselves the Junior Leaguers," I said matter-of-factly, as it suddenly dawned on me how these kids ended up with the same name as my team in the future.

"The Junior Leaguers featuring the Great Inflato!" Inflato said proudly, as he began to puff himself back up.

"We're stuck with Inflato, but what about you?" asked InvisiBoy. "Will you be part of our team?"

"Of course," I said. "And I already have a mission for us."

Half an hour later, we were back in Telomere Park, approaching the water tower. It was now beginning to get dark, and a shiver ran down my spine as I noticed that there were lights on around the base of the Time Tipler. I warned my new teammates to be silent as we inched our way closer.

When we got up near the base of the tower, we could see immediately that the Commune for Justice was already there. And who were they presenting the stolen meteorite to?

"It's Professor Brain-Drain," InvisiBoy hissed in alarm.

We all watched silently as the Professor gleefully examined the meteorite.

"Thank you so much, my fragrant friends," he began. "Once I've made the final preparations, I will, as promised, use it to transport you all to the land of perfection of which you've all dreamed."

"A place where no one ever has to work?" asked Hammer.

"A place where parents can't ruin my life?" added Aquarius.

"A place where duties are easy to shirk," said SkyDiamond.

"A place without bathing, and a place without strife," Bliss concluded with a strum on his ukulele.

Professor Brain-Drain just grinned enigmatically.

"Yes," he finally responded. "Something like that. And once I've proven it works"—Professor Brain-Drain's cackle began to build from deep in his lungs—"I'll destroy the people of Superopolis in a way they'll never forget."

Fortunately, the inherent illogic of that statement caused me to pause just as I was about to streak over and steal the meteorite back from the Professor. In that fraction of a second I had a sudden and horrible realization: I had no choice but to let Professor Brain-Drain go ahead with his horrible and fiendish plan.

CHAPTER TWENTY-EIGHT

The Secret Origin of the League of Ultimate Goodness

It was a sobering reality. I *had* to let Professor Brain-Drain proceed with his plot, and two days from now, I, as Meteor Boy, would have to be there to prevent it. It was the only way I would ever get back to my own time.

So it was up to me to make sure that events occurred exactly the way I knew they must in order for the future to turn out the way I knew it did. (Man, that's a statement that makes me dizzy just saying it!) And here I was, stuck for at least two days twenty-five years in the past. I had a lot to take care of, and I was going to need the help of my newfound friends.

"C'mon, guys," I said as I began to back away from the scene we had just witnessed. "We have to get away from here."

"Huh?" Funnel Boy responded in surprise. "Shouldn't we attack Brain-Drain?"

"We have plenty of time," I whispered. "He won't put his plan into action for another two days yet."

"How do you know?" asked Inflato.

Just then Professor Brain-Drain spoke aloud: "Now that I have the meteorite, I need just two days to finalize my plans. Then good-bye Superopolis!"

"Whoaaaa!" all three boys said at once. "How did you know?"

"It would take too long to explain," I replied in the understatement of the quarter century to come. "Let's get out of here."

As we neared the exit of Telomere Park it was now dark, but a full moon hung in the sky just above the tops of the Carbunkle Mountains. It was Friday night. I had left my own time on Tuesday, October fifteenth, but here, twenty-five years earlier, the fifteenth was a Friday. My new friends were eager to spend their weekend as sidekicks to the League of Goodness. We all agreed to meet first thing in the morning at Needlepoint Hill to see if we would actually have the chance.

"Until tomorrow, fellow Junior Leaguers," I said with mock seriousness as I blasted into the air.

They continued standing there shouting and waving as I speedily ascended. When they were out of sight, I turned and headed for Needlepoint Hill. I didn't have the luxury of waiting until tomorrow.

I arrived at Pinprick Manor at about eight o'clock. Even though it would have been a breeze to fly right up to the front door of the house, I instead used the elevator hidden at the base of the hill. There, I punched the button indicating the main headquarters level, and the car began to rise.

When it reached its destination, the silence within the car was broken the instant the doors began to part. Hurtling straight toward me was the Amazing Indestructo at an incredible speed, flames belching from behind him. It wasn't the rocket pack strapped to his back that was making all the noise, though—it was the high-pitched, girly scream erupting from his mouth as he came barreling right at me. I instantly ducked, and it was a good thing. He missed the top of my head by barely an inch as he smashed against the inside back wall of the elevator and crumpled into a heap.

"I told you there was no hope," I heard Lord Pincushion mutter as he and the Bee Lady rushed to help. "This buffoon will never get the hang of the controls."

"But he's the perfect person to test it," she protested. "See? He can't be hurt."

She was right. AI was already getting to his feet, an excited, dopey grin on his face. It was then that they finally noticed me standing there.

"Good heavens!" said Lord Pincushion. "How did you enter our inner sanctum? You really shouldn't be poking your nose where it doesn't belong."

"I'm sorry," I said, "but I think I might be able to help you all out."

"Indeed?" said Pincushion. "And how, pray tell, might you go about doing that?"

"Hey, kid," AI interjected as he got back on his feet, "don't be giving away any trade secrets. Remember, you work for me."

"I don't work for you!" I spun around and glared at him. "And you've got a lot of nerve trying to stop me from helping the league at the very same moment they're giving you the ability to fly. Are you completely shameless?"

I couldn't believe how I was talking to the Amazing Indestructo, a hero who had been my ideal for most of my life. Of course, that was before I actually met him. I had already learned how to push his buttons, though, as I now saw his eyes tear up and his lip begin to quiver.

"You're right," he began to sob. "I'll never be a success, and I don't deserve to be."

"Well, that second part is true," I said, "but the fact of the matter is you *are* going to be an incredible success."

"I am?" he said, raising his head back up expectantly.

"He is?" the Bee Lady and Lord Pincushion said in unison.

"Absolutely," I insisted. "You're helping to make it possible already by outfitting him with this rocket pack."

"It's an invention I've been working on for years," the Bee Lady pointed out. "But this has been my first chance to test it. Anyone else who tried it would get burned to a crisp."

"Not me," boasted the Amazing Indestructo. "I'm indestructible!"

"We know," I said. "Anyway, I think I have a proposal that will be a win-win for all of you."

"Child, we are at your disposal." Lord Pincushion bowed deeply as the sharp objects stuck into him clinged and clanged against each other. "Please follow us into the recreation room and you can address us all together. It may be your last chance if the bank has its way and forecloses on our headquarters next week."

We crossed the wide-open headquarters and passed into a room at the far end of the hangarlike space. Inside, we found the Animator and Zephyr watching TV. Or rather, we found them watching MagnoBox, who appeared to be broadcasting a game show.

"The answer is planter's wart," the Animator spoke to the screen.

"The answer is toe fungus," insisted Zephyr almost simultaneously.

"Planter's wart is correct," a voice on the screen confirmed.

"Bah," hissed Zephyr.

"Pardon the interruption," said Lord Pincushion as we entered. "But this lad would like our attention as he explains to us how, with the aid of Indestructo here, we might save ourselves from financial ruin."

"Uh, the *Amazing* Indestructo," AI corrected.

"Amazing-ness must be earned," Pincushion replied dismissively.

"That's true," I jumped in, trying to ignore the fact that I was standing before some of the greatest heroes in history. "But it will happen. In fact, it's inevitable. Just think about it. He's got a power that absolutely guarantees that he's going to be around fighting crime for decades."

"It's true." AI beamed. "I'm indestructible!"

"Yes, we know," sighed Lord Pincushion.

"And what he lacks in depth and character," I continued, "he more than makes up for in superficial charm and looks."

"Indeed," Pincushion admitted as the Bee Lady and the Animator nodded.

"It's a visual age," agreed MagnoBox, whose face had now replaced that of the game show host on his screen. "More and more, people are beginning to believe anything that they see on television. Doctors smoke Carcino Lights, the healthy cigarette! Someone who looks good on TV can be hugely successful even if he has nothing else going for him."

"He's right!" The Amazing Indestructo nodded his head vigorously. "I have all sorts of plans to publicize myself on the air."

"But so far you haven't found any networks interested in promoting you, have you?" I hazarded a guess.

"Well, no," admitted AI.

"But would they say the same thing if you brought them a show called *The Adventures of the League of Goodness, featuring the Amazing Indestructo?*"

"Hmm," pondered AI as the idea sank in. "I see your point—especially if it were called *The Adventures of the Amazing Indestructo and the League of Goodness*. Although it needs something to punch it up a little— maybe an adjective or two."

Lord Pincushion sighed and rolled his eyes.

"I would go insane dealing with this imbecile," he insisted.

"But you wouldn't have to," I explained. "You can work with him for as short a time as you like. AI just needs an established name to launch his own career. And he's shameless enough to make tons of money off it."

"I *am* standing right here," he pointed out.

"I know it's not ideal. But you're ready to retire," I continued, ignoring AI, "and you have a high-profile team name but no money."

"Sadly, I see your point," he agreed as he absent-mindedly flicked an ice pick sticking out of the side of his head, setting it vibrating. "Pinprick Manor is only days away from foreclosure."

"So join forces," I insisted. "Stay active a little bit longer to get the new team up and running, and then you can retire with a steady and growing stream of income from royalties refilling your empty bank account. You can continue living here for decades to come."

"It's not a situation to be proud of," admitted Lord Pincushion as he pondered his situation, "but it's a better one than I could have hoped for. You're a very wise boy."

As Lord Pincushion and the Amazing Indestructo shook hands on the deal, I suddenly felt queasy and sat down on the couch. I was happy that I had helped save the League of Goodness from bankruptcy. But I was *not* pleased to realize that I was the one directly responsible for launching AI on his own successful career. The fact that I had no choice in the matter was small consolation. It was what *had* happened, so it was what *must* happen for me to return to the same future I had left. But it was just one more unbelievable realization at the end of a long day of unbelievable events. I barely even noticed as I drifted off to sleep right there in the League of Goodness headquarters.

CHAPTER TWENTY-NINE

Hero for a Day

The next day, I became what I had always thought I wanted to be—the sidekick of the Amazing Indestructo! Of course, it's funny how quickly your greatest dreams and aspirations can change. A couple of weeks ago, I would have begged AI to have me as his sidekick—and I would have gotten nowhere. But here he was, pleading with me to take on the role. Reluctantly, I agreed—for the simple reason that I knew I had to.

And I'd be lying if I didn't admit I had a blast. I had a power—an amazing power! Nobody knew that it wasn't really mine—and I didn't really care. I fought crime with the Amazing Indestructo, the League of Goodness, as well as the Junior Leaguers. For the first time in my life I felt like a real hero—and I loved it!

The day began when my new friends, Funnel Boy,

Inflato, and InvisiBoy, showed up at Needlepoint Hill. It was the noise they made that woke me up.

"Meteor Boy, Meteor Boy!" I heard them shout. It took me a moment to realize they meant me. As I lifted up my goggles to rub the sleep out of my eyes, they jumped onto the couch on either side of me. They were holding a newspaper.

"Look at this!" Funnel Boy said, shoving the paper in front of me. Below the fold was the picture of the four of us (and a camera-mugging AI) holding the meteorite. It was the identical picture I would find as a clipping twenty-five years later.

"I'm the most famous kid in Superopolis," gushed Inflato.

"Yeah, but the story is all about Meteor Boy," InvisiBoy informed Inflato, annoyed with him, but showing no jealousy at all when he turned back to me. "They go on and on about how you saved the meteorite."

"Do they mention me?" AI barged his way into the conversation as he turned away from the Saturday morning cartoons he was watching on MagnoBox's screen.

"Yes," said Funnel Boy. "After they mention Meteor Boy saving the meteorite, they mention that you lost it again."

"That can't be right," AI said with concern as he grabbed the paper from our hands. That was when I noticed the other headline on the paper. "League of Goodness Retires," it blared in enormous type.

"This can't be good," I said.

Lord Pincushion noticed the headline at the same moment.

"Good heavens," he said, inhaling sharply. "The press must have overheard our comments yesterday about declaring bankruptcy."

"But now you're not going to," AI said, shrugging, "so what does it matter?"

"Don't you see?" scolded the Bee Lady. "All the criminals in Superopolis are going to take this as an open invitation to do whatever they want."

"MagnoBox," Lord Pincushion called. "Show us what's going on out there."

Switching from cartoons, MagnoBox revealed the full scope of his power as he began broadcasting live images of what was happening around Superopolis. It was as bad as the Bee Lady had predicted. The city was in chaos. Apparently, every villain, and everyone who had ever thought of being a villain, had read this morning's headline. The jewelry

district was so crowded that getaway vehicles were double- and triple-parked. Manhole covers were exploding everywhere as who knows what was happening in the sewer system. Megalomaniacs of every shape and size were attempting to seize city hall. Purse snatchers were having their stolen purses snatched before getting a chance to even see what they had snatched themselves. The most positive thing we saw was that, at least at some banks, the criminals were waiting quietly and patiently in lines for their turn to hold up the tellers.

As MagnoBox switched from one scene of pandemonium to another, I heard myself speak: "We've got to do something."

"This is it!" shouted AI. "It's time for Superopolis to meet the Amazing Indestructo and the League of"—and here he paused for only a second—"ULTIMATE Goodness."

I can't even begin to describe the look of horror on Lord Pincushion's face, but he said nothing. He knew there was no time to waste arguing.

Within minutes we were all soaring toward downtown Superopolis. Zephyr had whipped up a wind that carried the entire league, as well as their three new sidekicks. I, of course, was flying, and the Amazing Indestructo blasted through the air, wearing the Bee Lady's jet pack for the first time in public. He was still a little shaky using it but catching on fast.

Our first stop, appropriately enough, was the museum. It may have lost a meteorite the night before, but now it was losing its entire collection. Panic set in immediately among the museum looters as the league touched down. While bees chased off some of them, Lord Pincushion confronted others with blades drawn for battle. Meanwhile, other villains were surprised to find that some of their pilfered items were jumping right out of their hands and running back into the museum on their own. The Animator was the only hero I knew of who could create a stampede of statuary, pottery, and fossils.

My three new friends were having the most fun of all. Funnel Boy was producing larger tornadoes then I had yet seen from him, as Zephyr used his own power to concentrate the winds, magnifying Funnel Boy's ability. They currently had a villain with multiple arms caught in a whirlwind. As, one by one, each of his hands let go of the objects he'd stolen, Inflato and InvisiBoy were catching them before they hit the ground.

The Amazing Indestructo was striking terror into the hearts of villains as he blasted forward and backward with the aid of his new jet pack. But their terror in no way matched the look of fear on AI's face as time and again he nearly crashed into not only the criminals, but the museum building itself.

He looked like he needed some serious help, but I had just spotted a thief making off with the famous Magma Marbles. This was a collection of really cool-looking marbles that had been found inside a huge rock spit out of Mount Reliable. They came in all sizes and colors, and were still one of the most popular exhibits at the museum in my own time. Only now they were all in the hands of one of the most oddly dressed villains I'd ever seen. At first I had thought a mummy was escaping from the museum. But then I realized this guy was wrapped completely in adhesive tape from head to foot. The only parts of him that were exposed were his face and his hands. And his hands were full of marbles.

I swooped toward him at a medium speed, but it was still enough to catch him by surprise. He threw his hands up to ward me off, but the funny thing was that he didn't drop a single marble. They remained stuck in his grasp as if they were glued to his hands.

"Drop those marbles!" I ordered.

"Sorry, can't do that," he said, shrugging apologetically. "They don't call me Stickyfingers for nothing!"

I had to agree it was an appropriate name. The only question was how would I get the Magma Marbles away from him? My new teammates saw the problem and came to my aid. Inflato and InvisiBoy attacked Stickyfingers from either side, attempting to grab the marbles from his hands. The villain lunged first for InvisiBoy, who vanished just as Stickyfingers tried to grab him. As he turned back to his other side, Inflato expelled a sharp blast of air to evade the villain's adhesive hands.

As the thief went for Inflato, InvisiBoy suddenly reappeared and managed to pluck one of the marbles from his grasp. Stickyfingers immediately swung back around only to see InvisiBoy vanish. The marble he

had plucked away had not vanished, though, and I swooped down to retrieve it just before it hit the ground. Back and forth this went, with InvisiBoy and Inflato recovering a marble or two at a time. Every time InvisiBoy vanished, though, I had to retrieve whatever marbles he had rescued. It seemed odd that he couldn't hold them while he was invisible, but I didn't have time to think about it.

Stickyfingers seemed dumb enough to keep falling for the same maneuver indefinitely, but then Funnel Boy entered the picture. InvisiBoy, Inflato, and I all backed off as a twister sprang up around the startled villain. It grew quickly into a decent-sized funnel cloud, trapping Stickyfingers inside and setting him spinning. The winds were so strong that soon the marbles started shifting slowly and sluggishly off his hands and onto the tape that made up his costume. Within moments his entire body was covered with marbles, with only a few remaining stuck to his hands.

"Inflato, grab for a strip of his costume," I hollered above the torrential winds.

Puffing himself up proudly, Inflato lunged at a flapping strip that was already coming loose. He missed it the first couple of times, but then got a firm hold. The moment he did, Funnel Boy stopped his miniature cyclone, and Stickyfingers went spinning off like an out-of-control top, losing more and more of his wrapping with every turn.

"Quick, get the tape," InvisiBoy cried as he and

Funnel Boy began gathering up the long strip of tape that was now decorated with nearly the entire collection of Magma Marbles.

Stickyfingers, meanwhile, had been stripped of both marbles and costume and was running away in just his underwear.

We all shook hands and congratulated ourselves. Even Inflato had learned the benefits of teamwork. For the first time he wasn't trying to overinflate his own role. "Excellent work, lads," Lord Pincushion announced as he approached us. The rest of the league was chasing off the remaining thieves and returning the stolen objects to the museum. "You've shown you have what it takes to work as a team. That idiot may actually have been right in bringing us all together."

"Was someone talking about me?" AI asked as he cut the power from his jet pack and executed a reasonably competent landing. "We're going to be an enormous success if we keep this up!"

MagnoBox interrupted. "No time to rest on our laurels," he said. "Look what's happening at the seaport. The Felonious Feline has infiltrated the Fulcrum Fisheries!"

Quicker than you could say that five times fast, the League of Ultimate Goodness was on its way!

CHAPTER THIRTY

The Boy Who Knew Too Much

By the end of the day I was exhausted, but in the best possible way. I had battled villains, prevented thefts, thwarted jaywalkers—in short, I had been a hero! With nothing but successes behind us, the new League of Ultimate Goodness returned to Needlepoint Hill, while the Amazing Indestructo flew off to meet with a business manager who he was thinking of hiring to run and finance his new operation. This person, of course, was the Tycoon. Thankfully, the idea to hire him was AI's own. I don't know if I could have lived with myself if I had also been responsible for bringing him and AI together.

At headquarters, the Junior Leaguers sat on the couch watching a replay of our exploits on MagnoBox's screen. The Animator, who was watching as well, made a suit of armor bring us a tray filled with bowls of potato chips and mugs of root beer. We were all laughing at a replay of the Amazing Indestructo flying headlong into a huge vat of chicken broth at the Super Dooper Soup factory. On that mission we had prevented the theft of an entire railroad car full of oyster crackers, despite also having to rescue AI. As we watched him flailing around in the broth, the elevator doors opened and the real AI appeared.

"I found this pinned to your mailbox," he said tossing an envelope to Lord Pincushion, who was sitting at a grinding wheel sharpening his various blades. "At first I thought it was for me, but it turned out to be yours. It's a bill."

Lord Pincushion picked up the envelope and removed a letter from inside.

"Good grief," he said. "It's a demand from that farmer who we saved from the clutches of the Boll Weevil. He claims we tore up an acre of his turnips and he wants restitution."

"But we saved his life!" the Animator said.

"People disgust me," Lord Pincushion said with resignation as he dropped the envelope. "I shan't miss this life once we retire."

The Amazing Indestructo, oblivious to Lord Pincushion's problems, came and sat down on the couch, grabbing himself a handful of potato chips.

"What's on?" he asked, shoving the chips into his mouth. When he saw an image of himself flailing

around in a giant vat of chicken soup he practically choked. "That wasn't my fault," he protested. "Once the Bee Lady adjusts the thrusters, I'll be flying as smoothly as Meteor Kid here."

"His name is Meteor Boy," Funnel Boy said with irritation.

"Isn't it about time for you kids to go home?" a clearly annoyed AI asked as he stood up and blocked MagnoBox's screen which was now showing us four kids pulling him out of the soup.

"We do have to get home," InvisiBoy agreed, "but first we need to make plans for tomorrow."

"Tomorrow?" I said in surprise.

"Yeah," Inflato said. "Professor Brain-Drain's plan. You're the one who told us it was set to happen tomorrow."

"We have to make plans," InvisiBoy added. "It's up to us to stop whatever he's plotting to do with that meteorite."

And then I remembered what Coach Inflato, as an adult, had told me. He had blamed Meteor Boy for altering his and my other friends' lives for the worse. But I had seen no sign of any of them in the few clear snippets of MagnoBox's replay.

"What's this about Professor Brain-Drain?" Lord Pincushion interrupted.

"We spied on him last night and heard him talking about an evil scheme he's planning for tomorrow," Inflato informed him.

"The League has to stop him," Funnel Boy insisted.

"Indeed the League must," Lord Pincushion agreed. "But Professor Brain-Drain is incredibly dangerous. I don't think we should be exposing you children to that kind of peril."

"It's their decision," AI interjected. "We can't stop them if they really want to help."

"Of course we can," Lord Pincushion said sharply. "They're children and we're adults. At least some of us are, anyway."

"But we're part of the team," Inflato practically whined. "We have to help."

"We're the ones who discovered the plot," InvisiBoy insisted. "It's only fair to let us see it through."

"Perhaps." Pincushion nodded, a look of concern on his face. "Be here by noon tomorrow and we'll figure out how to handle this."

My teammates knew the discussion was over for the night and they followed Lord Pincushion to the elevator. I stayed where I was. After all, I didn't know where else I could sleep tonight. I glanced across the room to where the Bee Lady was working away at AI's jet pack with a wrench and a screwdriver. As my friends stepped into the elevator, I went in the opposite direction.

"That's quite a device," I said as I watched her tinker away at the source of the Amazing Indestructo's powerful new ability.

"Thank you, kid," she said, genuinely pleased. "I've been working on this thing for years. I always thought it would come to nothing because no one would be able to use it without frying their backside in the process. Then the lunkhead showed up. He's annoying, but at least this is one invention that won't turn out to be a waste."

"Do you have many inventions you haven't been able to do anything with?" I asked.

"I'll show you one of my favorites." She set down the jet pack and reached for something under her workbench. It took all my control not to gasp at what she pulled out.

"This was of no use to the league," she said, shrugging, "but I had a wonderful time creating it. I call it a Collide-a-scope. Here, take a look."

Taking the object from her, I held it up to my right eye and began to turn it. I knew what to expect, so it was no surprise when the images inside came hurtling toward me.

"That's really cool!" I said, trying to sound like I had never seen anything like this before. The Bee Lady stared at me.

"No one's ever looked through it and not flinched," she said, partly in awe, partly with irritation. "Kid, you've got nerves of steel."

"Thanks," I said, blushing slightly. "It's an amazing toy. You should do more things like this."

"I'd love to," she said matter-of-factly, "but Pincushion never had any interest in commercializing the league. It sounds, though, like the Amazing Idiot is going to change all that. In most ways it probably won't be for the best, but it *will* give me the chance to try more toy making. I'm looking forward to that."

"I know you're going to be great at it," I confirmed. "Kids are going to drive their parents crazy bugging them to buy your toys."

She looked at me curiously, and I suddenly worried that I had given away too much. I couldn't let her know I was from the future. After all, even in my own time, the league had been unaware that Professor Brain-Drain's device was a time machine. But it turned out that the look of concern on her face had been prompted by something else that I had said.

"And where are your parents?" she asked. "You slept here last night, and you've spent the entire day with us."

I had anticipated this question, and I had prepared for it as best I could.

"My parents are away for the weekend on an

279

important mission," I explained. "For the first time, they thought I was old enough to take care of myself for a couple of days, but to be honest, it's been really scary being in the house alone."

The truth was, I had no idea if I would make it back home safely and see my parents again. The worry and concern on my face looked genuine because it was, and the Bee Lady's motherly instincts took over.

"Well, I would question any parent who left a boy your age, even one as clearly capable as you, alone for a weekend. But I have no intention of making you go home to an empty house," she informed me. "I insist you spend the night here again. I just hope your parents aren't worrying about you," she added as she went to get me some blankets.

Then it hit me. My parents must be worried sick! I had been gone for over twenty-four hours and they had no idea where I was. If everything worked, I would be back in my own time in about twenty hours. But what was going to happen when (and if) I returned? An idea hit me. I hopped off the couch and approached Lord Pincushion. He was studying the small chunk of prodigium with a magnifying glass.

"Excuse me," I asked. "Could I borrow a piece of paper and a pen?"

"Certainly, my good lad," he said as he handed me a sheet of paper from his desk and retrieved a pen from his chest. "Here you go."

I sat down and began to write:

Dear Lord Pincushion:

You are receiving this letter more than two decades after I wrote it. It is being delivered to you on the Sunday before the 25th anniversary of my disappearance. Right now you are meeting me as Ordinary Boy, but as difficult as it is to believe, in just two days, I will travel back in time twenty-five years. There, you and the League will be introduced to me as Meteor Boy. You also know what will happen two days after that. What you haven't known until now, however, is that Professor Brain-Drain's device is a time machine. I interrupted his original plan by stealing the prodigium meteorite he used as his power source. The Professor himself calculated that I was flung twenty-five years into the future, which, if he is correct, means I will be reappearing this coming Thursday in Telomere Park at precisely 4:35 in the afternoon.

If I may, I would ask just one favor. By Tuesday evening my parents will have no idea what has happened to me and will be worried sick. Their names are Thermo and Snowflake, and I would be extremely grateful if you could let them know what is happening. Also, if my assumption is correct, and I return Thursday afternoon with the meteorite, Professor Brain-Drain will be there,

prepared to use it to complete his plan, what-
ever it may be. Despite what you have read in
the papers, he is not dead. If for some reason
I do not reappear, please let my parents know
that I love them very much.

With many thanks,
Meteor Boy/Ordinary Boy

PS: You may reveal that this letter men-
tions me, but say no more. This is imperative
for events to unfold the way they must. The
fabric of time depends on it. I'll understand.

PPS: Thank you for the fondue. I've
never tried it before, and it's delicious.

I reread the letter to make sure I wasn't forgetting
anything important, then I folded it up. Glancing
around, I noticed the envelope that Lord Pincushion
had dropped when he received his bill. Picking it up, I
was pleased to see the message written on the front of
it: *Please deliver to the leader of the League of Goodness.* I
folded the letter, sealed it in the envelope, and examined it again. It still needed one more thing. I took the
pen, and, mimicking the writing on the envelope as
best I could, added: *Many thanks! Meteor Boy.*

The Bee Lady was still off gathering up some bed-
ding for me, so I snuck over and retrieved the Collide-
a-scope. As I knew it would, the top came off when I
turned it in the opposite direction, dividing into two

equal pieces. I slipped the envelope inside, closed the scope back up, and returned it to its proper place.

As I settled myself on the couch, worry kept me awake. I possessed all this knowledge of what was going to happen tomorrow, but couldn't share it with anyone. I knew the League of Goodness wasn't going to figure out what Professor Brain-Drain's device was until Lord Pincushion read my letter twenty-five years from now. I knew I couldn't tell them now without altering both the present and the future. I knew that I would vanish at 4:35 tomorrow afternoon, but I had no way of knowing if I would get back to my own time, or what I would find waiting for me there if I did. And finally, I knew that the futures of my new friends were destined to change as well. Was there some way I could alter their fate? More importantly, even if I could, should I?

Eventually, I drifted off into a fitful sleep.

CHAPTER THIRTY-ONE

Betrayal

I awoke the next morning to find the Amazing Indestructo sitting at a table in the kitchen area of league headquarters eating a bowl of cereal.

"How do you think my face would look on a cereal carton?" he asked as he held the box up to his head for comparison.

"Crunchy," I said as I stretched and yawned. "Where is everybody else?"

"The league had an early morning emergency," he explained. "They were just getting ready to leave when I got here. I told them we should let you sleep and that I'd keep an eye on you."

"You're too selfless," I said with a sarcasm he missed entirely. As I sat down, AI handed me the box of cereal and then proceeded to pick up the morning newspaper he had been reading.

"Look at this coverage," he gushed as he flashed me the front page of *The Superopolis Times*. LEAGUE HERE TO STAY! the headline blared in huge type.

"I've put together quite a team, haven't I?" he commented, already convinced that this had all been his doing. "And I'm going to make the biggest star out of you . . . with the exception of me, of course."

"Of course," I agreed as I scanned the front page. It was full of photos and stories about all five members of the league with multiple pictures of the sidekicks, including two different ones of me. There was only one person not pictured.

"Where are you?" I asked AI. I admit it, I was trying to goad him.

"Huh?" he said as he grabbed the paper from my hands. I got up and looked over his shoulder as he scanned the front page up and down.

"There you are," I finally said as I pointed to a small scrap of type three quarters of the way through the main article.

"'And the group will now be known as the League of Ultimate Goodness (featuring the Amazing Indestructo),'" he read as his face got redder. "Pincushion is behind this somehow," he fumed.

"That will change," I reassured him. "In time you'll have a team where no one gets any attention except you."

"But even you kids got more coverage than me," he complained.

And then I saw my opportunity. I had wrestled all night with the question of whether I should try to affect the events that would happen today. If I left things as they were, my friends' lives would be changed forever, and not in a good way. But if I succeeded, I might alter my own future, and that definitely wouldn't be good either.

I had made up my mind, though, in the only way a hero could. It wasn't going to be pretty, but thanks to AI, I now knew what I could do to keep my friends from putting themselves in danger later this afternoon.

"Maybe you should rethink the idea of having kids on the team," I said as casually as I could. "The truth is that kids as sidekicks is a trend that's beginning to fade. You represent a new age of crime fighting. You need to set a new standard. Every second-rate hero has a junior sidekick. Why not be different?"

"I see your point," he pondered. "But what about you?"

"That includes me, too," I replied. "I'm only interested in making you the success you're destined to be. I know the greatest hero when I see him, and all I care about is that Superopolis gets the champion it deserves."

I practically gagged while I was saying it.

"Go on," pooh-poohed the Amazing Indestructo as he actually blushed. It took me a second to realize that what he really meant was "Go on!"

"Let kids idolize *you*—not the kids battling evil alongside you. You're the best there'll ever be," I tried to say with a straight face, "and sidekicks, including myself, will just deflect attention from you."

"No, no, no, we'd be great together." He shook his head as he produced a document that I now realized was his sole purpose for being here this morning. "My new partner, the Tycoon, even drew up a contract just for you. It's a great deal!"

Yes, for him, I'm sure it was. I took it from him and read it over. Sure enough, I would basically be signing all rights to my name and likeness to him in perpetuity. What a creep!

"I'm not going to sign anything," I said as I pushed it back at him. I wanted him to fire all of us.

"If you sign it, I'll make you my sole sidekick and get rid of the others," he promised.

I was so enraged that he would think I could be bribed to sell out my friends that I was almost tempted to throw my cereal bowl at him. Then it hit me. This might be the only way to prevent my friends from being at Telomere Park this afternoon. I wasn't happy that AI was going to think he had succeeded in bribing me, but it was an opportunity I had to take advantage of for the sake of my new friends.

"Okay, I'll do it." I sighed reluctantly. I took the contract, signed it, and handed it back.

"It'll be worth it, kid," he promised me as he quickly rolled up the contract. "And now that you work for me, maybe you should go take a shower. You smell like you haven't had a bath in two days."

I sniffed myself and realized he was right. Getting up from the table, I headed for one of the bathrooms and found myself a towel. As I got out of my costume, I carefully set my jet pack off to the side.

Turning on the shower, I got underneath the spray and thought about what I had done. I felt like I had betrayed my friends, but it was my only chance to keep them from harm this afternoon. Half an hour later, I came out of the bathroom, clean and back in my costume. AI was still sitting at the table eating.

"Have my friends gotten here yet?"

"Yes and no," AI answered as he continued eating. "Yes, they were here, but no, they probably aren't your friends anymore."

"What do you mean?" I asked in alarm. "What did you say to them?"

"I told them how you forced me into firing them. They weren't very happy about it."

"You told them *I* made you do it?!" I said as my temper began to boil. "It was *your* decision. Take some responsibility for once in your life!"

He went silent, his eyes blinking rapidly, and then his lip began to quiver. It was a signal I had become familiar with.

"You're right." AI began to blubber. "I always take credit for the successes, but shift the blame to others."

Unbelievable. I still couldn't get over what a cry-baby AI was. I could almost feel sorry for someone so pathetic. Almost.

"They made this for you." He continued sobbing as he handed me a small cardboard poster.

I recognized it immediately. It said: THE JUNIOR LEAGUERS. FRIENDS FOREVER: FUNNEL BOY, INVISIBOY, THE GREAT INFLATO, AND METEOR BOY. It was the poster I would find pinned up in the team's headquarters at school twenty-five years from now.

Then it hit me. How was it going to get there? I hadn't even been there. In fact none of my new—now ex—friends had even mentioned it to me. And time was running out. Well, someone had to leave it there, along with the newspaper clipping and the chunk of meteorite. Grabbing the poster from AI's hand, I went over to Lord Pincushion's laboratory area and retrieved the box holding the meteorite fragment. On my way to the elevator, I stopped and tore out the picture of us from the front page of *The Hero Herald*. Without really even thinking, I also picked up a pack of the seeds AI had been trying to sell, along with one of Lord Pincushion's knitting needles, and added them to the box as well. With my collection of items, I got into the elevator and hit the button for the ground level. As the door began to close I could still see AI slumped over sobbing.

When the elevator doors opened back up, I stepped out to find my three former teammates waiting for me.

"There's the traitor," fumed Funnel Boy. "Thanks for nothing."

"W-what do you mean?" I stuttered, even though I knew *exactly* what they meant.

"You told AI to fire us," huffed Inflato, "just so you could be his only sidekick."

"That's not true," I protested. "I told him to fire all of us."

"But why?" asked InvisiBoy, who looked most hurt of all.

"Because . . ." I paused. What could I tell them? "Because I was trying to keep you from getting hurt."

"That's a pretty poor excuse," said Funnel Boy with a scowl. "We can take care of ourselves just fine."

"No, you can't," I responded. "Something bad is—" and then I stopped. I couldn't exactly tell them I was from the future. Then I noticed InvisiBoy staring at me with a peculiar look on his face. I was so agitated by it that I blurted out the first thing I could think of.

"Professor Brain-Drain is going to do something awful today, and if you don't stay away it will ruin the rest of your lives."

"Oh, yeah?" asserted Inflato. "We can handle Professor Brain-Drain by ourselves, can't we, guys? We were a team long before you barged your way in."

"Yeah, even if we *had* just met Inflato a few hours before we met you," Funnel Boy added.

With that, all three of them turned to leave.

"Please don't go," I begged, as my plan unraveled around me. "You're in danger."

"No way will we let you get all the glory," harrumphed Funnel Boy as he whipped himself into a dust cloud and whirled off in the direction of Telomere Park. Inflato frantically ran after him. Turning around, I found InvisiBoy just standing there looking at me suspiciously.

"You're not *from* here," he said matter-of-factly.

I didn't know what else to do so I replied, "No. I'm not."

And then he began running toward me as if he were going to tackle me. At the last second he vanished completely. He had been so close that I expected his invisible self to bowl me over, but there was no sign of him. I called his name for more than ten minutes before finally giving up.

Finally, I blasted into the air and headed toward my school. To my surprise, it was a building still under

construction. The gymnasium looked fairly complete, though, and it was easy to find the hidey-hole. I removed the panel with no trouble at all. Inside, I placed the items that I was destined to rediscover twenty-five years from now, and then closed the space back up.

Leaving the school I rocketed toward Needlepoint Hill. I needed the help of the League of Goodness. It was now 2:35—only two hours until I would meet my fate. In trying to alter the futures of my friends, I had only succeeded in leading them into danger. I had failed at my attempt to change the past, and now I knew I had no choice but to follow things through in the manner they were destined to unfold.

CHAPTER THIRTY-TWO

The Final Mission of Meteor Boy

Upstairs, MagnoBox confirmed right away the danger that my friends (or ex-friends, if we're being technical) were in. His face vanished from the screen to be replaced by what was taking place at that very moment in Telomere Park. We could see Funnel Boy and Inflato, who were doing their best to battle the Commune for Justice on their own. They were completely outnumbered, and soon multiple copies of SkyDiamond had them captive. InvisiBoy was nowhere to be seen, but given his power that was hardly a surprise. We all gasped as Professor Brain-Drain appeared on the screen.

"I should drain the intelligence of these young scalawags right now," he said as his index finger inched toward Funnel Boy's forehead. "But they may come in handy as hostages, at least until my plan is executed."

"That cad!" Lord Pincushion exclaimed. "We must rescue those boys."

Moments later I was seeing exactly what I had witnessed as a black and white rerun on MagnoBox's screen. Only here it was in full-color—and happening to me. As in the replay, there was no sign of my friends as we neared the Tipler. Professor Brain-Drain was standing in front of it and just as we sighted it, it began slowly to turn.

"You're too late," I heard Professor Brain-Drain cackle as he had once before. "My Tipler has begun turning and when it reaches full speed, Superopolis will be destroyed."

Moments later, MagnoBox reacted the way I knew he was going to.

"What's . . . happening?" he said as his face began to blur and the image on his screen turned to snow. "Super . . . sized . . . headaches . . . need . . . Buffer-o!" Zephyr set him down on the ground where he dropped his head, his hands pressing the sides of the screen.

Knowing he would be okay, I turned back to Professor Brain-Drain and gasped as I saw the number that was displayed on the Time Tipler's panel. In MagnoBox's replay, it had been the number 25. But here it was showing something entirely different—a much larger number—the number 65,435,772. And the lever was set not for the future—but the past! No wonder he needed so much power. Professor Brain-Drain's plan was to transport all of Superopolis more than sixty-five million years into the past! But why?

"We have to stop him!" I yelled to the Bee Lady. "We have to reset the number on the Tipler to twenty-five."

"But why?" she asked. "What is this thing?"

"I can't explain," I said frantically. "All I know is that the number on that screen has to read twenty-five, or the consequences could be cataclysmic."

"Leave it to me kid," she responded. "But you've got a lot of explaining to do once we've taken care of things here."

The Bee Lady immediately swung into action, redirecting an enormous swarm of bees to fly over to Professor Brain-Drain, driving him away from the Tipler. They then circled around him, trapping him in place. A smaller swarm headed for the control panel, but instead ran up against some sort of electromagnetic force that was beginning to form around the Tipler. Just as I was about to panic, though, they began doing the oddest thing. The bees formed into a single line and began moving in a swirling pattern around the Tipler. They appeared to be moving *with* the rotational force rather than against it. With each circle around the machine they came in closer until they finally reached the number pad.

There, at the command of their mistress, they punched the buttons that changed the number on the screen from 65,435,772 to 25. Professor Brain-Drain, completely surrounded by the main mass of bees, hadn't noticed a thing. But the bees had only done half the job—the lever was still set for the past. I needed it set for the future. Moving it was too big a job for a swarm of bees. Before I could figure out a solution, though, a more important problem arose.

"Look! There are the boys!" Lord Pincushion shouted.

They were in the clutches of the Commune for Justice. The five hippies had seen the arrival of the League of Ultimate Goodness, and like any good cowards, they were making a break for it. The only problem is they were taking Inflato and Funnel Boy with them as hostages. Or so they thought.

"I'll deal with these misfits," Lord Pincushion volunteered. The two boys were surrounded by six

SkyDiamond duplicates, running as fast as they could to reach a rainbow band that arced off into the sky.

Drawing six short blades from various parts of his body, he strode to within a dozen yards of the captive boys, held one of the blades out in front of him by its tip, and then squinted one eye as he judged the distance and speed of his targets.

"Oh my gosh!" I started to gasp. "He's not going to—"

"Shhh." The Animator calmed me. "Don't disturb his aim."

Sure enough, Lord Pincushion let the blades fly, and one by one they flew straight and true to their targets, shattering each of the crystalline figures holding Funnel Boy and Inflato captive.

"My turn!" The Animator almost giggled as he clapped his hands rapidly.

He stepped forward and with just a twinkle of his eyes, the rainbow, which had been intended as a means of escape whipped around and encircled the startled hippies. The Animator took complete control of the inanimate band and used it to wrap up the members of the Commune for Justice in a multicolored prison. All the villains were now out of commission.

"I appear to be just in time!"

I turned to see that the Amazing Indestructo had finally arrived on the scene.

"No," Lord Pincushion replied dryly. "Just in time would have been about two hours ago. But since you're finally here, why don't you do us all a favor and stop this device—whatever it is."

"There's no stopping it now." Professor Brain-Drain danced and chortled with fiendish glee from within the cloud of bees that entrapped him. "Disaster is only minutes away."

"We'll see about that," AI snorted, barreling toward the cylinder. At this point it was moving so fast that it was practically a blur. AI plunged straight at it as if he intended to knock the enormous structure on its side. Instead, despite using his full force, the icon of indestructibility was hurled back with an equally powerful force. He landed in a heap right at the feet of his astounded teammates.

"Something's not right," he said, shaking his head. "There's some kind of impenetrable barrier wrapped around that thing. What are we going to do?"

"Why don't you use your new rocket pack to fly up to the top and remove the meteor?" suggested Zephyr. "Perhaps the electromagnetic disturbance is weaker up above the tower."

"Are you kidding?" AI said. "Look at the way that rock is glowing. The thing is practically radioactive!"

"Oh, good heavens, man," Lord Pincushion said in disgust, "you're indestructible."

"No way," he insisted.

"I can do it," I said, knowing that my destiny, for good or for ill, was at hand.

The entire League of Ultimate Goodness turned toward me, looks of concern creasing their faces. The only person who looked happy was AI.

"See," said AI, "the kid wants a chance to prove himself."

"You're pathetic," countered Lord Pincushion sharply.

"This job is mine," I suddenly heard Inflato shout. "I should have been AI's sidekick, not Meteor Boy."

Before anyone could stop him, Inflato darted for the tower. But the repulsing force was spreading. The army of bees became disturbed and began bolting in confusion. Just as Inflato got as close to the tower as he could, Professor Brain-Drain was suddenly free. Having no other immediate protection, he grabbed hold of Inflato, taking him hostage. Holding a single brain-draining finger near the frightened boy's head, he made his demand.

"Back off, do-gooders," he ordered, "or I'll drain this kid's brain until he's only as bright as an inner tube. Just stay back for another two minutes until my Tipler is at full strength and then I'll let him go."

"The cad," I heard Lord Pincushion utter as I came up beside him.

"I know how I can get to that meteorite," I told him. "If I fly in a tight spiral motion from the bottom to the top, I can duplicate what worked for the swarm of bees. By the time I reach the top I'll be close enough to grab the rock."

"Anything is worth a try," said Lord Pincushion, "but your attempt could cost your friend his intelligence. Wait until I resolve that situation first. You'll know when to act."

With that, Lord Pincushion strode out to meet the enemy with nothing to protect himself except a knife, a saber, a javelin, an ax, two corkscrews, two butcher blades, three daggers, four army knives, four skewers, six types of forks, enough steak knives for eight place settings, and one dueling foil, which he proceeded to withdraw from an area near his spleen.

"Come forward and face me like a gentleman, you scoundrel," he challenged.

"Ah, the leader of the League of *Ultimate* Goodness," Professor Brain-Drain taunted. "You've signed away your future and your self-respect, Pincushion, all because you made the mistake of assuming that the people of Superopolis would be there to support you after everything you've done for them."

"The public may have disappointed me," he acknowledged, "but a true hero never disappoints the public."

"A true hero, like the one standing behind you?" scoffed the Professor as everyone turned to the Amazing Indestructo. He had a "what? who, me?" sort of look on his face. "He sees himself taking your place as my greatest foe, never understanding that it was your intelligence that made you a threat to me. He's merely a powerful buffoon who is shameless enough to let children do his dangerous work."

"Hey, you're talking like I'm not even here," AI protested.

"It's true he's a buffoon," Lord Pincushion agreed, "but I'm a man of my word and I can't go back on it now. I can, however, finish you off here and now before I go into retirement. And I have every intention of doing so. Prepare to defend yourself."

"If only I could," the Professor said, grinning, his finger creeping ever closer to the nervous boy's head, "but I left my weapon collection at home."

"Then, by all means, borrow one of mine," Lord Pincushion offered, whipping off his top hat to reveal a hatchet sticking straight up from his skull.

Before Professor Brain-Drain could react, Lord Pincushion flung the hatchet straight at him. Luckily for the Professor, he ducked just in time and the hatchet clattered against the colander on his head. But in the process he lost his grip on Inflato, who ran for his life.

I knew this was my sign and I hurtled myself toward the tower with all the speed I could muster. I reached it in a second and began circling the electro-magnetic field as closely as I could. Spiraling around the Tipler, I began moving higher up and closer to the tower with every loop. But something wasn't right. The Tipler appeared to be moving even faster with every one of my revolutions. I actually appeared to be enhancing the device's power. Even worse, I saw that the lever was still set to send me twenty-five years even further into the past.

"Meteor Boy! Stop!" I heard Lord Pincushion holler as he began running toward the Tipler, his fencing sword still in his hand. Unfortunately, Inflato came running from the opposite direction and crashed right

into him. With a look of complete surprise on his face, Inflato got to his feet. But surprise turned to horror as he looked down at the fencing blade sticking into his stomach. Only the tip appeared to have pierced him, but he quickly grabbed the blade to remove it.

"Inflato, no!" Lord Pincushion gasped, but he was too late. The instant Inflato pulled it out the air rushed out of him like from a burst balloon. Before anyone could grab him he began scudding around, rocketing this way and that in no predictable pattern. At the very same instant, I reached the top of the tower and my tightest revolution. The giant metal cones were beginning to tip. The meteorite was within my grasp. I reached out and grabbed hold of it, and in that instant the electromagnetic force vanished—just as Inflato collided with the lever.

I heard Professor Brain-Drain let out a howl of despair as the collision shifted the lever from the left all the way to the right. Then there was a sudden blinding flash, and everything went dark.

CHAPTER THIRTY-THREE

Forth and Back

A split second later I was back in my own time. I knew it was my own time because of the ten-story-tall layer cake that I was hurtling toward at a good two hundred miles per hour. I couldn't have been more grateful for its presence, though, because I instantly realized I no longer had the Meteor Boy jet pack, or its controls. I must have lost them when I was catapulted through time. I was, however, still holding the prodigium meteorite. Its added weight helped propel me smack into the side of the cake at a point about fifty feet off the ground.

I must have plunged fifteen feet into the spongy and still surprisingly moist cake. I figured I must only be a few feet away from bursting out of the other side, and I briefly toyed with the idea of eating my way out. But when I turned around and saw that I

had left a clear tunnel behind me, I scooted around and began making my way back, rolling the meteorite in front of me.

Reaching the edge, I looked down at the crowds and realized it had to be Thursday afternoon. I saw my classmates over in one area displaying their science fair experiments as parents and teachers milled about them. I saw my father's team just below me with their thousands of normal-size pies and cakes all set up for their bake sale. Uncle Fluster's ice cream truck was parked nearby with no customers anywhere near it. On the platform in front of the tower, the Amazing Indestructo was posed between Mayor Whitewash and Professor Brain-Drain, who was still dressed as the artist Crispo, while half a dozen members of the League of Ultimate Goodness stood alongside. Every last person down there was looking up at me.

I realized that Crispo had just removed the shroud that had covered his "project" and that the giant water tower in Telomere Park was rotating at a steadily increasing speed. After all, it made sense. The only thing the professor was missing from his plan was the meteorite in my hands.

As if he had read my mind, Bliss suddenly dropped down in front of me, hanging on a rainbow rope, and grabbed the meteorite from right out of my hands. I looked up just in time to see the entire Commune for Justice arcing away on a rainbow toward the dish sitting atop the tower—the same one I had stolen the meteorite from five minutes and twenty-five years ago. Professor

306

Brain-Drain began chortling and cackling as he jumped up and down for joy. AI and the members of the League of Ultimate Goodness stood with their mouths hanging open, oblivious to Crispo's odd behavior.

Apparently, everyone was too busy looking up at me. I immediately spotted my mother and father who had enormous expressions of relief on their faces.

"OB! You made it back!" I heard my father shout. "Thank heavens, Lord Pincushion was right!"

"Don't worry about me," I hollered back. "Stop Professor Brain-Drain!"

"Oh, don't worry about him," my father shook his head. "He must be dead. We've had a trap ready for him for days, and there's been no sign of him."

I guess a paint-spattered lab coat and a shower cap *was* enough to fool the citizens of Superopolis. I should have been more specific in my letter.

"Crispo is Professor Brain-Drain!" I shouted as loudly as I possibly could.

As I said it, Bliss deposited the meteorite on the top of the tower and the Time Tipler began to pick up speed dramatically. Everything I had done—my trek through time, my two-day career as Meteor Boy, my disgust at having helped turn the Amazing Indestructo into the city's most financially successful hero—had all been for nothing. Professor Brain-Drain was back in possession of the prodigium meteorite and was once again preparing to transport Superopolis sixty-five million years back in time.

To my relief the Amazing Indestructo grabbed

Professor Brain-Drain by the collar and hoisted him into the air.

"This can't be Brain-Drain," he insisted. "He's dead."

"Look under his shower cap," I yelled down.

AI reached up and yanked the big poofy cap off Crispo's head, revealing Professor Brain-Drain's tell-tale trademark colander. The entire crowd let out a gasp.

"B-but you're supposed to be dead," stammered AI.

"Many of us have returned from the dead today," Brain-Drain hissed, "including your former sidekick."

"That can't be. He's just a kid I hired . . ."

"Yes, the exact same one you hired twenty-five years ago," confirmed the Professor. "How else do you explain him showing up here with the same meteorite he was stealing when he vanished?"

"It *is* him!" the Amazing Indestructo cried. "I wasn't responsible for his death after all!"

"Not yet, anyway," teased Professor Brain-Drain. "He looks like he could fall from that rather large pastry at any moment."

"No! Don't—" I began to yell, but AI paid no attention. He set Professor Brain-Drain down and launched himself into the air toward me. By the time he reached me, the Professor had made it over to the time-setting panel and punched 65,435,797 onto the number panel. He had added twenty-five years to the number I had seen in the past to account for the time that had elapsed since then. The lever was still set to the past, just as it had been when it sent me back in time two days earlier.

"Don't worry about me," I screamed at AI as he lifted me from the hole in the cake. "Stop Professor Brain-Drain! He's going to transport all Superopolis sixty-five million years back in time!"

"I'm not going to suffer another twenty-five years of guilt over you," said AI as he, in the way only he could, performed a heroic rescue for the absolutely most selfish of reasons. "The league can take care of Brain-Drain."

If only that were true. As AI lowered me to the

309

ground, I watched six members of the League of Ultimate Goodness go into battle with the five hippies plus the six duplicates of SkyDiamond. They were overcome in a matter of seconds. Most of the other adults created a protective barrier between the kids from my school and the villains up on the stage. But not *all* the parents. One group of heroes saw their chance and sprang into action—the New New Crusaders!

"Dad!" I hollered. "Stop the machine! You can't let it reach its top speed."

But how could he stop it? I asked myself. I had just witnessed another group of heroes attempt the same thing twenty-five years in the past, and they had failed. And I no longer had the jet pack that might have allowed me to steal the meteorite yet again. This situation was not looking good.

Sure enough, the Big Bouncer hurled himself at the Time Tipler . . . and bounced right off it. The electromagnetic barrier was beginning to form, and there was no way to get at the machine. Windbag had taken a deep breath, but all he was succeeding in doing was blowing the entire League of Ultimate Goodness and a handful of hippies off the stage. Meanwhile, the Amazing Indestructo had managed to swoop in close enough to grab Professor Brain-Drain, but he didn't even seem to mind. He just kept cackling as if he had pulled off the biggest evil scheme of his career—and he might just have been right.

The Time Tipler had become a blur, and I looked

up just in time to see the cones begin to tip. A moment later a flash of energy erupted from the tower and spread out in all directions as far as I could see. It was a blast of power that dwarfed the tiny burst my rock had generated when it had sent me back in time.

As soon as the concussion had passed, I looked up, and to my amazement and distress, realized that the entire range of the Carbunkle Mountains had vanished. But that wasn't nearly as frightening as the pack of dinosaurs that had suddenly appeared in our midst, who were looking at us as if dinner had just been delivered.

CHAPTER THIRTY-FOUR

The Return of the League of Goodness

A velociraptor had already locked its eyes on me and stalked my way with cool detachment. Then, out of nowhere, a cloud of bees descended from the air and surrounded the dinosaur's head. I glanced around and saw swarms of bees surrounding all the dinosaurs. It didn't take a genius to know where they had come from.

A moment later, the Bee Lady came putt-putting her way up one of Telomere Park's cement pathways, which, like everything else, had been transported back in time along with us. Right behind her was Lord Pincushion and the Animator. But it was the army with them that really got my attention. Marching in ranks behind the Animator were dozens of empty suits of armor that I recognized from the halls of Pinprick Manor. Just as the bees began to tire, the disembodied knights took over and began battling the dinosaurs, who found their sharp teeth useless against the metal.

"My apologies for our tardiness," Lord Pincushion said as he tipped his hat to me, revealing a dagger sticking from the top of his head.

None of them looked as they had when I last saw them only an hour ago. Then, they had been in their early fifties but still very active. Now I saw three elderly heroes in their late seventies. But they had an aura of excitement about them that reminded me of their younger selves. These were heroes ready again for action.

The New New Crusaders and the League of Ultimate Goodness were still doing battle with the Commune for Justice. The Amazing Indestructo was still holding Professor Brain-Drain, who had a big grin on his face. My classmates and their parents, along with the school faculty, finally remembered that they had superpowers and started fighting back against the dinosaurs as well. Stench had just lifted one above his head and hurled it into another oncoming lizard. Another was attempting to snap at Plasma Girl, who kept reducing herself down to a goopy puddle and then re-forming herself a few feet away. All I could see of Halogen Boy was a bright glow that was warding off a trio of dinosaurs who were blinded by his brilliance. Tadpole was caught in a trickier situation. He had used his tongue to pull the legs out from under one velociraptor, but he didn't know that another was sneaking up right behind him. Just as I was certain it was going to pounce, it went stiff. Tadpole swung around to find that Miss Marble had just saved him.

As I watched the dinosaurs begin to panic and run, I turned to Lord Pincushion and the Animator, who were standing beside me. The Bee Lady also puttered up to join us.

"I'm sorry you only found out the truth recently from my letter," I said to them. "I should have told you all twenty-five years ago, but I was afraid I would alter the course of history."

"Oh, we knew the truth shortly after you disap-

peared," the Bee Lady said casually as she lit up a cigarette.

"Indeed." Lord Pincushion confirmed. "But I regret to say I continued to harbor doubts until you arrived on our doorstep with your letter."

I'm sure I was standing there with my mouth hanging open. I was dumbfounded. Who had revealed the truth to them?

"That letter *was* a clever idea," the Animator smiled at me. "We would never have thought to notify your parents on our own."

"How clever could I have been?" I finally found my voice, as I indicated the disaster surrounding us. "Everything is a mess!"

"Oh, but things are certain to improve," Lord Pincushion reassured me as we watched Tadpole and Miss Marble shaking hands. "We've already been told how everything will turn out."

"But how? And by whom?" I said, perplexed.

"Why, the same person who told us twenty-five years ago to show up at this place and time prepared to do battle with dinosaurs," Pincushion explained. "We don't normally bring along the armor when we leave the house."

I didn't know what to say. Who was manipulating all these events?

"Of course, things will get worse before they get better," Lord Pincushion calmly informed me. "Take a look."

He removed a long, sharp pointer that had been stuck through his neck and used it to direct my attention

toward the sky. Even if it had been broad daylight, there would have been no way to miss it. The fact that dusk was setting in made it all the easier to see. Heading straight for us was a gigantic fireball.

"It's enormous!" I said in alarm. "What is it?!"

"It's a meteor, of course," said Lord Pincushion. "A gigantic one. It will be striking this very spot in under an hour. And unfortunately, this is one meteor that Meteor Boy could never stop."

"Meteor Boy's career is over, anyway," I admitted.

"I lost my jet pack when I shot into the future."

"I know," said the Bee Lady. "I found it after you vanished. I held on to it for twenty-five years, until I could return it to you."

"But then who invented it?" I said, so perplexed I almost forgot about the giant meteor.

"I have no idea." She shrugged.

"Don't think about it." Lord Pincushion shook his head sharply. "It will only give you heartburn."

"So how *do* we stop it?" I said, trying my best not to sound helpless.

"We don't," he replied. "What we need to do is return to our own time."

I glanced up to the top of the Time Tipler and saw that the large chunk of meteorite had vanished. And then I remembered how a trip of a mere twenty-five years had left my own small chunk of prodigium reduced to a pebble. Clearly, the power required to transport all Superopolis back sixty-five million years had totally used it up.

"The meteorite is gone!" I said in alarm. "There's no power source left to return us to the future!"

"I think the kid's right, Pincushion," said the Bee Lady nervously, squinting through her cat's-eye glasses at the empty dish atop the water tower.

"Indeed," he agreed as he paused and absentmindedly inspected a meat thermometer protruding from his left arm. "That does present a bit of a problem. But I have faith that the boy will figure something out."

"Why is it always my responsibility!?" I shouted.

317

"Surely you don't expect one of *them* to provide a solution?" Lord Pincushion stated sharply, indicating the heroes surrounding us.

Unfortunately, as I had come to realize was often the case with Lord Pincushion, he had a point. The League of Ultimate Goodness was being utterly humiliated at the hands of the hippies, while my father's team, the New New Crusaders, wasn't faring much better. The other heroes were all too busy fighting off dinosaurs or protecting the other kids. And all the while, Professor Brain-Drain just continued laughing as AI stood there helplessly holding him aloft, not sure what else to do. Watching the egghead of evil so gleeful got me completely steamed.

"Well, I know one person who can figure a way out of this," I fumed, storming off toward the Time Tipler.

Professor Brain-Drain spotted me coming.

"Ah, there's the junior do-gooder who made all this possible," he said, chortling. "I must admit, it took me a moment to realize that you were, in fact, Meteor Boy when I met you backstage. It wasn't until you used my Tipler to escape to the past that it all came together. Happily, despite your valiant effort, my master plan has worked, with only a minor twenty-five-year delay."

"There's one other little glitch you might want to consider," I said, pointing to the meteor that was now beginning to dominate the darkening sky.

It was never easy to tell what was going on behind those thick glasses of his, but Professor Brain-Drain did not seem at all panicked.

"Why do you think I brought us all here?" he said with malicious glee. "That is the meteorite that created what we know to be Superopolis. When it hits, it will do so with such force that it will create the Carbunkle Mountain range and the plain where Superopolis will eventually rise."

"But why bring us back here?" I demanded.

"So that Superopolis can be destroyed by the very thing that created it," he answered matter-of-factly. "Surely you see the beautiful symmetry of my plan?"

"But you'll be destroyed, too!" I said.

"One must sacrifice for one's art," he said. "Of course, there is always a way to escape any fate, if one can only think of a solution."

I turned to AI. "Can you fly out there and stop it?"

"Are you nuts?" cried the Amazing Indestructo, setting the Professor down. "Look at the size of that thing!"

"You're indestructible!!" I yelled at him.

"What about all these other heroes?" AI protested. "Why can't they handle it?"

"You've made that impossible by choosing such feeble wits as your teammates," the Professor pointed out just as the Human Compass ran by us pursued by one of SkyDiamond's duplicates.

"North is this way!" he shouted to us.

"I rest my case," Professor Brain-Drain replied. "But, as I said, there is always a means of escape. And if the Amazing Indestructo here can fly up to the dish atop my Tipler to retrieve what is left of the prodigium,

I'll show you all the solution."

"Sure," AI said, blasting up to the top of the water tower. He returned with a small rock—all that remained of the once-large meteorite.

The Professor stepped up to the control panel and pulled the indicator lever from the past position to the future, leaving the number 65,435,797 on the screen.

"Now give me what's left of the prodigium," the Professor demanded.

"AI! Don't!" I warned him.

"How can a piece this small transport all of us forward in time sixty-five million years?" AI asked as he handed it to Brain-Drain, ignoring me completely.

"It can't," he replied with an enigmatic grin on his face. "But it will transport *me*."

Professor Brain-Drain darted into the interior chamber of the Time Tipler, locking the door from the inside. I ran to the window just in time to see him place the chunk of meteorite into the small power chamber. The cylinder, which had continued to rotate slowly, immediately began to pick up speed. I didn't know if the small Tipler chamber would generate an electromagnetic barrier and force me away from the tower, so I acted quickly.

As loudly as I could, I slammed the outer lock in place. This got Brain-Drain's attention, and his sinister face appeared in the window. It didn't take him long to see the danger he was in and he immediately unlocked the door from the inside—not that it did him any good. He could only watch helplessly from the window as I grabbed the time lever. I almost felt guilty about how much I enjoyed the look of horror on his face when I switched the lever from the future setting to the past.

A moment later the warping of space-time flung me from the platform and I landed with a soft but solid thud on the grassy ground. I vaguely remember staring up at the cones as they once again began to tip. After that, I must have blanked out—just as the Time Tipler hurled Professor Brain-Drain another sixty-five million years further into the past.

CHAPTER THIRTY-FIVE

Cretaceous Park

When I opened my eyes I had no idea where I was. It was dark out and there were people huddled all around me. At first I thought that I must be at school because I noticed Principal Doppelganger and Miss Marble standing there. My team was also gathered around, and I noticed looks of relief on the faces of Stench, Hal, Tadpole, and Plasma Girl. But when I saw the Amazing Indestructo, the Bee Lady, and Lord Pincushion, it quickly came back to me where I was. And then I heard two familiar voices calling my name.

"OB? Where are you?"

"Here he is!"

The panic in my mom's and dad's voices vanished in an instant as they elbowed their way (carefully) past Lord Pincushion, both attempting to hug me at once.

"Well, I guess you figured out the mystery of Meteor

322

Boy," my mom said with a mix of laughter and tears.

Meteor! It suddenly reminded me of the danger we were still in. I looked past my parents and saw that the meteor was now dominating the sky to such a degree that it appeared at least ten times bigger than the sun.

"What are we going to do?" I said. "That meteor is going to destroy us all in less than an hour! And we have no power source to activate the Time Tipler so it can return us to our own time! And for some reason, people think I know how to get us back there, but I don't have any idea!!"

I honestly thought I was going to start crying—which may have been worse than getting crushed by an enormous meteor—but then Principal Doppelganger said something very odd.

"No one expects you to fix this all by yourself," he said mysteriously, as he stretched out a hand to help me to my feet. "And I think someone is on his way who can help you."

He gestured toward the entrance of Telomere Park. I squinted into the darkening night, unsure of what I was seeing. There was a disturbance of some kind, and it was coming our way. I could mark its trail primarily by the leaves and branches being flung wildly into the air. But the object itself soon became clear. An enormous tornado nearly twenty feet high was moving toward us. As it finally stopped, directly in front of us, I realized there was only one person it could possibly be. As the winds began to dissipate, a lone individual was left in its wake. It was Funnel Boy. Except he was

324

no longer a boy. He was now a fully grown criminal—Cyclotron. For a moment he just stared at me with the strangest expression on his face.

"You look exactly like you did the last time I saw you," he finally said.

"I should," I replied, not knowing how else to react. "That was only a couple of hours ago, my time."

"I was told that you might need my help."

That was an understatement. Most of the dinosaurs had fled and the Commune for Justice was finally being reined in by the combined efforts of the League of Ultimate Goodness and the New New Crusaders. I had no idea, though, how any of them could help stop the oncoming meteor.

"We don't need the help of an evildoer," AI shot back huffily.

"Why?" I asked, turning to him. "Have *you* decided to fly out there and stop that thing?"

The Amazing Indestructo stood silently with an *oops* look on his face before finally replying, "Well, there's no reason not to let him try, I guess."

I heard a faintly mumbled "despicable" from the direction of Lord Pincushion.

But how would Cyclotron save us? No funnel cloud could possibly stop a meteor.

"But what can you do to help us?" I asked.

"That's for you to figure out," he said. "Someone told me twenty-five years ago that this was going to happen and that you and I together would be able to prevent it."

"But how?!" I blurted out in complete frustration. All this someone-sometime-told-me-something-some-such was driving me crazy. "And can't someone just give me a straight answer?"

"Maybe you have something in your pockets," Principal Doppelganger suddenly spoke up.

I slipped my hand into the right pocket of my Meteor Boy costume and retrieved the last remaining pebble of prodigium in existence—the remnants of the piece that had first brought me to the past. I stared at it for a moment, but nothing came to me.

"It's only the size of a chocolate chip," I said with a sigh. "It's not powerful enough to return even one of us to our own time."

"Try your other pocket," suggested Principal Doppelganger. "But make sure you hold on to that tiny rock."

I looked up at my principal suspiciously as my hand dipped into my left pocket. As my hand wrapped around its contents, an idea materialized in my brain. It was the Oomphlifier and if it still carried a charge, I knew how to get us all back to our own time.

"Here, take this," I said, handing the device to Cyclotron. "But don't do anything until I give the word."

I ran back up to the platform, where the Time Tipler had slowed to a moderate rotation, which was the best it could do with no prodigium to power it. I grabbed the direction lever and switched it from the past to the future. The number 65,435,797 still appeared on the panel. That done, I darted back to Cyclotron.

"Now, all you need to do is whip up a tornado around the Tipler and press the button on the Oomphlifier. It will increase the level of your power almost a million times, which I'm hoping will get the central cylinder of the Time Tipler spinning fast enough to return us to our own time. Ready to give it a shot?"

I hoped that the answer was yes. The meteor was now so close that I knew we had only one chance at this.

"Let's give her a spin," Cyclotron said confidently.

Turning to face the Time Tipler, Cyclotron closed his eyes and concentrated. A funnel cloud immediately began to develop around the cylinder of the tower. It began to spin faster and faster as he got the device spinning at the top speed he could manage on his own. It was moving fast, but not fast enough to activate the time machine. I looked up once again at the meteor which now filled most of the sky. I knew only minutes remained before it hit.

"Now," I said nervously. "Try it now."

Cyclotron pressed the button on the Oomphlifier. Instantaneously, the speed of the funnel cloud ratcheted up to the fastest cyclone on record—and then got even faster. We all began backing away as we felt the pressure from the circular winds start to suck us in. And still the speed got faster. And then faster still. The cylinder was spinning at a speed that looked equal to what the prodigium had been able to generate.

The meteor was now so close that not only could

we hear it but I could swear we could feel the enormous heat from it as well—or maybe that was just my dad's hand on my shoulder. Cyclotron only had seconds left. And then I saw it. The cones on top of the Tipler began to move. With one final burst of willpower and speed, Cyclotron gave it his last bit of effort, and the cones tipped sideways. The last thing I saw was a flaming ball heading right for us.

CHAPTER THIRTY-SIX

A Wrinkle in Timing

When I opened my eyes again, I expected to see a blinding fireball. Instead, all I saw was a full moon rising in the still-dusky sky high above the once-again-present Carbunkle Mountains. We had made it back to our own time.

Heroes and villains alike were also just shaking off the effects of the journey across sixty-five million years. There was even one stray dinosaur that had failed to flee with its fellow reptiles and was now looking very out of place.

The members of the Commune for Justice used the momentary confusion as an opportunity to resume their attack. But they had seriously underestimated the level of irritation that had built up in people who had just been whipsawed through time, threatened by dinosaurs, and almost crushed by a meteor. I don't know who threw the first one, but a large custard pie came hurtling out of the crowd, smacking Bliss right in the face. From there it turned into a free-for-all.

The thousands of pies and cakes my father's team had produced were used up within minutes, and the entire Commune for Justice was rounded up and hauled off to jail. The equally confused dinosaur was taken away to the Superopolis Zoo.

"See, my boy," I heard Lord Pincushion say as he came up beside me. "I told you everything would turn out just fine."

I turned to confront the founder of the League of Goodness with a fact that I now realized was undeniable.

"That's only because a witness to all this is going to go back twenty-five years and make sure everything happens the way it's supposed to," I said. "And I think I know who that person is."

"InvisiBoy?" I said, addressing the air around me. "It's time to show yourself."

There was a pause and deathly silence as a crowd began to gather around me. For a moment, I thought I was going to look like an idiot. Then InvisiBoy materialized before me. He was the same age as I had last seen him, and he looked very frightened and nervous.

"Your power isn't invisibility, is it?" I asked him as gently as possible.

He looked anxiously at the people around us.

"N-n-no," he finally admitted. "My power is the ability to shrink myself to the size of a speck. People have always just assumed that I was invisible and I've never told anyone otherwise."

"You've been hitching a ride with me since you confronted me outside Pinprick Manor just five hours ago," I said. "Haven't you? Never guessing that it would carry you twenty-five years into the future."

"I also think I accidentally unlatched your jet pack," he admitted meekly. Then he started sobbing as a greater realization hit him. "How am I going to get back home?!"

"He has to get home." I turned to see Cyclotron step up between Lord Pincushion and my mother. "After all, he's the one who is going to tell me what my part has to be in this twenty-five-year mission."

"Then you're not a villain!" I said, a wide grin spreading across my face.

"Of course not," he replied.

"But you've been committing crimes for over fifteen years," the Amazing Indestructo piped up.

"Think about it, you idiot. I've never actually stolen anything," Cyclotron said. "But it's true I've rarely missed a chance to embarrass you in whatever way I could."

AI looked as if he were about to protest, then wisely shut his mouth.

"InvisiBoy returned from this trip to the future and told me the role I was going to have to play in saving Superopolis from its worst crisis. In order to ensure that the Tipler would be reassembled, I had to gain Brain-Drain's trust and play a part in helping those mindless hippies complete their task."

"If it hadn't been for you, they wouldn't have retrieved even one of the cones," I confirmed.

"True," Cyclotron agreed, "and I wouldn't have been hired by Brain-Drain to help them if I hadn't been a believable villain."

"You remained focused on a single mission for twenty-five years?" said Lord Pincushion with awe. "Zephyr would have been immensely proud of you."

"I told him my mission early on, and he always supported it," Cyclotron revealed. "Even when I seemed to become a villain, he always knew the truth."

"But how will I get back to tell you all this?" exclaimed a very panicky InvisiBoy.

"He has to," the Bee Lady agreed. "It's the only way I'll find out as well."

"I think I know," I said as I fished the tiny pebble from my pocket. "This last remaining piece of prodigium is too small to use even in the interior chamber of the Time Tipler. It utilized almost ninety percent of its original size just to transport me twenty-five years to the past."

"So what use is it?" AI asked dismissively.

"Shut up and let my son talk," my dad said.

"What we need is a smaller time machine."

I walked over to where my class's science fair experiments were on display. On the way, I stopped by Uncle Fluster's ice cream truck to borrow three sugar cones and the wire rack that held them. As I approached the science exhibits, I saw that the crowds were wandering back to them and most of my classmates we're back explaining them to the passersby.

I noticed Puddle Boy's and the Spore's pea plant, which, in a matter of days, had been completely choked off by a layer of mold and moss that had also spread across their card table and halfway up Puddle Boy's leg.

I passed by Plasma Girl's and Little Miss Bubbles' tea and fruit juice experiment, set up like a fancy party. The Animator was sitting with them enjoying a cup.

Then I saw Cannonball, who had Halogen Boy standing on a table as one by one he stuck balloons on my friend, utilizing Hal's natural electric charge to demonstrate static electricity.

The next table was what I had come here for. Melonhead was manning it, but all that was on display was a potato with wires and two dials.

"Where's my time machine?" I demanded. I had

left it at school on Tuesday and I panicked that Melonhead may not have brought it.

"I jutht thet it off to the thide for a thecond," he protested as he got it out of a box underneath the table. "Here it ith." I exhaled a sigh of relief.

As everyone watched me intently, I placed the wire rack onto the potato-chip-can cylinder and then inserted a sugar cone into each of the three rings that extended from it. I then opened up the power chamber of the phonograph and pulled out the battery and the wires connected to it. I replaced the battery with the pebble of prodigium. My impromptu invention only needed one more thing.

"Melonhead," I asked graciously, "may I have the use of your potato clock?"

"Thertainly!" he said, as surprised as anyone that it may be useful.

I removed some of the wires sticking out of the potato and proceeded to rewire them into the phonograph controls. It was tricky, but I managed to set it the way I needed it.

"Good heavens, son!" Lord Pincushion said with astonishment. "Is that what I think it is?"

"It's a miniature Time Tipler," I confirmed. "I've recalibrated Melonhead's potato clock so that each minute represents a year. One of the dials indicates the past, the other the future. All I have to do is set the hands on the past dial to twenty-five minutes, and it should be ready to transport InvisiBoy back to his own time."

"Ingenious," Lord Pincushion responded.

"It wath all my idea," Melonhead claimed with a spatter of seeds.

"Are you ready?" I asked InvisiBoy.

"Yes," he said with as much confidence as he could muster.

I instructed InvisiBoy to set himself dead center on the tip of the phonograph spindle inside the can in order to avoid the effects of the rotation. He shrunk himself down to a speck on my finger, and I transferred him to the interior of the cylinder. Once I was sure he was in place, I switched the turntable on.

The can began spinning faster, and then faster yet. The prodigium was doing its thing. Within a minute the speed was so great that the cylinder had become a blur. Finally, just when I was beginning to doubt the thing would work, the sugar cones tipped. A moment later, the prodigium vanished and the turntable returned to a normal speed.

"Did it work, OB?" my dad asked.

"It must have," I replied confidently.

"But how do you know, lad?" asked Lord Pincushion.

"Because if it hadn't worked, Principal Doppelganger wouldn't be standing here," I motioned to my principal. "After all, how else could InvisiBoy have grown up to become him?"

CHAPTER THIRTY-SEVEN

Applied Science

Considering how bad things had been looking just one day earlier (or 65,435,797 years earlier if you want to be technical) everything had turned out reasonably well for everybody. The New New Crusaders made such an impression with their gigantic cake that they finally landed themselves a sponsor—the Maximizer Snack Cake Company!

There were some happy winners of our science fair. With the absence of Crispo, the Amazing Indestructo was the only remaining judge. First place went to Limber Lass and Lobster Boy for their water beaker xylophone. I'm sure the fact that they used it to perform AI's theme song played only a small part in their victory. Second place went to Transparent Girl and Foggybottom for their hardly scientific but deliberately pandering "exploration" of what makes AI the most impressive hero ever. Melonhead's and my fully functional time machine got third place.

And both Cyclotron and Principal Doppelganger were finally able to go back to being exactly who they were. I don't think my principal was completely happy that his power was no longer a secret, but he shouldn't have worried. No kid was going to do anything they shouldn't when there was a possibility that their principal could be shrunk to the size of a speck and observing everything they were up to.

Principal Doppelganger admitted to me that shortly after he returned to his own time, he had started acting incredibly reckless, knowing full well that he was destined to survive to adulthood. He got more and more out of control until, finally, Zephyr and Funnel Boy had convinced him that he could actually harm himself and throw everything out of whack. With their help, he staged a disappearance, and reinvented himself as Doppelganger.

Eventually, he embarked on a career in education with the sole purpose of putting himself in a position to pair me and Melonhead for the science fair. Just to be certain, he also gave Melonhead the idea of creating a time machine, not knowing I had already thought to do it on my own. I don't blame him, though. He had to make certain we would invent the means for his younger self to get back home.

Even my own team, the present-day Junior Leaguers, got a chance the very next day at school to utilize the science they had learned. Only one week after this whole strange adventure had begun, we were back in gym class, and once again divided into the same teams for dodgeball.

That was where the resemblance to the previous week's game ended. From the moment Coach Inflato blew his whistle, my team was on the offensive. Stench and Tadpole immediately teamed up with Limber Lass, using her as a slingshot to fire balls into the opposing team. In addition to the added speed, they put topspins and backspins on the balls, using their new knowledge of how objects move through the air to completely fool their opponents. The Quake, Melonhead, and even Transparent Girl were taken out in only a matter of moments.

Plasma Girl and Little Miss Bubbles had learned how the acid in fruit juices could easily clear up any cloudiness in iced tea. Using that knowledge, they coated one of the dodgeballs in lemon juice just before hurling it at Foggybottom. As soon as the ball struck the cloud surrounding him, his fog covering evaporated just long enough for Tadpole and Stench to smack him with one of their slingshot balls.

The first member of my team to be taken out was Halogen Boy, who got hit from behind by Sparkplug. Before he headed to jail, I whispered some advice in his ear. On the way, he stopped to congratulate Sparkplug with a handshake. In that instant, the same static electric charge that Cannonball had forced him to demonstrate at the fair, succeeded in short circuiting Sparkplug's own electric field. I saw my opportunity and hurled a ball that found its target with nothing to stop it.

A moment later, I got hit myself by the Spore. Even as I headed to jail, I felt confident that we were going to win this game. Hal was still there, and the moment I arrived, a ball came flying back. It bounced off his hands and onto the stage.

I jumped up and followed the ball back to the hidey-hole where I had found the items that had set this whole chain of events in motion. I lifted off the panel and crawled inside, finding the remaining items I had left there—a packet of seeds and Lord Pincushion's knitting needle. I picked the needle up, thinking it was high time I returned it to him. As I emerged from the cramped space, I barely noticed the dark figure standing in the shadows.

"It's a good thing I was riding along with you when you placed these items here," Principal Doppelganger said stepping forward. "If I hadn't been, no one would have known to guide you to their discovery."

"You threw that ball up here on purpose last week," I stated. "And then made sure it rolled through the hole in the panel."

"I had to," he explained. "That's why I asked Inflato to have you kids play dodgeball, even though it's against school policy. I knew it would provide the opportunity I needed to steer you back here."

"I'm sure he didn't mind," I said. "He seems to enjoy inflicting misery on us."

"Sadly, yes," the former InvisiBoy sighed. "But he's really not a bad person. For twenty-five years he both blamed you for his failed career, and felt guilty over your disappearance. Nothing Funnel Boy or I said to him could convince him otherwise."

"In reality, he saved my life," I admitted. "If he hadn't struck the Tipler's lever, I would have been sent back twenty-five years *further* in time."

"We tried telling him that, but he just wouldn't believe our story."

"It *is* pretty far-fetched," I said with a smile.

"Indeed," Principal Doppelganger started to laugh for the first time that I could ever recall. "Now get back out there and win your game. I allowed for one more dodgeball game to give your team a second chance. After all, I stacked the previous game against you."

"You told Cannonball who to choose for his team?" I said with annoyance.

"He couldn't have figured it out on his own," the principal admitted. "And I had to make sure you ended up in jail."

Even more determined to avenge last week's defeat, I returned to the game. It couldn't have been going better for us. The Banshee let out a tremendous scream just as the Human Sponge's ball collided with her forehead, and even Puddle Boy managed to raise a cloud of mildew with a well-aimed shot at his science fair partner, the Spore.

In fact there was only one person left to get—Cannonball, himself. Tadpole and Little Miss Bubbles each held a ball, Stench had a third. The fourth came bouncing back to me. Halogen Boy had gotten out of jail, but Lobster Boy had taken his place. I handed the ball to him despite barely being able to hold it with his claws. I figured he was owed this shot. On my signal, the balls were thrown all at once. Cannonball made for a nice fat, round target and even Lobster Boy was able to hit him. Thanks to the force of Stench's ball, the creep crumpled beneath the onslaught. Our victory was complete.

Even as my team erupted in cheers, a figure appeared at the entrance to the gym. The cheers were suddenly stifled as my classmates couldn't believe who they were seeing. It was none other than the Amazing Indestructo, here at our school. The shouting, which had been confined to my team, now spread to almost the whole class as they ran to mob their favorite hero.

I did not join them. But as I watched the hubbub, another person stepped up next to me. It was Coach Inflato.

"I finally figured it out," he said. He appeared remarkably calm for him.

"Coach Inflato," I started to say. "I hope that now you understand why I . . ." but that was as far as I had gotten.

"That's okay," he interrupted. "I finally realize why AI chose just you as his sidekick. My abilities would have taken too much attention away from him. He needed someone who wouldn't overshadow him, and of course he saw that in Meteor Boy."

I looked at the knitting needle in my hand, and then at the Amazing Indestructo. I suddenly knew how I could repay Inflato for saving my life, while doing it in a way I could feel good about. As he went on and on, insulting my abilities, I jabbed him in the leg with the needle.

The air burst out of him instantly as he ricocheted around the gym—up and down, and over and around. He finally came to rest at the feet of the Amazing Indestructo. Ignoring the kids still clamoring about him, AI helped our completely deflated coach onto his shaky feet.

"Say, I'd forgotten how impressive your power is," he told his long-ago sidekick. "We should talk sometime. You could have quite a future with the League of Ultimate Goodness."

Coach Inflato couldn't have looked prouder.

"But first I need to have a talk with this young man," AI continued, looking directly at me.

My first thought was to run, but I was curious as to why he had come to see me. I should have known it would involve money.

"Well now," he said as he walked me over to a quiet corner of the gym, "I just thought we should have a little chat about how we move ahead in promoting the Meteor Boy line. Sales are already through the roof, and once we get you on TV, things should go bonkers."

"Aren't you forgetting something?" I reminded AI. "I never signed a contract. I only agreed to play the role last Tuesday as a favor to Whistlin' Dixie."

"True," said the Amazing Indestructo in a way that indicated he had something up his sleeve, "but I have another contract." And sure enough, he pulled one out of his sleeve. "It's a twenty-five-year-old contract that I have with Meteor Boy himself. You should know, you signed it as Meteor Boy. And a contract is a contract."

I stared at him silently wondering what I had ever been impressed by. His smile got broader as he sensed his victory over me.

"Clearly," I finally said, "you have never—even in

twenty-five years—actually looked at the contract. Because if you had, you would see that you have no rights to the name, image or likeness of Meteor Boy, and you never will."

With that I turned and walked away from him as his eyes scanned the contract. When I heard his strangled cry of rage, I knew he had reached the bottom of the page where, twenty-five years earlier, I had signed with the name—Ordinary Boy.

(b) This Agreement expresses the entire understanding of the parties, and cannot be amended except by a written instrument signed by both parties. Without limiting the foregoing, this Agreement cannot be modified by any invoice, confirmation or delivery memorandum.

Amazing Indestructo

Ordinary Boy

Amazing Indestructo

Meteor Boy

Ordinary Boy returns for
more extraordinary adventures in

THE EXTRAORDINARY ADVENTURES OF

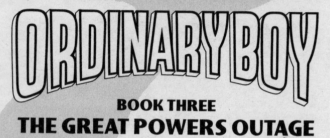

ORDINARY BOY

BOOK THREE
THE GREAT POWERS OUTAGE

PROLOGUE

Great Ball o' Fire

The meteor was hurtling toward me and there was nothing I could do to stop it. I tried launching my body into the air, willing myself to fly, but with no luck. The fireball got closer and closer, and just as it was about to hit I raised my arm to ward it off, knowing it was futile.

And then I woke up, safe in bed, drenched in a cold sweat. It took me a moment to realize I had been dreaming. It was the cool air of the October night drifting across my skin, raising a field of goose bumps, that finally convinced me there wasn't a flaming meteor coming.

But there *had* been, less than two days earlier. In fact all Superopolis had been facing complete destruction at the hands of Professor Brain-Drain.

The evil genius had succeeded in his plan to transport the entire city sixty-five million years into the past to the very moment when the site that would become Superopolis had been formed by the impact of an enormous meteor. His plan had been for the city to be destroyed by the same event that created it.

The neat symmetry of his plot hadn't distracted me from the realization that it was up to me to stop him. With the help of a villain named Cyclotron, and one of Professor Brain-Drain's own gadgets, I had used a little ingenuity of my own to return Superopolis to the present just in the nick of time. In the end, Cyclotron turned out not to be a villain after all, and Professor Brain-Drain was marooned one hundred and thirty million years in the past.

That's the short version. Along the way, in the guise of the legendary hero Meteor Boy, I also spent a couple of days twenty-five years in the past battling evil. Wait a minute—let me clarify that. I wasn't disguised as Meteor Boy—I *was* Meteor Boy, one of the most powerful young heroes in the history of Superopolis. The irony of all this is that I'm actually the *least* powerful hero in the history of Superopolis. They don't call me Ordinary Boy for nothing.

You see, Superopolis is a city of heroes—and villains—and every one of them has a superpower.

Except me. But, thanks to a trip through time courtesy of Professor Brain-Drain's Time Tipler and a mysterious jet pack that allowed me to fly at tremendous speeds, I had the thrill of spending two days battling crime as Meteor Boy—and I had loved it!

During my adventure in the past I made the acquaintance of the League of Goodness, Superopolis's first and greatest team of heroes. The team's leader, Lord Pincushion, provided me hospitality and an opportunity to fight alongside him and the rest of the league. I'm not so sure I did him much of a favor in return. I introduced him to the Amazing Indestructo.

The thing you need to know about AI (that's what everyone calls him for short) is that up until a couple of weeks ago, he was my absolute favorite hero. He's totally indestructible, which gives him a pretty good advantage over any villain, and he's turned the hero business into a hugely profitable enterprise. Between his TV show, toy lines, packaged food business, and dozens of other endeavors, AI has become incredibly wealthy. The problem is all those things come ahead of actually battling crime. He's really kind of a creep, to tell the truth. It took me a while to realize it, and most of the population still hasn't figured it out.

The only part of my trip to the past that still makes me a little queasy is the fact that I was the one

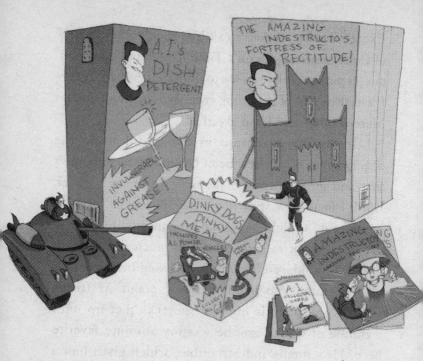

who suggested AI join forces with the League of Goodness. It had been for the best of reasons. The league was bankrupt from the expense of fighting crime, and the Amazing Indestructo needed a well-known name to launch his own career. The league provided the name, and AI soon provided the money.

Sadly, it didn't take long for AI to drive the founding members out of the league and replace them with the most incompetent array of nitwits you could imagine. He changed their name to the League of *Ultimate*

4

Goodness, and set himself up to be the team's most impressive member.

My own father had tried to join the LUG a bunch of times. He never realized what a compliment it was that they wouldn't have him. His name is Thermo. He has the ability to generate enormous levels of heat in his hands. For most of my life he had a job at Dr. Telomere's Potato Chip Factory heating their massive fryers. But prior to that he had been part of a superhero team called the New Crusaders.

That's where he met my mom, Snowflake. She can freeze anything solid just by looking at it. She has a great job at the Corpsicle Coolant Corporation, although I've never really known what she does there. Here's the entry for CCC in the *Li'l Hero's Handbook*. The handbook has sections on all the people, places, and even some of the things in Superopolis. I carry it with me constantly!

Because of the money my mom makes, Dad was able to quit his job at Dr. Telomere's and return to crime fighting. He joined some of his former teammates and they're calling themselves the New New Crusaders . . . and, no, that's not a misprint.

Of course, there's one thing I miss about his old job, and that's the unlimited supply of free potato chips. Boy, do we eat a lot of them! So does everyone in Superopolis. In fact, the only business more

5

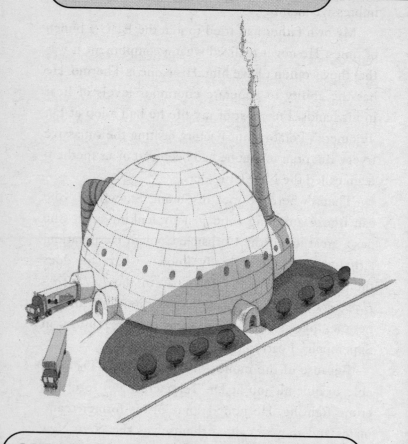

CORPSICLE COOLANT CORPORATION

From its earliest success when it applied for—and received—a patent on winter, CCC has dominated the market for subzero products. Their Chilled Gills line of frozen fish and their Frigi-Fries line of frozen potato products have all been hits. Equally successful is their Vegicles line of frozen vegetables, despite the notable failure of their advertising campaign to convince kids that their vegetables were made by elves who lived in a magic igloo.

successful than the Amazing Indestructo's is Dr. Telomere's chip factory.

I'm sure it drives AI crazy, but there's nothing he can do about it. Nothing beats the salty, fried goodness of a bag of Dr. Telomere's potato chips.

Mmmm . . . potato chips. With that pleasant thought I felt my eyes drifting shut once again. But only a moment later I was reawakened by a familiar voice.

"Thank you for saving me, O Boy."

I opened my eyes and found myself atop Crater Hill in the center of Telomere Park. It was still the middle of the night. I was dressed in my Meteor Boy costume, and standing in front of me was the cartoon figure of Dr. Telomere, a potato chip wearing a derby hat, pince-nez glasses, and a bow tie. The thought that I was dreaming again never even occurred to me as I talked with the advertising spokescharacter of Dr. Telomere's Potato Chip Company.

"You're welcome," I answered, as if talking to a potato chip was a routine situation. "But how could I have saved you if you're not real?"

"Aren't I?" he replied with concern as his gloved hands patted at his potato chip body. "Oh dear. Then are any of us real?"

"I'm real!" I insisted. "I think."

"Only because of *that*, boy!" The potato chip pointed to the night sky. "Only because of *that*."

I looked up and there it was again—a huge flaming meteor heading right for me. I turned back to the potato chip, but he was gone—replaced by the sinister, cackling presence of Professor Brain-Drain. I jolted awake—once more back in my bed. But the image of the fireball stayed with me. I may have escaped it, but it *had* hit the piece of land where Superopolis now sits. The effects of a collision of that magnitude must have been enormous. Now wide awake, I couldn't help but wonder if an event like that might still be affecting things even all these millions of years later.

CHAPTER ONE

Tossed Salad

I couldn't believe what I was seeing. A group of vegetables had just robbed the Mighty Mart! I know that sounds ridiculous, but it was true. Even now, an enormous stalk of celery was crossing the parking lot heading right for me. Okay, so maybe it wasn't *really* a giant piece of celery (not that such a thing was impossible in Superopolis), but it *was* a guy dressed like one. And he was trying to get away with a large bag of Maximizer Brand Booster Bars.

But just as he tried to escape with his loot, a powerful blast of air knocked him to the ground, courtesy of the hero Windbag. As the startled vegetable struggled to get back on his feet, a large ear of corn pushing a shopping cart filled with Maximizer Brand Superdoodlers tripped and fell on top of him.

"You're stepping on my leaves, Colonel Corncob," yelled the celery. "Watch where you're going!"

I almost started clapping as my father, the mighty Thermo, strode up to the crumpled vegetables and lifted Colonel Corncob off the flustered stalk of celery.

"The only place you'll be going, Celery Stalker, is prison!"

"Tarnation!" hollered Colonel Corncob as he got a taste of my dad's power. "I'm feelin' hotter than a peck of pipin' peppers!"

A second later, some of the Colonel's kernels exploded in my father's grasp. Amid the confusion, the Celery Stalker made his escape. He didn't get far before another hero grabbed him and hoisted him effortlessly into the air.

"The Levitator!" I cheered, as my dad's teammate used his power to levitate the human-size celery stalk. Wrapping his hands around the villain's ankles, he began swinging him around in a circle.

"Batter up!" He laughed as he spun the Celery Stalker faster and faster.

"And here's the pitch!" someone added from across the parking lot.

There, another member of my dad's team, the Big Bouncer, was rolling toward a horrified-looking onion. Actually, only his head looked like an onion—or more precisely, a shallot. Regardless, as the Big

10

NAME: Levitator, The. **POWER:** Can make anything weightless just by touching it. **LIMITATIONS:** Except himself. **CAREER:** Following the disbanding of the New Crusaders, the Levitator became a dietitian whose happy clients always held his hand when weighing in. **CLASSIFICATION:** An all-around lighthearted guy.

Bouncer smashed into him, he went flying toward the swinging stalk of celery. The Levitator smacked the onion-headed guy with the Celery Stalker, and he went flying across the parking lot, leaving a shower of Maximizer Brand Fudge Brawnies, raining down on the startled onlookers.

With everyone's attention focused on the shower of snack cakes, an irritated-looking chickpea came running up to my father.

"What da heck are youse guys doin'?!" he sputtered in frustration. "Da script says dat we's s'posed to be roughin' youse guys up at foist."

"Oh, sorry, Garbanzo," my dad said, raising his hands defensively as he backed away from Colonel Corncob, who was now missing several kernels from his body.

"Dat's da *Great* Garbanzo to youse," the cigar-chomping chickpea responded with disgust as he motioned forward another member of his "gang." "Now let da Broccoli Robber here rough youse up some."

The Broccoli Robber was definitely a guy in a costume. His fists were sheathed in big, poofy gloves that looked like broccoli florets. He nervously approached my dad and began punching him feebly. My father almost looked sorry for the guy.

"You could at least *act* like I'm hurting you," the Broccoli Robber whined between breaths.

"Oh, sure," Dad replied. "Sorry about that."

"I'm powerless . . . against . . . broccoli," he said in what was supposed to be a weakened voice. He then fell to the ground beneath the Broccoli Robber's blows.

"Man, your dad is a lousy actor."

I turned to my best friend, Stench, who was standing beside me.

"Yeah, I know," I admitted. "Your dad is actually pretty good though."

We both looked over to where Stench's dad, Windbag, was on his knees in front of the guy with the onion head. He was bawling his eyes out.

"No, he's pretty bad, too," Stench said. "That guy's head actually *is* an onion and he's making my dad's eyes water."

Looking around I realized that none of the members of my dad's team, the New New Crusaders, were very good actors. The Levitator was practically throwing himself at the feet of the Celery Stalker, who could barely maneuver in his unwieldy costume. Not far from them Colonel Corncob was trying to lasso the Big Bouncer, who was standing completely still to make the task easier.

"Now youse guys see da effects dat vegetables can have on youse." The Great Garbanzo laughed as he got everyone back on script. "Youse heroes is too weak to even fight back!"

13

Okay, so maybe this wasn't the most honest representation of the "dangers" of vegetables. But, then again, no one here was trying to sell vegetables.

"Must . . . increase . . . strength," my dad said robotically as he reached for one of the scattered packages of Maximizer Brand MaxiMuffins.

Ripping off the wrapper, my dad gave a performance he didn't need to fake as he shoved the muffins into his mouth. A moment later he slowly got to his feet and delivered another wooden line.

"I feel my energy returning," he said. "Listen up, New New Crusaders. These Maximizer Brand snack cakes can give us back the strength these vile vegetables have sapped from us."

The Broccoli Robber backed away nervously.

"And the first thing coming off the menu"—Thermo smacked a fist into his hand—"is broccoli."